Alexander Innes Shand

The Life of General Sir Edward Bruce Hamley

K.C B., K.C.M.G. - Vol. 1

Alexander Innes Shand

The Life of General Sir Edward Bruce Hamley
K.C B., K.C.M.G. - Vol. 1

ISBN/EAN: 9783337332396

Printed in Europe, USA, Canada, Australia, Japan

Cover: Foto ©Andreas Hilbeck / pixelio.de

More available books at **www.hansebooks.com**

GENERAL
SIR EDWARD BRUCE HAMLEY

K.C.B., K.C.M.G.

BY

ALEXANDER INNES SHAND

WITH TWO PORTRAITS

IN TWO VOLUMES

VOL. I.

WILLIAM BLACKWOOD AND SONS
EDINBURGH AND LONDON
MDCCCXCV

READERS of this biography will find in its pages
the names of many distinguished soldiers and
civilians to whom I have to return heartfelt
thanks for time and trouble most generously
bestowed. More than one of the former who
could speak with exceptional authority on somewhat delicate subjects have preferred to remain
anonymous. But there is a friend to whom I
feel bound to recognise a very special debt of
gratitude. Colonel Gleig was the lifelong associ-
ate and confidant of Hamley from days of cadet-
ship at Woolwich. He has supplied the personal
recollections which could have come from no other
source. His acute critical faculty and his rare
professional knowledge have been ungrudgingly
exercised in a searching examination of the
proofs; and to him I am indebted for guidance
and suggestions in the matters that are more
strictly military and technical.

Most important of all was the help of Miss Barbara Hamley. The adopted daughter and literary executrix of her uncle not only placed freely at my disposal all his diaries, note-books, and confidential papers, but, associating herself with Colonel Gleig in the thoughtful revision of the chapters, suggested much that was essential to an intimate acquaintance with the real character and innermost life of a man who had won the devoted attachment of all who knew him well, but who was fated to be grievously misunderstood and misrepresented.

OAKDALE, EDENBRIDGE, KENT,
    May 1895.

CONTENTS OF THE FIRST VOLUME.

CHAPTER I.

THE HAMLEY FAMILY.

CHAPTER II.

THE ARTILLERY SUBALTERN.

CHAPTER III.

IN GARRISON AT GIBRALTAR.

CHAPTER IV.

THE CRIMEAN CAMPAIGN.

CHAPTER V.

IN SCOTLAND.

CHAPTER VI.

PROFESSOR AT THE STAFF COLLEGE.

CHAPTER VII.

LIFE AT THE STAFF COLLEGE.

CHAPTER XIII.

THE BULGARIAN DELIMITATION COMMISSION.

CHAPTER XIV.

THE BULGARIAN DELIMITATION COMMISSION—*continued*.

CHAPTER XV.

ON THE BOSPHORUS.

ILLUSTRATIONS TO THE FIRST VOLUME.

LIFE OF SIR EDWARD B. HAMLEY.

CHAPTER I.

THE HAMLEY FAMILY.

INTRODUCTION—THE HAMLEYS OF HALWYN—THE OGILVYS—ADMIRAL HAMLEY—HIS SONS—EDWARD'S BOYHOOD—EARLY TRAITS—ILLUSTRATING A MURDER TRIAL.

To write the Life of Sir Edward Hamley might task the powers of any man. Few but himself could have done satisfactory justice to his versatile genius and to the various sides of his character. We should have been glad, indeed, had he left an autobiography; yet in any autobiography he would have done himself but imperfect justice. We should have heard but little of the delightful personal traits which give life and colour to an autobiography; and we should have learned still less of the adventures and hair-breadth escapes which came often enough to him in the course of his campaigning. It was only incidentally, and in the familiarity of unreserved conversation, that he would recall the thrilling experiences he seemed to have wellnigh forgotten. To do him the justice he would have denied himself, his biographer ought to have many qualifications to which I make no manner of pretension. I can only plead — if I may be forgiven the indispensable personal allusion — that although in later years I was privileged to enjoy his intimate friendship, I shall nevertheless do my best to be impartial. No one could have had less patience than himself with a chronicler who should ignore his failings or his foibles.

As a staff officer of artillery in the Crimea, and as the commander of a division in the Egyptian campaign of 1882, his services were of a very distinguished character. But it is as scientific master of the art of war that his claims to professional distinction are most conspicuous and exceptional. As Professor of Military History, and subsequently Commandant of the Staff College, he had the charge of teaching and training the intellectual *élite* of the army. These congenial occupations were singularly favourable to the conception of his great work on 'The Operations of War.' It has passed through five successive editions, and has ever since it appeared been the recognised authority on strategy and tactics. It is difficult to overrate the military genius and position of a man who writes a text-book, not for the use of mere scholars and students, but for skilled veterans of unrivalled practical experience. He becomes the standing counsel of leaders in the fields which are to decide the fate of kingdoms and the future of nations. In other departments of literature, light or serious, Hamley was equally at home. His command of style was extraordinary, and his pen was as sure as swift; in fact, his was a brain which ever sought relief in some fresh form of activity, and his mental energy rose superior to circumstances. So in all the horrors and hardships of the Winter Campaign he found leisure for the series of graphic letters which dramatically told the story of the siege. He threw off brilliant stories, which were succeeded by a delightful novel; he was a graceful poet, an admirable translator of French verse, and, after he had come home from the East, he was perhaps the most valued contributor to 'Blackwood's Magazine.'

It is characteristic that, with all this variety of work, we learn little of the man from his writings. His opinions are unmistakably expressed, but his individuality is kept in the background. Yet so dexterous an artist must have known well that judicious egotism would have greatly heightened the effects. I believe the truth to be, that to the last, whether in person or with the pen, he could never overcome a constitutional shyness, which strangers certainly would never have suspected. Reserve was often mistaken for coldness, and did him much injustice. Only those who had the privilege of his intimacy, and who, moreover, enjoyed opportunities of frequent intercourse, saw Hamley at his brightest and best. He was never more fascinating than on the rare occasions when he was led on to indulge in personal reminiscences. He had an extraordinarily quick and almost nervous sense of humour, and no story ever lost by his telling it. He had travelled much, officially and otherwise; and his habits and pursuits had brought him into contact with all manner of men. Subtle foreign diplomatists might have been surprised to learn how shrewdly he had read their characters and purposes. It is to be regretted that he was not more of a letter-writer; but with the solitary exception of his friend John Blackwood, he had no regular confidential correspondent.

Sir Edward Bruce Hamley, though he never boasted of it, was proud of his descent from Cornishmen and Shetlanders. He showed any latent pride of ancestry by the fondness with which he used to allude to Bodmin and the Shetland Isles. Yet he had only revisited his birthplace, since he left it for Woolwich, in the course of an occasional Cornish tour. Those who hold to the doctrines of heredity might have found illustrations to prove their case in the latest generation of the Hamleys. They had the stalwart frames and the indomitable resolution of the Cornishmen; as, on the other hand, they had something of the adventurous romance of a race which had settled among the descendants of Norwegian Vikings. The Hamleys—there are various spellings of the name—had been domesticated in Cornwall from the time of the Conquest. With the list of their Cornish lands they filled a page in Domesday Book. Those great possessions had gradually dwindled. But even in the beginning of the present century they still possessed the family estate of Halwyn, in the parish of St Mabyn. Latterly the Hamleys had had ill-luck, even to the destruction of their sepulchral monuments in the quaint little church of St Mabyn. Unfortunately, towards the end of last century the church had become ruinous, and it was necessary to rebuild. The restorers of that age of vandalism were even more ruthless than now, and more utilitarian and eco-

nomical. At the time an illegitimate member of
the House of Hamley chanced to fill the offices of
sexton and clerk. He heard with dismay of the
proposed demolition of the interior of the chancel,
and even dared to threaten the vicar with the
vengeance of the knight of the shire if "he so
much as touched one veather of an hangel's
wing." However, the vicar had his own way,
and demolished the monuments with their guard-
ian angels.

Hamley was descended from the old Scottish
house of Ogilvy through his mother Barbara.
The first of the Ogilvys to settle in Shetland was
John Ogilvy, a surgeon in the Life Guards of
King James, who went there after the battle of
the Boyne. He belonged to the Ogilvys of Milton, a branch of the House of Findlater, and
he married Elizabeth, daughter of John Niven
of Luning, who brought him a dowry as a co-
heiress. There was no one of Scott's novels—
and they were his favourite reading—in which
the descendant of the refugee took greater pleasure
than in 'The Pirate,' although he preferred many
of the others as works of art. He delighted in
the descriptions of the roosts and voes, and of the
free-handed hospitality of the fiery old udaller.

Bodmin and the Hamleys have been immemori-
ally connected. It was their "county town" in

the reigns of the Plantagenets. Edward and his brothers were born in one of the older houses, though the family removed a few years after his birth to a residence in the outskirts. He always retained a warm affection for the picturesque old borough, with the two leading thoroughfares of Fore Street and Back Street, and the labyrinths of steep lanes and sunless passages. A letter written to an aunt from a mud-hut before Sebastopol is filled with local allusions which were sure to delight the old lady. The Hamleys had been dying out, as they had been losing their lands, but the grandfather left a vigorous and promising family. The sons, for generations, had been in the habit of serving the King, and Edward's father entered the navy. When he married, he naturally settled at Bodmin; but during the long war he was almost constantly at sea, and the visits to his Cornish home were few and short. Not many months before his own death, Sir Edward happened to mention to the present writer all he knew of his father. Few naval officers had done more useful work : he had seldom to make interest about going to sea, and he died a Vice-Admiral, although, as with Rittmeister Dalgetty, promotion " came dooms slow." He saw much dashing service in the way of cutting out vessels from under batteries, and capturing privateers and smugglers. For long and in successive ships he was flag-lieutenant to the Hon. Captain Cadogan, who was famous for putting his ship's companies in the way of peril and prize-money. In 1806 Lieutenant Hamley specially distinguished himself at the capture of the Dalmatian stronghold of Zara, which had fallen into the hands of the French. He landed in command of the attacking force, and hauling the ship-guns up the hills with seaman-like skill, compelled the surrender of the fortress. The Austrian Emperor showed his gratitude by sending the Lieutenant the Cross of Leopold and a medal of gold, with an autograph letter couched in most flattering terms. The letter was lost, but the cross and medal were treasured as heirlooms, and were in the possession of Sir Edward at his death. There was a sword, too, richly damascened, which had been given up in token of surrender by the French officer commanding the fortress. It disappeared like the letter when the home at Bodmin was broken up, and most unaccountably. Though, indeed, " Ned " as a child had done his best to lose it, for the future soldier seldom missed a chance of making prize of the tempting weapon when his nurse's back was turned.

The Admiral had four sons. Three of them went into the service. The fourth, who bears the family name of Wymond, and who still survives, was Collector of Customs in Vancouver's Island, and is now retired, living in British Columbia. Of the eldest, William George, who died a Major-General of Engineers in April 1893, a word or two ought to be said in passing. He served much of his time in the West Indies, and to his familiarity with their scenery, society, and customs we are indebted for some delightful novels and tales. It is the opinion of the best judges that, since Michael Scott gave us 'Tom Cringle' and 'The Cruise of the Midge,' there has been no brighter or more picturesque book on Jamaica than 'Captain Clutterbuck's Champagne.' He was Acting Governor of the Bermudas in eventful times. The blockade-runners of the American war brought over the yellow fever in chests of infected clothing. The epidemic came rapidly to a head, and its ravages were frightful. Though the islands were threatened by a Fenian descent, the Governor got rid of all the troops he could possibly spare. Each day he made a regular round of the hospitals, till in his turn he was stricken down. He recovered, but he never altogether rallied from the consequences of a prolonged and severe struggle. Though his figure was commanding and his appearance robust, his constitution had been already shattered as a young subaltern. Exposure during a severe winter had done the mischief. His tent was blown away night after night when he was employed on the Ordnance Survey in the Ross-shire Highlands, and he had been left shelterless till the morning. After his return from the Bermudas his life was one long martyrdom from sciatica and acute rheumatic pains, when restless days would succeed the broken nights. But nothing could sour that sweet temper or quell the irrepressible intellectual energy. Enfeebled by pain, he would pull himself together to write one of his thoughtful articles for 'Blackwood' when he was one of 'Maga's' regular contributors. We are reminded of Scott writhing on the sofa with cramp in the stomach, while dictating 'The Bride of Lammermoor' to Laidlaw or John Ballantyne. For his contributions under those distressing circumstances were playful and imaginative as well as grave; and, like Scott, his serene manhood would assert itself the moment the paroxysms were past.

To Charles, who entered the Royal Marines, and rose to the rank of colonel, Edward seems to have been specially attached. In any letters to members of the family he is always affectionately spoken of as Charley. Charles Hamley was on board H.M.S. Pique at the siege of Acre, and served with the Fleet in the

Baltic at the taking of Bomarsund. He was the author of several articles in 'Blackwood,' written from the Baltic.[1] But death cut short a promising career, and of Colonel Charles I shall have more to say when his sorrowing brother was in attendance on the deathbed.

Edward, who was born in 1824, was the youngest of the brothers. He was early addicted to hero - worship, and he said he used to look on those seniors of his as "tremendous fellows," when they were got up for church parade in gorgeous Sunday raiment. Strangely enough, he was five years old at his public christening; and his brother Wymond, who was received into the Church at the same time, was three years older, though both boys had been privately baptised as infants. The reason is said to have been that the ceremony was deferred till their father came back from one of his cruises, although that is scarcely a satisfactory explanation.

[1] "We have great pleasure in publishing the following graphic description of the Baltic in 1855. Another admirable paper from the same pen, 'Aland and the Baltic in 1854,' will be in the recollection of our readers. The writer seems to us a worthy brother-in-arms of our gallant friend who has, month after month, with a regularity which no hardship, no difficulty, no labour, could interrupt, sent us a continuous, lucid, and often eloquent narrative of all that has taken place in the Crimea since the landing at Eupatoria."—Editorial Note, 'Blackwood's Magazine,' August 1855, in "The Baltic in 1855."

The Church of England at the time took things remarkably easily, and Methodism had made good its footing among the Cornish farmers and miners. Ned while a mere child had the honour of being made the subject of a sermon. His nurse, who was a member of the communion of the Wesleys and Whitefield, had taken her young charge to the chapel, where a fervid cobbler held forth on Sundays. The preacher had the genius of his vocation, and seized on opportunities for improving an occasion as he saw them. Ned was wearing one of the gold-laced and tasselled caps which had moved his envy when worn by his elder brothers. The orator made it the text for a passionate invective against the pomps and vanities of this sinful world.

Hamley was always an adventurous little fellow. He used to tell his niece how one day he had found the horse of the family doctor hitched on to the garden gate. By help of the railings he scrambled into the saddle, cast loose the bridle, and trotted away. Luckily the steed had been sobered by age and rough exercise, and the pair were overtaken and brought back before they had gone very far. He had a narrower escape when he was tossed by a cow—"bunched," as they say in the Cornish dialect. When he was landed safely on his legs again, he calmly remarked that "he had been nearer heaven than ever he was in his life." Later in life he became one of the most enthusiastic of anglers. No distance was too great to go in search of his favourite sport; no day too long and no weather too discouraging. Already it was his chief delight to accompany his brother Charles in the fishing among the moorland streams, though those prolonged rambles overtasked his strength.

But whilst Edward was a very manly and venturesome boy, his precocious tastes even in childhood had set strongly towards literature. It is little wonder that his family thought him a prodigy. Precocious intellectual phenomena like Master John Stuart Mill have been forced on deliberate system in an unnatural atmosphere. The young Hamleys were much left to themselves; but their mother was a woman of intellectual ability as well as of high education, and she was in the habit of helping them in their school work, especially in their Latin exercises. In after years they always considered they derived their literary faculty from her. Though young Ned read voraciously, he might indulge his caprices unchecked like David Copperfield; and, as with David, all things were pure to the little boy. The fresh young memory is marvellously retentive, and he never afterwards forgot what he had read and enjoyed when young. In those days good books for children were so scarce that they were carefully studied and doubly prized. How he would revel in those childish recollections across a dinner-table at his clubs! The old simple books still came home to him more sympathetically than the most brilliant work of the hour, much as he may have admired its genius, and though possibly he was a familiar acquaintance of the author. Perhaps he had pored over 'The Arabian Nights' almost as industriously as over 'The Fairchild Family' and 'The Robins.' He was barely out of the nursery before he had begun to dream in the Forest of Ardennes, and to disport himself in the moonlit glades of "The Midsummer Night's Dream" with the fairies of his favourite Shakespeare. It may be mentioned, by the way, that he was reading 'The Arabian Nights' the very week of his death, and they were on the table near the sofa when he was lying in his shroud. From the "Nights" and Shakespeare he soon passed on to Scott's novels, which he devoured. He used to appeal to his mother for the interpretation of the Scotch phrases which puzzled him, and to the end of his life he always maintained them to be the best books that had ever been written. But the little volume that undoubtedly was his greatest favourite was the 'Evenings at Home,' by Dr Aikin and Mrs Barbauld. There was really nothing in the way of literature he so thoroughly enjoyed as 'Eyes and no Eyes' and 'The Transformations of Indur.' As to the former, he naturally objected, as critic and man of the world, that the intelligent young observer was too much of a prig, and that the listless Robert, if strong enough, must infallibly have punched his head. But for "Indur" he had unmitigated admiration. And, curiously enough, in the most benevolent of Brahmins Dr Aikin had painted Hamley's own prototype. For we are told that Indur "was distinguished not only for gentleness of disposition and humanity towards all living creatures, but for an insatiable curiosity respecting the nature and way of life of all animals."

Of no one could this be more truthfully said than of the writer of that most humorously sympathetic of articles, " Our Poor Relations," which naturally leads to the mention of Hamley's juvenile devotion to pets. Whatever may be their feelings in after-life, most schoolboys, like terriers, are the natural enemies of cats, and generally keep a stone in readiness to shy at the tribe of which sufferance is the general badge. With Hamley, on the contrary, the love of the cat was innate. The first of his feline friends became a local celebrity. Being naturally meagre and lanky, perhaps owing to a depraved taste for flies and cockroaches, this famous animal was christened John of Gaunt by the young admirer of Shakespeare. He survived so long and became so venerable of aspect, that he naturally grew into " time-honoured Lancaster." The Hamleys were then living in the country at Curland, and John would follow his young master like a dog, when he took his strolls abroad or went to school at Bodmin. There was a point where he would prudently turn aside into the hedge, patiently waiting for any length of time. There was a parrot, too, which became a valued intimate, though the beginning of the acquaintance promised indifferently, when the bird, sitting bodkin in a post-chaise, stripped all the gilt buttons off the boy's jacket.

Few of Hamley's personal friends, except the officers who were on his staff in his Eastern missions, knew that he was an extremely clever artist. No one was on terms of closer intimacy with him than Sir Frederick Burton, the distinguished Director of the National Gallery, and I have it on Sir Frederick's own authority that he had never heard that Hamley was a brilliant master of the brush. In this, as in all the other accomplishments of his later life, he had shown

his strong proclivities in boyhood. In fact, he
might boast of having been one of the first to
send illustrations to the newspapers. It happened in this way : Bodmin was an Assize
town ; the state entry of the judges, with offi-
cials and javelin men, was a grand event, and
the young Hamleys always made interest for
places in the Court - House during the trials.
Sir Edward was wont to recall a trial that made
a wide sensation and left indelible impressions on
his mind, — all the more so that the murdered
man was a special favourite of a venerable aunt
of his. The victim's name, which was Nevil
Norway, would have sounded well in a criminal romance. He was a prosperous timber and
corn merchant, resident at Wadebridge. One
Saturday evening, after attending Bodmin mar-
ket, he mounted to ride home. He never reached
it, although his horse did ; and when search was
made, the body was found in a hollow a few
paces aside from the road. Suspicion fell on two
brothers : their guilt was brought home to them,
and they confessed all the details of the murder.
They had lain in wait for their victim, and struck
him from his horse ; but all they gained by the
transaction was a couple of halters. They had
hoped to find a large sum in his possession; but as
it proved, he had banked the money at Bodmin.

Young Hamley sketched the prisoners and the witnesses, and sent the sketches to a local paper, which published them,—a very exceptional proceeding in those days, and which speaks strongly for their merit. But he had always a pleasant knack of caricaturing, and of giving the characteristic traits of a face with half-a-dozen scratches of a pencil.

CHAPTER II.

THE ARTILLERY SUBALTERN.

ROYAL MILITARY ACADEMY—CADET LAND—COLONEL GLEIG'S RE-
MINISCENCES — GAZETTED TO THE ARTILLERY — CANADA—
DR BENT — AN INDEPENDENCE DAY EPISODE — READINGS—
RES ANGUSTÆ—THE NORTH OF ENGLAND—TURN FOR CARI-
CATURING—FIRST LITERARY EFFORTS.

LIKE his brothers, Edward Hamley was educated at the Bodmin Grammar-school under the Rev. L. J. Boor. He seldom spoke of his school experiences; but Mr Boor would seem to have been an efficient master, and to have grounded his pupils thoroughly. Their literary tastes came naturally, but both William and Edward must have been indebted to Boor for a fair knowledge of the Classics. Thanks to their upbringing, their surroundings, and their inclinations, the vocation of both was unmistakably marked out. Both went to the Royal Military Academy. William was entered there at the early age of fifteen. Edward for some reason had the advantage of two additional years of schooling. For the reminiscences of his life at the Academy—and for some notes of Canadian scenes which are quoted in this chapter—I am indebted to his old friend Colonel Alexander Gleig, the eldest son of the late Chaplain-General of the Forces. By an odd coincidence, on which medieval astrologers would have put their own interpretation, Gleig and Hamley were born on the same day, and apparently under the same planetary influences. At least, from the time of their making acquaintance at Woolwich, they gravitated together irresistibly : no cloud ever came across their fast friendship; it was always to Gleig that Hamley most freely unbosomed himself; and it was to that lifelong confidant he bequeathed the many-drawered writing-table, at which the visitors to his chambers in Ryder Street have so often seen him seated. The acquaintance "soon ripened into the closest friendship, and I doubt if Hamley was on such intimate terms with any other man than myself, except with our common friend Dr John Bent, R.A., with whom both he and I were on affectionate terms from the year 1845 to Bent's death in 1874."

Seventeen was an unusually late age in those days for cadets joining the Academy. But Hamley's rare natural ability enabled him to make up for lost time and run rapidly through the curriculum. In a year and a half he had passed out with his commission. He had soon an opportunity of asserting his independence and vindicating his very decided individuality. At Woolwich, in those days, as at all other public schools, the rule of the seniors over the younger boys was autocratic and tyrannical. Things in themselves perfectly innocent were prohibited under penalty of a severe thrashing. For example, it was forbidden to walk arm in arm: the cadets who infringed the rule were declared to be " cool "; and coolness involved summary chastisement. Very soon after Hamley joined, he was denounced by an old cadet for " coolness," and ordered to come to his room after tea and bring a stick. There was no mistaking the meaning of the invitation, and there was no declining it. Hamley was a tall lad—as tall, perhaps, as ever he was—though, like his cat John of Gaunt, he was decidedly lanky. But he had the pluck, the determination, and the detestation of anything like injustice which always distinguished him. He was punctual to the appointment, and asked the old cadet what he was wanted for. It was a case where second thoughts would have been wise and silence golden. But the senior had committed himself and provoked his fate, and he was very soundly thrashed for his pains, with the cane which had been carefully selected to suit its intended purpose. Hamley had given offence to the older lads by his independent bearing, which showed itself, quite unconsciously to himself, in many ways. He had been tried and condemned in a *Vehmgericht* of the seniors, and the executioner had volunteered, as the vindicator of old cadet law, to bring the insolent novice to his bearings. Now the young revolutionist had literally made his mark, and thenceforth he was left to his devices. He quietly followed his own course, and there was no further attempt to influence it. Nevertheless he was noways aggressive; and he always allowed to others the liberty he claimed for himself.

Colonel Gleig writes :—

He was on good terms with his companions generally, but I don't remember that he particularly affected the company of any of them, except myself. In the last half-year of our life at the Academy, he and I occupied the same room, and it was there that we became sworn allies. He used to keep me awake half the night—we went to bed by bugle-call at ten o'clock—relating the adventures of " Christopher in his Sporting Jacket." I don't think he knew anything more at that time about the personality of Christopher than I did—which was nothing. But he told me how he had found some old magazines in his father's house (how little he anticipated the interest which ' Blackwood's Magazine ' was to have for him, and he for it, in after times !), and how he had read in them those delightful descriptions of Christopher North's fishing and shooting expeditions. He used to repeat the adventures to me as vividly as if he were describing his own.

The nights in that dormitory at Woolwich recall Dickens as David Copperfield, and the nocturnal readings at Mr Creakle's :—

He was always fond of reading, and always remembered what he read with the most astonishing accuracy. We used to have great literary discussions, lying in our beds in the dark. For, in a second-hand sort of way, I had picked up a certain amount of familiarity with Coleridge and Wordsworth, whose poetry my father used to read aloud to us; and I knew the names, and very little more, I suspect, of many of the writers of the day. Among these, however, Christopher North's was not one. After we joined the Royal Artillery at Woolwich, we were constantly in each other's rooms; and I remember perfectly that he read the Memoirs of Marshal Saxe, and used to talk to me of that hero's methods, and compare them with the little that either of us knew at that time about more modern tactics and methods of warfare.

The future master of strategy was already striking out a course of study for himself. It reminds us of the youthful Pitt, before he had sought a seat in Parliament, listening to a great oration by Fox, and suggesting in an undertone how each successive point might be met and answered. It has been said that Hamley, and perhaps not unnaturally, was comparatively indifferent to the more trivial details of regimental duty.

Yet he never neglected them, and he could always be trusted if anything serious was to be done, as might sometimes be the case, even in times of peace.

After leaving Woolwich, the subaltern, newly gazetted to the artillery, was sent to Ireland, and was quartered for a year at Charlemont. Old acquaintances are still living there who can remember the bright and buoyant young soldier. From Charlemont he was ordered to Canada, where he almost immediately availed himself of an opportunity for showing his soldierly qualities. When the battery had to change its quarters, and leave Quebec for London, which was then a dull though thriving "location," the men objected strongly. On the march up country they passed from grumbling to something like mutiny, refusing to carry their packs or even to move without them. The chief responsibility happened to fall on Hamley, and they were only reduced to some sort of order by his firm energy and unflinching resolution.

At London there was no great choice of companions, and it was very fortunate for him— possibly a turning-point in his career—that Dr Bent was stationed there. Otherwise he might have satisfied himself with his passion for field-sports, or at best with the desultory reading in which he must have always indulged. But Bent was a man of thought and cultivation, devoted to all manner of intellectual pursuits. Soon they were inseparable : so when Hamley would go shooting, Bent always accompanied him. They agreed to differ, thoroughly understanding each other. As to which there is a characteristic story. Hamley was striding forward, with gun on full cock, looking out keenly for the birds the dogs were drawing. Bent was stalking along at his elbow, absorbed in admiration of the scenery.

Bent. Look, Hamley, look !

Hamley (seeing nothing). Where ?

B. There !

H. Where ?   What is it ?

B. There, don't you see it ?   The sunshine on that bank.

H. Damn the sunshine !   I thought it was a quail.

B. Damn the quails !   Look at the sunshine.

The story is the more telling that Hamley was really a passionate admirer of scenery, as all his friends are aware who have had the pleasure of country rambles with him. He may have loved sport even more dearly than landscape and light effects, but it was his invariable rule to attend to one thing at a time. There is another characteristic Canadian reminiscence, which illustrated the fixed determination of purpose which always distinguished him. In this instance he kept his word to an obnoxious farmer; but the chronicler of " Our Poor Relations " must honestly have regretted the fate of the dog who discharged his duty somewhat too impetuously.

By the by, I ought to have mentioned an incident which occurred at London, because, like the part he played when cadet law was so emphatically repudiated, it was highly characteristic. He used to ride to his shooting-ground very often, and on one of his roads there was a particular farmhouse from which there used to dash out on all who passed a large and very savage dog. The animal had frequently attacked Hamley's horse, and caused him great inconvenience, encumbered as he was with a fowling-piece; and he had often complained not only of the dog but of his master, who, if he saw what was going on, never tried to stop it or call the dog off. Hamley resolved to abate this public nuisance, and when the dog attacked him again in presence of his master, who was deaf as usual to Hamley's appeal, he warned him that if the dog were not kept in he would shoot him. The man made an unmannerly reply, and dared him to do any such thing, to which Hamley answered, " Very well: now I give you fair notice; I shall shoot him."

Which he did on the very next occasion when the dog had broken loose and the master was looking on. Probably if it had not been a question of horse *v.* dog, and of a favourite horse who was his daily companion, he would never have committed himself to the rash threat. He was a youth besides, and hot in the temper. But later in life he never said what he did not mean; and when he once declared he would do a thing, that thing would infallibly be done.

On another occasion we see the future soldier and strategist extricating himself from a situation of danger and difficulty by a happy union of audacity and science. He had gone with a comrade to admire the Falls of Niagara, and they had crossed the river to Buffalo on the 4th of July. They had forgotten that the Americans were celebrating Independence Day. Buffalo, like most border towns, swarmed with roughs, and even early in the afternoon the patriots had been celebrating the immortal memory of Washington with bumpers of "Bourbon" and a variety of drinks. They "spotted the Britishers," who were walking up from the ferry, resented the unseasonable invasion, and began to jostle them. The youths of two-and-twenty were indignant at the unprovoked assault, and soon found themselves in the thick of a very serious row. They succeeded in retreating into a hotel; but they were beset, like the pilgrims in "Vanity Fair," by a mob that increased in numbers and fury. There were pleasant suggestions of tar and feathers and of riding upon rails, and it was clear that the rioters meant serious mischief. It was in vain that some Americans of the better class tried to persuade their countrymen to hear reason. A dozen of the most violent forced their way into the house, and things were looking very black. Then Hamley stepped forward to speak for self and friend. The speech was short, but much to the purpose, and nothing could have been more nervously masculine than the peroration : " Gentlemen, it's a cowardly thing for a dozen men to attack two. However, I have not the least objection to fight you one at a time ; I am quite willing to do that." What might have been the issue of the ordeal by battle it is impossible to say. Hamley, though tall, was still slightly built ; and although his constitution afterwards hardened so as to be only shaken and not shattered by the prolonged hardships of the Crimea, at that time he was far from robust. But the better-minded of the Buffalo folk kept the others in talk while the hotel-keeper assisted the escape of the foreigners. They promptly executed a movement to the rear through the back premises ; and " monstrous glad we were," says his friend, " when we found ourselves well out on the river on our return to the Canadian shore."

Hamley's circumstances, then and immediately afterwards, were singularly favourable to study ;

and at an age when many men seem to try their best to forget everything they may have learned, his education was steadily progressing. The heat of summer on the shores of Lake Erie is as intense as the winters are severe. It was in one of the hottest of summers that he found himself there with his two dearest friends. Gleig, who was quartered elsewhere, had got leave for a long visit. Each morning they made a very early party to bathe in the Canadian Thames, on which the Canadian London is situated. Hamley was in the habit of requisitioning the battery horses, which they rode full gallop down to the river, arrayed in little more than the airy costume in which they had tumbled out of bed. *Honi soit qui mal y voit* was their motto, and the primitive inhabitants of what has since become a fashionable town saw no scandal in the practice. After bath and breakfast, they were kept close prisoners by the sun. Prolonged siestas alternated with private readings; they were all three more or less argumentative and critical, as heat and languor would allow; and it is easy to conceive how those appreciative studies of " the best authors " must have helped to develop Hamley's tastes. Gleig, possibly as being the most effective reader of the three, was told off pretty regularly for duty. He can recall an incident and a very amusing coincidence which shows how close was the attention they paid, and how indelible were the impressions that were left on those fresh and susceptible memories. One day he was reading " The Bridge of Sighs," when he came to the couplet—

> " Perishing gloomily,
> Spurred by contumely."

He stretched a point in the pronunciation of " contumely," in order to excite Bent, who was listening to Hood's poem in his most exalted mood, an amiable intention in which he was quite successful. Bent, with his somewhat romantic temperament, took the matter up very seriously ; Hamley, who, like Childe Harold, was of lighter mood, chaffed and laughed. Years afterwards the old cronies had come together again one day on the banks of the Tchernaya, on another party of pleasure. Gleig was in command of one of the field-batteries ; and Bent had come to do duty as a medical officer of superior rank. Hamley, who was then on Sir Richard Dacres' staff, had taken out Bent to make a peaceful reconnaissance, and to give him a glimpse of the Russian positions. They made a long detour in walking their horses out, but in returning they passed within range of the enemy's works, when the Russians opened fire. Naturally they turned their steps in the direction that would most quickly take them out of range, and after a little while Hamley observed that they had been instinctively quickening their pace more than he thought was becoming. So he pulled up, and laying his hand upon Bent's shoulder to check him, said, " This won't do, Bent ; they'll say we are spurred by contumely."

" Well," was the retort of Bent, " that is better than perishing gloomily."

The triumvirate was broken up by Bent's death in 1874 ; but his memory was fondly cherished, and Hamley would always speak of him with the warmest affection, nor did he ever forget or ignore the great debt of gratitude for the direction his early friend had given to his studies and pursuits.

Such intellectual intercourse as that, with the solitary study from childhood to early manhood, was to bear abundant fruit. The *res angustæ domi* was to prove a blessing in disguise. The Admiral had many calls on his purse, and after the expenses of education at the Military Academy had been paid, Hamley was thrown on his own resources. Consequently he made his start in the service heavily handicapped. In those days confiding tailors and outfitters seem to have been in the habit of giving generous credit, and it may be presumed that they charged proportionately, if not usuriously. It was several years before the self-reliant young officer had shaken himself free from his debts. They weighed upon him, and he was eager to be relieved of the burden. With all his resolution, and with the adaptive power which was to turn his many talents to account, he would never have succeeded as soon as he did had he not been singularly favoured by circumstances. In garrison in Ireland, in Canada, and at first in England, he had compensations for having little of lively military society, for he could go very much his own way. There were no messes with lavish entertainments, and bands playing in the ante-room. By the way, to the last Hamley detested music at dinner, the rather that he was somewhat deaf on one side of the head. It was fatal, as he declared, to all pleasure in conversation; and the only occasions on which he was known to seem grudging, was when an emissary coming round with the plate at some public banquet or hotel *table d'hôte* appeared to add insult to injury. His personal habits were simple in the extreme; and although he afterwards became an intelligent connoisseur in *cuisine*, and delighted in giving little dinners and *soigné* breakfasts, he could make himself happy after a frugal meal through many a quiet evening, with his favourite books for the companions of his solitude. But as Scott remarks in his journal, after expatiating on the satisfactions of solitude, no man was ever meant to live alone, and even genius must be stimulated by converse with its fellows, and the assurance that congenial society is within reach. Hamley was generally fortunate in finding some comrade of whom he could make a crony. It was at Carlisle that he formed his intimacy with Gage, and I well remember that his feelings almost overpowered him on the eve of his going down to General Gage's funeral at the romantic seat of the family, which shelters under the Sussex Downs. At dinner the day afterwards he indulged half-abstractedly in many fond reminiscences of their long acquaintance; and during his protracted sojourn at Folkestone when his health had failed, there was no one whom he saw with more pleasure, or of whom he spoke with more kindness, than the widow of his old comrade.

On his return to England, after nearly four years spent in Canada, he was quartered first at Tynemouth and afterwards at Carlisle. It was then that, in City language, he contemplated a scheme for the liquidation of his liabilities, and for securing himself against pecuniary anxieties in the future. Probably the idea had long been simmering in his brain, for he must have been conscious of his intellectual gifts, and of his rare facility of expression with the pen. He determined to try his luck in the field of literature : and half a century ago that field was less crowded, and consequently more inviting, than now. He devoted himself to a course of incessant activity, and of almost ascetic self-restraint. The activity came pleasantly, for his energy was indefatigable, and there was never a man who had less of the lotus-eater about him ; but it must have been a sore trial in those northern counties to resist the seductions of sport. He brought good introductions, and might have made many acquaintances. He might well have been tempted by the shooting on the Cheviots and the Keeldar moors, by the angling in the Coquet or the Eden and the upper waters of the Tyne. He might have found endless historical subjects for his brush in such priories as Brinkburn, or such fortalices as Ford or Warkworth. So far as I can learn, he never cast a fly at that time, or opened a colour-box. He was set upon the single purpose of making a fair literary start.

Still, it may be remarked in passing that if he did not go abroad with colour-box and camp-stool, he did sometimes dash off sketches with pencil or pen and ink. As has been observed, he had a pleasant gift of caricaturing, which, although latterly he used it with great discretion, undoubtedly made him more than one unforgiving enemy. There would often be a laugh over a dinner at the Athenæum, when Hamley passed an envelope across the table on which he had scratched down the portrait in outline of some grave ecclesiastic or dignified judge. Perhaps the sketches were not more than clever. But it was always noteworthy that he gave prominence to the trait or the feature which seemed to indicate the inner nature of the subject. To use the word "victim" would do him injustice, for those sketches had no tinge of malevolence. He never exaggerated a personal defect, and what he caricatured was the character and not the man. One of the earliest, and apparently not the least successful, of his efforts is an excellent example of that. When he joined his regiment, among the most conspicuous figures at Woolwich was a colonel of Horse Artillery, an old Waterloo man. The veteran passed his time promenading in front of the barracks, surveying the soldiers who went by, with glances that made them tremble. He was the terror of the mess waiters, and indeed of all save his few intimates; and he habitually indulged in language of the most terrific character. No young officer would have dreamed of addressing him, yet it was surmised that his bark was worse than his bite, and that really at heart he was a kindly old fellow. Hamley drew him in that double aspect, and hit him off to the life; so much so that the sketch passed from hand to hand, and was shown at last to its subject by one of his familiars. The colonel chuckled, and was so much amused that he forthwith took the artist into favour, even occasionally condescending to challenge him to take wine—an honour he had never vouchsafed before to any youngster of similar standing.

But to revert to Hamley's beginnings in literature. Any intelligent aspirant begins by drawing, if he can, on his personal experiences. Hamley had no lack of immediate material. His first article was "Snow Pictures," which was the narrative of a shooting expedition from Quebec into the Highlands of Maine, in the company of some Indian hunters. It professes to be a letter from Lieutenant Michael South, and is more realistic than imaginative. In fact, for his matter he relied chiefly on his memory. Nevertheless there are effective pictures of his English companion, of the Indian guides, of the romantic scenery, the sport, and the bivouacs beneath the pines. This paper was soon followed by 'The Peace Campaigns of Ensign Faunce,' and both were offered to 'Fraser,' or 'Regina,' which was then at the height of its popularity, and the formidable rival of 'Maga.'

When he was busied with the biography of Faunce, at Carlisle in 1849, the anxious author read the opening chapters aloud, speculating with a friend on the chances of their being accepted. His satisfaction was immense when he knew that the novel had taken the editor's fancy. And he rejoiced with better reason than many of his aspiring *confrères* in Letters, who have found a first success pave the way to illusion and disappointment. He had fallen upon a veritable vocation, and had found inexhaustible sources of interest. Henceforth his circumstances were to be easy if not affluent, and he could write with a light heart and in the fulness of agreeable anticipations. In all his after work he was to show rapid and steady progress. His early efforts, as was natural, were crude enough. " No one has read the rubbish, I am glad to say," was his own subsequent criticism on the Campaigns of the Ensign. That was of course a *façon de parler*, and even in the maturity of his judgment he must have regarded his maiden effort with a certain pride. For notwithstanding looseness of construction in the plot, superfluity of gratuitous digressions, the pedantry of professional prolixity, and not a few florid affectations in the style—in short, in spite of the faults which are inevitable with a clever artist, at the outset the story was brightened by sparkles of wit and frequent flashes of rollicking fun. There are dramatic bits of description, and telling touches of satire. 'Ensign Faunce' had never the honour of a reprint, so we can only say "Peace be to his memory." But there and in the "Snow Pictures" there are the unmistakable signs of the excellences the writer subsequently developed.

CHAPTER III.

IN GARRISON AT GIBRALTAR.

LIFE ON THE ROCK—FIRST CONNECTION WITH 'BLACKWOOD'—
THE 'LEGEND OF GIBRALTAR'—'LAZARO'S LEGACY'—
'LADY LEE'S WIDOWHOOD'—LETTERS TO JOHN BLACKWOOD—
TRIP TO BARBARY—LADY FRIENDS—FUNERAL OF CAÑUELO.

In 1851 Hamley got his promotion, and had orders
to join his battery in Gibraltar. It was no unwelcome change from the quiet of Carlisle and the grey
skies of "Rocky Cumberland" to the sunshine of
tawny Spain and the bustle of a great garrison.
He revelled in the picturesque scenery on either
shore of the Straits, and his letters show how
heartily he enjoyed the riding expeditions into
the Sierra of Ronda and through the cork-forests,
with the streams brawling down over the cliffs
which skirt the coast from Gibraltar to Tarifa.
There were shooting trips to Tangiers, where Sir
John Drummond Hay had always a welcome for
sporting officers from the Rock. Tangiers and the
neighbourhood were very different then from what

they are now. The picturesque town was only accessible by the cattle-boat, which regulated its sailings according to weather and freight; and there were but two small hostelries, one kept by a Frenchman famous for his *cuisine*, and the other by a cleanly Scottish woman. If the visitor had not made arrangements beforehand, he might have to put up with rough accommodation. But the shooting was excellent: there were quail and snipe in profusion, and· battues for wild boar were arranged for within a short ride of the gates. So at Gibraltar Hamley had both sport and scenery in perfection, and whether he gave his mind to the one or the other, he always had pleasant occupation. But these expeditions only lent occasional variety to what might have been a monotonous existence. As every one knows, Gibraltar is a magnificent precipitous promontory, connected with the mainland by the sandy isthmus of the Lines. The Calpe Hunt, established in 1817, was the great excitement of the sporting soldier, and well-bred fiery little barbs were cheap and plentiful. ·But Hamley was a heavy man to mount, and, as we have seen, he had little money to spare. He did not care greatly for racquets, which were the standing resource of those who did not devote themselves to billiards and whist, cigars and siestas. What perhaps pleased him most was the animated panorama of Jews, Turks, and heretics, mingling with the Christians in a babel where every language was spoken. Nothing could be more interesting to the student of man and manners than the sun-burned types of all the races from Cairo to Fez, and Tetuan to Timbuctoo. Then there was something more than a colouring of romance in the venturesome audacity of the smugglers who did lucrative business with the " scorpions " of the Rock. The free port, which supplied all southern Spain with contraband goods, was perpetually being watched by the *guarda costas* from Algeciras, and sea-fights sharply contested and captures threatening international complications were incidents of continual recurrence. All this Hamley carefully noted as matter for immediate literary inspiration, and long afterwards a scene from the turmoil in the market-place was brought in most effectively by way of illustration in the scathing review of 'Lothair.'

For it was now that he fairly launched out on the literary career. The comparative seclusion of his successive quarters served him well in laying broad and solid foundations. In those days there were no circulating libraries, and the man who desired the newest books must borrow or buy. There was an excellent garrison library, which received, as we learn from one of Hamley's letters, a monthly box from Longmans. But the earnest student cannot read comfortably in public; he must live in familiar companionship with his volumes, however few they may be. So it was that Hamley came to ground himself thoroughly in Shakespeare and the old dramatists; in Milton, Dryden, Pope, and the modern poets; in Richardson and Fielding, and the classical novelists; in such unrivalled biographies as those by Boswell and Lockhart. He read again and again, mused and inwardly digested; and such was the remarkable tenacity of his memory, that had he been struck blind he might have been left poor, but by no means destitute. Alexandre Dumas boasts in 'Mes Bêtes' that the fidelity of his recollections spared him the necessity for references; and he proceeds to prove the point by making three egregious blunders. Hamley might have made the boast with better reason, and he might have ventured to transfer whole passages to his own writings without the trouble of verification. Moreover, he had the advantage of being always in admirable intellectual training. The Rock was wont to be renowned for unbounded hospitality, and the messes, to say the least, were extremely convivial. But Hamley was temperate almost to abstemiousness: he would pride himself on dining with half a pint of light claret even in the depressing London fogs. If he drank the less, perhaps he ate the more, and, thanks to his excellent digestion, his powerful and muscular frame was always well nourished. When he was bracing himself for a severe literary spurt, he would put himself for the time on short allowance. So at Gibraltar, although his attention to duty recommended him to the special notice of his chief, who selected Hamley for his aide-de-camp in the Crimean campaign, he got through a great deal of writing as well as reading. It was the more to his credit, that the climate is enervating and relaxing for eight months of the twelve, and that he resisted the seductive example of a society that let the world slide when not actually on duty.

In those days the monthly periodicals of any note might almost have been told off on the fingers of one hand. No one among them was more powerful or more popular than ' Blackwood,' which had gone forward, increasing the prestige it had gained through the versatile talents of Wilson and Lockhart, with a host of more or less able contributors. The rollicking ' Noctes Ambrosianæ,' with their exuberance of fun and frolic, had their faults—the faults chiefly of the exhilaration of youthful spirits, and of an impetuous fancy that was hard to bridle; but with their brilliant blending of wit and eloquence, pathos and humour, satire and tenderness, with their picturesque and Burns-like delineation of Scottish scenes and character, they had made a wide and deep impression.

As we have seen, "Christopher in his Sporting Jacket" had been the favourite of Hamley's boyhood. 'Blackwood' had early established a reputation for dramatic stories and bright social sketches and essays, as many of the most popular novels by celebrated authors had first appeared in its pages. Hamley's youthful admiration for 'Blackwood' had doubtless been deepened during his residences at Tynemouth and Carlisle, for 'Maga,' with its northern and national tendencies, was doubly a power to the north of the Trent. So we find him writing to John Blackwood in the spring of 1851: "As a boy it was my great ambition to be a contributor to 'Maga,' whose pages I used delightedly to study whilst yet in corduroys." We know not why he did not carry out his original intention of offering Blackwood 'The Peace Campaigns of Ensign Faunce': possibly his innate modesty held him back. Be that as it may, he was now to make ventures which more than realised his young dreams of ambition, for neither he nor his editor could have foreseen how long, how close, and how mutually advantageous this new connection was to prove.

'Blackwood' owed much to the brilliancy of its contributors; but the most brilliant of the contributors were the foremost to acknowledge how much contributions and Magazine owed to the editor. The late John Blackwood was so unassuming that few beyond his immediate circle recognised his rare and remarkable qualities. He and John Delane of the 'Times' had lived together as young men in London, in one of the houses between St James's Square and Pall Mall. After the death of Barnes, one afternoon Delane burst into their sitting-room with a "By G—! John, what do you think! I'm editor of the 'Times.'" To outsiders, the selection seemed hazardous, for Delane was as yet a lad. As he said long afterwards, with justifiable pride, in answer to a question as to whether he had not shrunk from the responsibility,—"Not I: and that is the worst of you young fellows of this generation; you are scared by the very shadow of responsibility!" Delane went to be dictator in Printing-House Square; and never, according to universal consent, was self-confidence more amply justified. His hastily scratched notes were models of pregnant brevity. He could give a lead in

a couple of lines, and there was a witty or
weighty suggestion in each hurried sentence.
Time was more than money, and never a second
went to waste. Blackwood, who had gone back
to Edinburgh to conduct the Magazine, was in
some things Delane's double, and in many his
antithesis. But as the one was the prince of
English journalists, so the other was *par excellence* the model magazine editor. He loved to
take life leisurely—he had no reason to do otherwise—and he wrote his letters deliberately and
methodically. But no point of importance was
ever overlooked, and as he made the feelings
and interests of his contributors his own, they
knew that their work was sure to be generously appreciated. They believed, besides, so
firmly in the sincerity of his friendship that
they forgave him any amount of frankness. He
was the centre of what was in the best sense
a select literary ring. It was not in any way an
unlimited mutual-approval society : the art of
log-rolling was as yet non-existent; but all the
members felt themselves united by a common
interest and a common bond of loyalty. Anon-
ymity was as yet strictly observed. But if one said
anything discriminatingly appreciative of another,
either the letter or an extract was duly forwarded.
And whether in his Edinburgh home, at Strath-

tyrum near St Andrews, or on his visits to London, Blackwood was the most genially hospitable of men. At breakfast, luncheon, or dinner when in town, he was always bringing two or more contributors together, so that the seeds of future friendships were being sown broadcast, and affinities came to be closely attracted by their common sympathies and tastes. All who have been habitually connected with the Magazine will own that they have been indebted to that connection for lifelong friendships and delightful intimacies, although the survivors have been paying the inevitable penalty—for death has of late years been busy in the companionship. Consequently, what has been said is no digression : on the contrary, it is essential to estimating Hamley's relations, not only with his old intimate and correspondent " the Editor," but with many others of his most cherished friends.

It is curious to note how quickly the relations with John Blackwood passed from the beginnings of ceremonious formality through successive stages of growing geniality, into terms of the most warm and cordial unreserve. Years were to go by before they met; but when they did meet, there were no barriers to be broken down between men who seemed superficially to have little in common. It was a pleasant sight to see them when they came together latterly in London after a separation. If they talked but little at first, both were brimming over with contentment. The twinkle in Blackwood's eye from beneath his shaggy eyebrows, and the puckering of the corners of his kindly mouth, were answered by the beaming smiles that softened Hamley's somewhat stern features. As they committed themselves to the glow of recollections, they were fairly carried away, till the listener might almost fancy himself assisting at a revised and modern edition of the "Noctes." So many of their common friends were, or had been, celebrities; each had his store of illustrative reminiscence; and there were the memories besides of many lively literary symposia between archi - episcopal St Andrews and the Staff College at Sandhurst.

The first letter to Blackwood was a formal communication as to some contribution of William, the eldest of the brothers, who was then in the West Indies; and so little did the editor then know of the Hamleys, that he confounded their personalities and Christian names. But the ice being broken, Hamley soon wrote again on his own account, sending the poem of "Michael Angelo and the Friar" on approval. The poem duly appeared; but it seems strange that Hamley, knowing that the special attractions of the Magazine lay in travel, adventure, and sparkling fiction, should not have followed up the earlier contributions to 'Fraser' with something in similar vein. Nevertheless, "Michael Angelo" was appreciated as it deserved to be. The dialogue is a really noble conception, and must have been suggested by the spirit of lofty ambition which always animated the writer. The minds of both painter and monk are alike set on immortality; but the friar is content to pursue the quiet tenor of his way, consoling himself for self-denial upon earth with the blissful assurance of a happy eternity. He ought, on conventional principles, to have had the best of the argument, when he asks why the layman, bound by no vows, should sacrifice the shadow for the substance, and barter contentment for fame. But in a fine climax he must bow his head and listen in reverential silence to the impassioned speaker, who has veritably seen in visions of the night that Judgment and the appalling *dies iræ* of which the pious recluse had but vaguely dreamed.

The poem was printed, but Blackwood, with his instinctive perceptions, had recognised in the new recruit possibilities that might be turned to more practical purposes. No doubt he had been referred to 'Regina,' and had looked back over the pages of 'Fraser' for the "Snow Pictures" and 'Ensign Faunce.' There is a letter dated Gibraltar, 11th August 1851 :—

DEAR SIR,—In your note to me you observed that a story of Gibraltar life ought to be amusing. I send you one, a "pretty slight drollery," illustrative of the scenery and the garrison life, pretty much as they now appear, though I have cast my tale at a more picturesque period. If you like it, and it suits your Magazine arrangements to publish it at once, the MS. is, I believe, ready for printing,—but if the publication is deferred, I should be glad to see a proof.

For Hamley had one great advantage in forwarding articles from distant quarters, which were often written under all manner of difficulties. His handwriting was admirably firm and clear, so that the arrival of one of his manuscripts was never the signal of a stampede in the printing-office with the compositors, as the irritated manager protested was the case with more slovenly contributors. And when once a piece of work had taken shape in his brain, he would dash it off with glowing facility. For example, his 'Diary of the Egyptian Campaign' is a model of lucid simplicity. The "Legend of Gibraltar" was the first response to Blackwood's request, and he says in one of the letters that it was thrown off in three evenings. Yet the thought and care which were given are evidenced in a hasty note :—

GIBRALTAR, *8th September*.

DEAR SIR,—Thinking over the story I sent you, the "Legend of Gibraltar," it struck me that the catastrophe was rather too sudden—that I had married my grandfather rather too unceremoniously. I now send another scene to throw it into better perspective. This will reach you in time for insertion if you are going to publish it in the September number—as I hope to learn from you by the mail that has just left England.—Believe me, yours faithfully,   EDWARD HAMLEY.

Whether the suggested alteration was made or no, I cannot say : it is clear that he followed with thoughtful anxiety the fortunes of the little story. His mind was speedily relieved. "The Legend" delighted the editor, and made a great hit with the public. The present writer can remember, when it appeared, the shouts of laughter it provoked in a country-house, and the eagerness with which it was passed from hand to hand. In fact it was a capital piece of genially satirical comedy, and one cannot help suspecting that the character of Major Flinders had been taken in some measure from the chronicler himself. The major is an ardent devotee of Shakespeare : the major takes a personal interest in the cookery of the savoury Spanish dishes : the major is loath to hurt a wasp : and when the horses are gored in

the bull-ring of Algeciras, his feelings get altogether the better of him. Indeed the major
seemed so realistic to one prosaically minded
soldier that, as his creator writes gleefully in
the letter acknowledging the cheque,—

"Fancy the Governor, a very matter-of-fact old gentleman, going out into the picture-gallery with 'Maga' in
one hand and a candle in the other to look for my grandfather Major Flinders, and expressing his wrath at not
finding him. He imagined the whole thing to be really
a veracious narrative."

Apropos to the portrait - gallery, there is a
charming touch as to a larger canvas, the masterpiece of an artist of the olden school, " representing
a council of officers held during the siege, where,
notwithstanding the gravity of the occasion and the
imminence of the danger, not a single face in the
intrepid assembly wears the slightest expression
of anxiety or fear, or indeed of anything else."
" The Legend " was quickly followed by " Lazaro's Legacy," and in this case the sequel was
certainly not inferior to its predecessor. The
writer recommends special attention to the Spanish phrases, and the " vulgarious talk " put in the
mouths of the inferior personages,—" for dreadful
are the pangs of an author when a pet sentence is
turned into nonsense or deprived of the point by
the alteration of an important letter." That " vul-

garious talk," which caused natural anxiety, was the most ludicrous and characteristic part of the story. Our old acquaintance, the major, is lively and entertaining as ever, and the matrimony into which he was rather shabbily betrayed has in no way staled his infinite jest. But surely the private broken loose from discipline was never better drawn than in the respectable Mr Bags and his worthy comrade Bill. Multiply them by many, and magnify their opportunities for evil, and we can realise the worst scenes of the Peninsular war after the storming of Badajoz and Ciudad Rodrigo. In the Gibraltar story there are no horrors, but only the ludicrous side of licence, although it was no joke to the unlucky victims. But the climax of cleverness is in the comically artistic way in which just retribution is finally distributed. The grasping old usurer is shelled and burned out of the stores he had accumulated against the extremities of the famine : and Mr Bags, who has invested his portable pillage in a cannon's mouth, sees the fruits of his industry scattered to the winds when the gun is discharged at the Spanish gunboats.

Sending off " Lazaro's Legacy," Hamley wrote : " We will now, I think, have done with my grandfather, for fear he should get tiresome." We can avouch that there were readers who sincerely lamented the major's premature decease; but Hamley dismissed him with the more complacency, that already he was engaged on a more ambitious piece of work, and soon his novel of 'Lady Lee's Widowhood' had taken complete form in outline. The author was impetuous and the editor was cautious. Hamley, adopting a dashing strategy, hoped to carry the Magazine by assault. He despatched a couple of parts of a story that would probably extend to ten, and sanguinely suggested that they should be printed forthwith if there were an opening. Blackwood admired and approved, but naturally hesitated to give his promising recruit *carte blanche.* Indeed, even when the fifth part of the story was forwarded, he writes as if the decision was still in suspense. In reality the novel was practically accepted, but the editor was frank and outspoken in his criticisms, and took exception to some of the details. It is interesting to follow the course of the correspondence, which shows, besides, the decision and foresight of Hamley's manner of working. Scott declares repeatedly that he could never stick to a plan: that his plot would change with the inspiration of the moment, and that his most disreputable characters invariably ran away with him. Hamley sends twice a minute description of the development of the plot and its incidents, and it did not undergo any substantial alteration. All was mapped out as methodically as any novel of Wilkie Collins or Charles Reade. Most men would have found their surroundings singularly unfavourable to light and sparkling work, for the imaginative temperament is generally stimulated by the bustle of active life and the society of congenial spirits. But Hamley congratulates himself on the ample leisure that was given by solitude and comparative isolation. In the midsummer of 1852 he says,—

I am now stationed with my company, in our turn, at Europa Point—a part of the Rock removed by a couple of miles from the town and very lonely—which is favourable to work. It is, moreover, much cooler here than in the city—something like ten degrees of difference—and therefore a far healthier spot in the summer, so that I am much pleased with the change, although my society consists chiefly of monkeys and rabbits, the aborigines of Europe.

Yet although he could easily dispense with the ordinary mess company, he sadly missed such familiars as Gleig and Bent, with whom he could have discussed his work and consulted. Moreover, he was fretted and hampered by the distance from literary headquarters. The mails were few and precarious; the rates of postage were heavy, and often important packets were forwarded by

private opportunities, with considerable doubt as
to the ultimate delivery.

Gibraltar, 14*th Sept.* 1852.

My dear Sir,—I was very glad to get your long-
expected note this morning, for it was exactly what I
wanted. I have no literary friend here with whom to
discuss my projects, for most of my companions in arms
are, to say the truth, much better judges of brown sherry,
black eyes, and Cuba cigars than of composition. This is
unfortunate; because talking over characters and incidents
gives them a reality, which they want so long as they are
confined to the brain that imagined them. I will now
give you a sketch of the design, and I am glad to observe
that your objections are such as would disappear in the
course of the story.

Two main features in the plot are taken from real life.
A certain peer was lately here in his yacht, who, in youth,
for some offence noways dishonourable, as I believe, was
turned adrift by his father. He enlisted in the Life or
Horse Guards, and served as a trooper for some time under
a feigned name; afterwards a commission was procured
for him by his mother's friends in a regiment serving in
India; and now, by his father's death, he enjoys a title
and estate.

From this I took the idea of Corporal Onslow. I
thought I had sufficiently indicated, from his first appearance at the Heronry, that he was by chance in a position
below his station.

.   .   .   .

Finish it I certainly shall, because so much being done,
the idea would haunt me till completed; and, moreover, I
think the capabilities of the design such, that, if well executed, it would have certainly an original, perhaps a strik-

ing, appearance. And if, as I said, you will take the pains to give me the benefit of your opinion, I shall take it as a great favour. Meantime I shall look at the whole by the light you have already thrown out. The Corporal seems particularly to stick in your throat: but besides the instance I have given, where truth is stranger than any fiction, I could name others, where gentlemen have served in the ranks. What would you say to the *Honourable* Mr C—— being flogged at Chatham for some blackguardism he had committed, while serving in a line regiment in which he had enlisted?

Mr Blackwood's objections to the dashing scapegrace, who had enlisted and received promotion in the — Light Dragoons, must have been overruled, for Onslow figures as he was originally conceived. It may be remarked, by the way, that Lever paid Hamley the compliment of transferring him to his ' Davenport Dunn ' as Conway " the Crusher." Hamley bowed more submissively to minor protests. Living a garrison life, he would appear to have forgotten that ' Maga ' lay on the tables of manses and parsonages, and that the decorous classes were its most valued patrons. For in his next note is this paragraph :—

You shall not have to complain any more of " full-flavoured " passages. I remember one in the first part, in Bagot's interview with the Squire, which I thought at the time you might object to: at the same time it was characteristic, and gave reality to the scene. I hope you will not require much to be blotted out.

Nevertheless he possessed the susceptibilities without which neither novelist nor poet is likely to attain distinction.   He writes in another letter :

I shall be very glad to get proofs of the early Nos., and will carefully correct them; but I hope that the alterations you speak of will be as few as possible, as I have a great horror of tooth-drawing and amputations. However, many things will strike you as reader that may have escaped me as writer.

Thackeray may be quoted as a distinguished exception, but very few novelists, whether soldiers or civilians, have been capable of illustrating their own works. Hamley himself sketched the illustrations to the first edition of ‘ Lady Lee,’ and very deeply was he interested in having them satisfactorily rendered by the engraver. As a characteristic specimen of Hamley’s sketches in comical vein, we reproduce here the humours of “ Doddington Fair,” and give at the end of the chapter, “ Trying the Trotting Mare,” which formed the vignette on the title-page of the novel. This is one of several letters on the subject of the illustrations :—

Gibraltar, *9th Dec.* 1853.

My dear Blackwood,—The etching is extremely well copied in every part, except the principal one—the lady’s face. Besides the fault in the mouth you notice, and have requested him to alter, the line of the nostril goes too much upward to the eye, aiding the downward turn of the mouth

Doddington Fair.

in giving a disdainful look. The eyes are two blots, and should be made lighter. These alterations the engraver could easily make. An additional line outside Julius's right shin to make the leg thicker, and another ear to the cat, wouldn't cost him two minutes' work, and would be an improvement. All the rest is excellent, and so the engraver seems to think from the prominence he has given to his name, which would have been better placed at the bottom of the page. The two faces I feel most doubtful about his rendering are Orelia's in "the Restoration" and Kitty's when Bagot is holding her chin: both are mixed expressions, requiring much nicety to catch.

By that time, and, indeed, considerably earlier, the "Dear Sir" had passed into the "Dear Blackwood," and thenceforth the letters multiply in something like arithmetical progression, and the friends, indulging in much playful badinage, speak their minds with the utmost freedom. The care, the thought, and the correspondence bestowed on 'Lady Lee' were amply rewarded. The novel was warmly received: it has gone through five editions, and the writer had the satisfaction shortly before his death of seeing it renewing its youth in a cheaper and more popular form. The success it won was so well merited, that we must always regret that Hamley did not follow it up in a field in which he excelled. Often latterly, when the time hung wearily on his hands, he thought seriously of occupying himself with another novel. But with him, unfortunately, it was a case of *ce n'est que le premier pas*, and he stood hesitating over the trouble and drudgery of thinking out a satisfactory scheme. Had he followed Scott's great example, and dashed boldly *in medias res*, he would have fallen back into a pleasant pursuit, and novel - readers would have been great gainers. For all the critics, with the solitary exception of the 'Spectator,' were agreed that in ' Lady Lee ' there was wonderful freshness with a rare lightness of touch. Nothing can be more ludicrously dramatic than some of the scenes, such as the free fight in the streets of Doddington — which was Bodmin — or the mess dinner at " the Bush." Possibly Lady Lee herself and her dignified friend Orelia have some of the stiffness of lay figures, though there are life and nature enough in the third of his feminine triumvirate. But the soldiers, and especially the sporting soldiers, are hit off to the life, which is the more noteworthy that Hamley's habits had never taken him to Tattersall's, and that he had been quartered far away from Newmarket and the Shires. Bagot Lee is a masterpiece in his way, and yet the jovial old reprobate is so cleverly and pleasantly drawn that we cannot withhold a sneaking sympathy, when his sins have at last found him out and landed him in the depths of despair. Yet here again, as in the " Legend of Gibraltar," we see Hamley vindicating himself, when he asserts the dignity of his profession in the nobler military types. We doubt not that the novel was all the more appreciated by Blackwood for the buoyant vivacity and the perennial flow of fun by which it is distinguished. No man had more profound faith in the literary judgment of " the Editor " than the late Colonel Laurence Lockhart. But the humorous author of ' Doubles and Quits ' and ' Fair to See ' used always to say that he mistrusted " the Editor's " passion for light comedy. " He will laugh," Lockhart would declare, " till he forgets to criticise : but it is lamentable when jokes chance to miss their mark—and then the public don't care to be always grinning."

Hamley seems to have stuck very steadily to the desk in the intervals of duty when in garrison, nor did he indulge much in social frivolities. But he frequently took short leave—one spring he spent several weeks in the Sierras of Granada —and there is a characteristic description of a shooting expedition to Barbary, which came off in the Christmas week of 1853.

Gibraltar, 12th Jan.

My dear Blackwood,— . . . Our trip to Barbary was rather disastrous. In the first place, we were roused a morning or two after our arrival by a report that our cutter, which we had left snugly moored to the river's bank the night before, was in danger of being swept away by a flood, and rushing out half-naked we had the pleasure of seeing her borne down the current to the sea, where she sank. Luckily there were no stores on board except most of our shot. Then we had infamous weather and bad sport. Christmas day we spent in a tower belonging to the Bashaw, unable to move for the weather. Our stores were almost exhausted, for we had intended to be back by Christmas, and we had the prospect of remaining all night without fire, light, or anything to drink. Luckily somebody groping about discovered a candle-end, with the assistance of which we fished out a bottle of brandy, so we made a festive evening—rather dismal, I must say, but that is not unfrequently the case even with Christmas parties at home, with all appliances and means to boot, which we had not. To crown our misfortunes, we started in a trading vessel for Gibraltar, which first went aground and was afterwards becalmed, so that we spent three days and nights getting across (tho' the distance is little more than thirty miles), and had very little to eat, nothing to drink, and never took our clothes off the whole time. Letters which we found on our return wishing us " a merry Christmas " we could afford to laugh at then, being comfortably established in our quarters ; but such compliments at the proper time would have sounded like very cutting irony. I'm afraid there were very few merry Christmases this year in Gibraltar, for our supplies being cut off in great measure from Spain, the poorer classes are in great distress, painfully short both of fuel and food, and the troops have salt provisions four days in the week.

At Gibraltar he appears to have had few male friends and no intimates. It was eminently characteristic of him that, next to the children, who were irresistibly attracted to him, he took most readily to sympathetic women. He always delighted in feminine society, though his confidence was not given very readily. But it is evident from his letters that he unbosomed himself with more unreserve to ladies than to any man, with perhaps the exceptions of John Blackwood and Colonel Gleig. I am indebted to two of the good friends he made on the Rock for sketches of the unassuming and studious young captain. Miss Jones, now Mrs Harry Smith, knew him well, and afterwards they kept up a desultory correspondence. These are her rather abridged recollections :—

Captain Hamley was very thin and angular, and looked much taller than he was. He was a very reserved, quiet man, and though liked had few if any intimates. He went out into society a good deal, but always as a looker-on rather than taking part. He did not dance much, though he went to every ball, and he did not dance well. He came to the Rock with the reputation of being very clever, satirical, and given to drawing caricatures. I never saw but two—one of himself and one of me. He spent a great deal of his time in writing, and largely availed himself of the garrison library. He had at one time very pretty quarters high above the town, and took great pride in his garden. Most people stood in awe of him, owing to his silent ways and stiff manner, and from his taking but little part in things around him, and never taking the trouble to talk, except to a few. He was, however, much thought of for his talents, and acted as judge-advocate on more than one important court-martial. His constant companions in the town were his cats, and out of the town his dog Cañuelo (Spanish for cinnamon), a brave setter. He rode much, alone with his dog. He was a good horseman, fearless, but with a perfect understanding with his horse. He joined all the large riding-parties that were a feature in Gib. life in those days. He had a most tender heart behind his stiff manner, and many were the kind acts he did to the wives and children of his company.

Mrs Stopford, a daughter of Sir John Burgoyne, says very much the same, remarking that she always refused Hamley for round dances, as he danced them indifferently, and there was an awkward disparity in their heights. But when she sat out with him, as she was always delighted to do, he made himself extremely agreeable; and young as she was at the time, she saw how much there was in him. As for Mrs Smith's portraiture, it is Hamley himself—in course of evolution—as Gleig had sketched him at the College and in Canada, and as we knew him afterwards, even when he had mixed much in the world and had attained the highest ranks in his profession. And Mrs Smith relates one eminently characteristic incident, which would have made a capital subject for one of his own stories of Gibraltar.

One night there were strange noises on the heights, and mysterious lights were seen flitting about one of the upper batteries, which were left unsentinelled. The drums beat to arms, the garrison was alarmed, and a search expedition was sent out to scale the rock. It came upon a funeral. The faithful Cañuelo had died suddenly, and his mourning master with his servant were laying the departed to rest in a spot believed to be safe from disturbance.

TRYING THE TROTTING MARE.

CHAPTER IV.

THE CRIMEAN CAMPAIGN.

APPOINTED ADJUTANT TO SIR RICHARD DACRES—DEPARTURE FOR THE EAST—SCUTARI—LETTERS TO MISS JONES—AN ACCIDENT —VARNA—'THE CAMPAIGN OF SEBASTOPOL'—HAMLEY AT INKERMAN—IN THE TRENCHES—LITERARY MERITS OF THE 'CAMPAIGN'— DESCRIPTION OF THE ALMA — CRIMEAN SCENERY—LETTERS TO JOHN BLACKWOOD—ON THE EVE OF THE REDAN.

IN noticing the years that Hamley passed on the Rock, I have dwelt almost exclusively on the beginnings of his literary work, partly because evidently it greatly preoccupied him, and partly because his letters to his friend and publisher are chiefly concerned with the literary pursuits into which he had thrown himself with characteristic enthusiasm. But it would be doing him gross injustice to suppose that he was in any way neglectful of his professional duties. Literature only occupied his leisure : and throughout his life his indomitable determination of purpose

was directed to the attainment of military distinction. The best of his brilliant intellect was
given to subjects which were to serve as a preparation for the great work on which his reputation as a consummate master of strategy is
solidly established. There are many passages in
the letters in which he apologises for the delay
of promised contributions on account of the exigencies of military service. Then he will congratulate himself on the immediate prospect of
" ample leisure," and write more industriously than
before, in the excitement of exchanging one form
of activity for another. But there was no more
earnest soldier in the garrison, as assuredly there
was none more intelligent. He was to receive a
very flattering proof of the way in which his services had been regarded by his superiors, from the
man who was most capable of appreciating them.
For months the storm-warnings in the North had
become more threatening, and the Mediterranean
garrisons had been excited by anticipations of
stirring times and of an expedition to the East.
Hamley had more than once written, with the
natural impatience of a young and aspiring officer,
on the vacillating and dilatory policy of Lord
Aberdeen. Subsequently, in the exercise of
more deliberate judgment, he shows very clearly, in the first chapter of ' The War in the

Crimea,' that it was Russia and not England which had been drifting into the war. But whether the Czar or the English Premier was to accept the responsibility, in the beginning of 1854 war with the Russians was a foregone conclusion. Colonel Dacres, afterwards Sir Richard Dacres, was the Commandant of Artillery at Gibraltar. He had been informed that he was to command a division of artillery in the expeditionary force, and apparently he lost no time in offering the adjutancy to Hamley. The first notice of it is in a letter to Blackwood, dated 8th March :—

GIBRALTAR, 8th March.

MY DEAR BLACKWOOD,—This must be a short and hurried note, for I am in a great bustle at present. Two prospects present themselves to me. First, Colonel Dacres, who is to command a division of artillery in Turkey, wishes me to accompany him as Adjutant, and has written both officially and privately applying for me in the strongest terms. As he ought, according to all precedent, to appoint his own Adjutant, there would seem no doubt of my success but for a private hint that another man had been talked of at Woolwich, where nothing is done without a job; but we hope the other man is only meant to come in in case of Colonel Dacres not wishing to take an officer from here, which the *official* notification of his appointment authorised him to do.

To-day's mail brought me the chance of another adjutancy, at Woolwich. This I have accepted in case of not getting the other; but whether the end of the month will see me on my way to Constantinople or to Woolwich, it is impossible to foresee.   I hope the former.

There is no direct correspondence as to the appointment, but his niece, Miss Barbara Hamley, happens to remember a conversation when Sir Richard Dacres, then well stricken in years, recalled the circumstances with a significant detail.   What Sir Richard said was to the following effect: "I had been struck by your uncle's abilities, and at that time I sent for him.   I said, 'Hamley, I should like to take you with me to the Crimea, if you know French well.'   The answer was, 'If you will only take me, sir, I shall set to at once and learn.'"   Dacres was satisfied with the assurance: Hamley went to work next day, and his subsequent translations of the verses of Voltaire show how thoroughly he had inspired himself with the spirit of the language.

But it would seem to have been his destiny to find obstacles cropping up on each occasion when advancements or appointments were offered him, however conspicuously his qualifications might mark him out for some special post.   Now, his suspense was relieved in little more than a fortnight; and while actively occupied over the urgent business of kit and outfit, he is already changing front in his literary schemes, and shaping his strategy according to the change in his circumstances.

GIBRALTAR, *25th March* 1854.

MY DEAR BLACKWOOD, — To-day's mail decided my movements. I am to go to Turkey as Colonel Dacres' Adjutant. We have received no intelligence as to the day of our departure for the East; but as private letters say the Artillery were embarked on the 18th, we shall probably see them here before long. In the meantime I am busied with preparations.

Will it be asking too much if I beg you to strike a rough balance of the edition of 'Lady Lee,' supposing it to be not yet all sold? Horses, and equipments, and bills on leaving Gibraltar will demand more ready cash than I have, and if you could conveniently, during the month of April, put £100 or thereabout to my credit with Messrs Cox & Co., Craig's Court, I should take it as very kind. I am ashamed to talk of money matters to you, who have always been so liberal, and would not now do it on any account but that I think the sale of the 1000 copies you spoke of will already have secured me more than the sum I mention; and considering the exigency, you will, I know, excuse my saying anything on the subject.

I shall let you know of our movements in Turkey; and if I can write in an extended form on the subjects of interest which will present themselves, without overstepping the bounds of official reserve, you shall have some letters from the field and incidents of the campaign for 'Maga.' I had projected and commenced some papers, which were to have taken the form of a biography of an imaginary hero, with some discussions on art; but of course my present prospects put an end to all ideas requiring time and thought to develop them. I hope I shan't lose the thread of the design before I come back; but at any rate I shall get a fine supply of new ideas on active service, which will come in with good effect hereafter, so that, even in a literary point of view, I expect the campaign will be not without profit to me. On other accounts I have every reason to congratulate myself on the field which opens to me; and my position on the Staff will be more agreeable and advantageous than that of a regimental officer. I shall see service against enemies more creditable to contend with than Chinese or Caffres, and, in fact, think myself very lucky. The selection itself is flattering. My friends in England will, I fear, be much disappointed, for they expected me home immediately to take the Woolwich adjutancy; but that of course I did not allow to weigh with the appointment I have been so fortunate as to get.

Before he embarks on the transport which was to take him to the East, I may go back to a playful letter which explains his views as to matrimony—views which, perhaps unfortunately for him, he was never to realise. At any rate, his immediate prospects confirmed him in his previous resolutions; though he had reason to envy his friend's matrimonial happiness, when he had made the acquaintance of the lady, to whom some of the most lively of his more confidential letters were to be addressed.

GIBRALTAR, 1st February.

MY DEAR BLACKWOOD,—First let me congratulate you warmly on the event you apprised me of in your last. By the time this reaches you, you will have made some progress in your honeymoon, and will have realised the first bloom of the happiness you promised yourself. That it may go on increasing steadily in permanent qualities after the novelty is worn off is my sincere wish and expectation. Thanks for the hope that I may some time join the ranks of you married men. I hope so too; but it is scarcely desirable while I am knocking about the world with no more prospect of settling than the Wandering Jew. Bardolph, you know, was of opinion that "a soldier is better accommodated than with a wife," and I am inclined to agree with him. At the same time I have observed that old bachelors in the army are generally miserable and not very respectable beings: this you will easily understand, as the experience of the last week or two will have caused you to look on bachelors with great compassion.

There are some amusing notes to Miss Jones from Scutari and Varna. He had one special reason for writing to her, for he had bought her favourite riding-horse, and Jim was one of his chargers through the campaign. Jim had been sent to bid farewell to his mistress, the evening before he was shipped for the East. The first of the letters is from Coolali Barracks, on the Asiatic shore of the Bosphorus. Hamley sends by way of souvenir a flower he had gathered from the grave of Achilles on the plains of Ilium, and then he passes from classical sentiment to the commonplace in a lively description of his quarters:—

We are in a huge cavalry barrack that the Turks have vacated to make room for us, leaving it perfectly bare and empty, except of fleas and cats, both of which swarm in every room. Of course the society of the latter visitors quite compensates *me* for the annoyance of the others.

There is a Turkish commandant who is to have his head cut off, without judge or jury, in case the building is burnt; so whenever we want anything, we set fire to some straw in the passage, and the old gentleman, rushing in, followed by his pipe-bearer, in a dreadful fright, immediately complies with all our demands. But the straw is all burned now, so we must devise some other means of persuasion. I am writing on a table made out of a door which I pulled down in the passage, which is the only article of furniture except a chair I brought with me, and a hammock hung in the corner, which has broken down three nights successively. But I have spent little time in my room, for the Colonel and myself have been fully occupied with looking after the force here—about 700 men and the same number of horses: splendid animals they are, and deserve all our care.

It is lamentable to turn to the pages of his Crimean Narrative, where the tender - hearted writer deplores the fate of those " splendid animals," as they died by inches of starvation and overwork in lingering agonies.

He was unexpectedly detained in the Coolali barracks by a mishap which he describes in an affectionate letter to an old relative at Bodmin. The accident was an awkward one, and might have had more serious consequences, had it not been for the sufferer's robust constitution. As it was, it troubled him in the Crimea from time to time, although never actually incapacitating him :—

I was enjoying capital health, when on the 8th of this month [June] I met with a most unfortunate accident. The division had gone out for a march, and as I was riding past some infantry in a narrow lane, General Adams' horse struck out and kicked me on the shin, breaking the bone. I was lifted off my horse and laid down by the roadside for the surgeons to examine my leg, and the Prince [the Duke of Cambridge] sent his servant to the camp for a party of the Guards to carry me home, which they did on a garden-door. My leg was set, and is now doing uncommonly well. I have never had much pain nor any fever, and my health and appetite are as good as before. The worst of it is that the army is on the move for Varna, so that I shall be left almost alone here and miss the opening of the campaign. In six weeks more I hope to be with them again, and many people think that there will be no fighting before that. Sir De Lacy Evans told me he did not think we should see the Russians these two months. I hope not, as then I shall not lose any of it, and shall not regret my accident so much.

Sir De Lacy Evans' prognostications were more than realised, and the invalid's convalescence was not delayed by any worry as to missing opportunities of distinction. In little more than the six weeks he was out of the hands of the surgeons, and had gone on to Varna to join his chief. For a letter from Varna Bay of the 26th August describes the fearful outbreak of cholera which had fallen like a Black Death on the camp and the fleet, and which he has dramatically described in his volumes on the war :—

Whatever befalls, it is better that the fine army should fall in the field than be destroyed by sickness and climate. I don't observe any great enthusiasm among the troops; but that will come, no doubt, with the first sight of the enemy.

That he kept his own health so well must be attributed in great measure to the cheerfulness with which he accepted inevitable hardships. A letter from the lines before Sebastopol, written in mid-winter, gives a humorous account of the subterraneous luxury in which the writer was living :—

The Colonel and myself are now underground in what you would consider a very inferior kind of cellar, but which we look upon as a very superior residence. It is made by digging a deep trench and roofing it with poles and branches. It has a chimney, which is a comfort when it does not smoke, and a nuisance when it does. This we prefer to living in tents, especially as tents are liable to be blown away,—an event which happened at daybreak on the morning of the 14th, in the great hurricane, when in every camp might be seen a multitude of wretches sitting up in bed half-naked, holding their fluttering bed-clothes, while their effects were borne away on the tempest towards Sebastopol. This cannot happen to us now: the only thing to apprehend is, that as our roof is nearly on a level with the ground, some runaway horse or drunken soldier may blunder through it on to our table or beds.

We get on pretty well, though the Colonel frets a good deal after his wife, and clean shirts, and cream in his coffee. I have an uncommonly nice cat, and it is a great addition to our circle.

It was fortunate for the ardent reader that, in the fulness of occupation, he was comparatively indifferent to books. Literature of any kind was even more hard to come by than the delicacies which were sometimes within reach of a well-filled purse. He talks of *fêting* his birthday and the arrival of his friend Bent with turbot, turkey, and champagne, and he goes on :—

Mr Wright, the senior chaplain, of whom I see a good deal (owing probably to my serious turn and reverential demeanour), has a great number of books which have been sent to the army from home; but on looking at the backs of them, I suspect some old ladies and gentlemen have been weeding their libraries, and getting a reputation for benevolence at small expense.

Finally, though in defiance of chronology, another letter to Miss Jones may be quoted, written from Leith Fort after his return, showing the trouble and cost he incurred for his furry favourites, and the staunchness of his friendship for his " poor dependants." It proves, too, how firmly he could attach women to him, for Lady Dacres did him a troublesome piece of service, which few men so self-contained would

have dreamed of asking, unless in the assurance
that the trouble would really be a pleasure :—

My cat Topsy has had some marvellous adventures.
She was left in Lady Dacres' charge, and was put in a box
with a small family to be conveyed on board ship at Balaklava. On the way the cart was upset, the box broke, the
family dispersed, and Topsy in a panic ran up a drain,
and could not be got out before the ship sailed. Lady
D. came home inconsolable. The subject was still too
painful to both of us to be dwelt on, when I saw her and
Sir Richard during my late visit to town. Judge of my
surprise at receiving a note from her, to say that Topsy
and all her family were safe, and just about to arrive in
England.

But for a time, with such exceptions as these,
the personal narrative is merged in the letters
regularly despatched from the Crimea, which appeared in ten successive numbers of ' Blackwood's
Magazine,' and were republished as ' The Campaign of Sebastopol.' Notwithstanding that he
wrote more deliberately in ' The War in the
Crimea ' in 1890, it is to be regretted that the
earlier volume has long been out of print. Even
now one can read with all the excitement of a
romance what Kinglake has styled that soldier-
like narrative. Nothing can be more impressive or more picturesquely dramatic than those
rapid pictures dashed off on the spot, of the ter-
rors of a war and the horrors of a slow siege. No

detail escaped him which can give life and vivid colour to the story: the general situation with its shifting scenes is seized and indicated with rare lucidity; and the predictions he hazarded as to the course of events are wonderful examples of scientific prescience. When he wrote on the subject again after the lapse of a generation, he could declare that he had nothing to correct or explain away. He was one of the first of the modern war correspondents—and certainly one of the most remarkable. There is no need for drawing contrasts or comparisons. But it is to be remembered that writers of unsurpassed brilliancy like Russell were specially sent out to the Crimea for the purpose, and the letters to their journals were their sole business. Hamley, in the brief and precarious intervals of active duty, dashed off his flying despatches under the most unfavourable and depressing conditions. They were penned after long days in the saddle, under breezy canvas or in dripping mud-huts by the light of a flickering candle, when fatigue was getting the better of him. These letters were carefully preserved and bound in a volume by Mr Blackwood. They are closely written on either side of sheets of letter-paper. Yet there is scarcely an erasure and seldom an alteration. It is the same in his Diaries of the Egyptian Campaign, and nothing demonstrates more conclusively that he had the genius of authorship. The thoughts shaped themselves in his brain, and the words flowed from his pen with scarcely sensible effort. In that respect he was the antithesis of his friend Kinglake. Though their styles were so widely different, each valued the remarkable qualities of the other. Kinglake, though he had some slight contempt for any workmanship at all hasty or superficial, would often speak with hearty admiration of Hamley's intuitive perception, and the instinctive precision with which he arrived at satisfactory results; as Hamley, in 'The War in the Crimea,' bears honourable testimony to the indefatigable industry of Kinglake, and the care with which he arranged his information, so as to make battle details intelligible as they had never been before, even to those who had fought or commanded in the actions. Kinglake would polish and revise, till proof-readers and compositors were driven to the verge of lunacy: Hamley needed barely to revise at all, and we read his work, like the Waverley Novels, almost as originally written.

It is perhaps not surprising that the author of the "Legend of Gibraltar" and of 'Lady Lee' should describe picturesquely, even when writing under difficulties. But we are specially struck in the third of the letters by the acute intelligence

with which the future author of 'The Operations
of War' indicates the novel features of the campaign on which the Allies were about to enter.
He explains how the old conditions of warfare had
been modified by the presence of steam. It was
possible now to advance with a floating base of
operations which accompanied the march, and
to dispense with the drain of guards for long-
drawn lines of communication, liable to be cut at
any point by the enemy. Of course some appre-
ciable risk is inseparable from the most carefully
planned operations, and had a reverse in the field
been followed by such a hurricane as sank the
vessels in Balaklava harbour, the transports
would have been scattered, embarkation would
have been impossible, and a mishap might have
resulted in disaster. So, when things were approaching a crisis, he discusses and criticises the
various designs attributed to the chiefs of the respective armies, which, as the adjutant of Dacres,
he had exceptional opportunities of learning. He
sets forth the arguments urged, as was supposed,
by Niel and the French Emperor, by Pélissier and
Lord Raglan : he gives them impartial consideration, and, so far as may be, he is confirmed by
actual history, by Kinglake and Todleben, in the
opinions expressed, on the spur of the moment,
with modest confidence. Latterly he had lost

faith in Lord Raglan. There can be no indiscretion now in quoting a passage from a private letter, dated 28th May 1855, when he may have been suffering from liver, and was apparently out of temper. At least he speaks as disrespectfully of the policy of the Premier as of the strategy of the Commander-in-Chief :—

My Lord R. goes on in his old careless fashion. He is a most courteous old gentleman, with an extraordinary faculty of letting the most important affairs slip off his mind like water off a duck's back, without any uneasiness. I hope fortune will befriend him and us in our future enterprises, for he is past mending as a General.

As to Lord Palmerston, he remarks :—

I am disappointed in old Palmerston. He seems to meet every difficulty with a joke, replying like Jack Falstaff "with a fool-born jest," as if Grimaldi had taken Kemble's place in a tragedy.

Generally, however, he made the most generous allowance for the difficulties of the Ministers, and of the high military and naval officers who were responsible for the conduct of them, whatever may have been his own views as to the right method of conducting the war or of the wisdom or unwisdom of particular operations. Writing deliberately for the public, he never loses his head amidst the hardships and horrors of the campaign. He may incidentally blame

Lord Raglan for being influenced by Sir Edmund Lyons in his unfortunate preference of Balaklava to Kamiesch, when the French general had offered him freedom to choose. But the choice once made, Ministers, generals, and soldiers were alike the victims of circumstances, or at least of that sudden change of plan which had transferred the war from the banks of the Danube to the Tauric Chersonese. Everything, as he repeatedly points out, turned upon a sufficiency of forage. He does not even blame Commissary-General Filder, who was given up as a scapegoat, when the Commissary's forethought was subsequently impeached by the M'Neill Commission. Filder had been making his arrangements to supply an army upon the Danube. The decision to make the descent on the Crimea took him and every one else by surprise. A stream of transports began to set towards Balaklava, and great quantities of supplies, most of them practically unavailable, were either landed or in the holds. For after the beginning of the rains there were seven miles of mud between the harbour and the front. The horses were dying of starvation or disease; transport was being brought almost to a standstill; and consequently the troops had to do terribly severe duty on short rations, and wellnigh in rags. As the numbers dwindled rapidly from day to day with disease and exposure, the strain on the survivors became more exhausting. Yet in a letter written in the depth of the winter, Hamley maintains that even had all the horrors been foreseen, that winter campaign would still have been wise. For though Sebastopol lay open to the north, the losses of the Russians in their efforts to relieve it were immensely out of proportion to those of the Allies. English prisoners sent into the interior had reported that at one time the road from Sebastopol to Simpheropol was literally strewn with corpses. Hamley, on the strength of authentic returns quoted by Lord Lansdowne in the House of Lords, estimates the total Russian losses at 240,000 men.

In a summer siege we must have fallen into Niel's plans and invested the place, with unknown masses of the enemy pressing on the rear of the besiegers. In fact, the conclusion is that the game of war is always a calculation of chances, and at best a choice of difficulties. In this case, though the soldiers at one time were dying like rotten sheep, and although Hamley has described with vividly painful realism the scenes in the overcrowded hospitals at Scutari to which sufferers were looking forward as an earthly paradise, he holds, nevertheless, that our strategy was amply justified by the results. Essentially a soldier, and never sparing either himself or his subordinates, as will be seen when he was commanding a Division in Egypt, he had no notion of making war with rose-water. So he quotes with approbation the speech of Marshal Vaillant on the respective qualities of Canrobert and Pélissier as commanders, as he sympathetically appreciated Pélissier's sturdy independence and iron resolution :—

Pélissier will lose 14,000 men for a great result at once, while Canrobert would lose the same number by driblets, without obtaining any advantage.

As he sums up in 'The War in the Crimea' :—

The army once before Sebastopol and dependent on a military system so deficient in much that is essential, no arrangement or forethought within the scope of human intelligence could have averted the disasters which followed.

Apparently a few years before his death, for the notes are on paper stamped with the address of his rooms in Ryder Street, he drew out some memoranda which may have been intended as material for a memoir. They are only too brief, but at least they give a list of the engagements at which he was present, and make exceptional mention of his remarkable escape at Inkerman, when, as he says, he had given himself up for lost :—

At the beginning of the Crimean war, Colonel (now General Sir Richard) Dacres, being appointed to the command of a division of artillery in the field army, selected me to accompany him as his adjutant. In that capacity I served (in the 1st division of the army, commanded by the Duke of Cambridge) at the landing in the Crimea, in the action on the Bulganac, at the battle of the Alma, where my horse was wounded under me by a cannon-shot; at the action of Mackenzie's Farm, at the battle of Balaklava, and at the battle of Inkerman, where my horse was first shot by a musket-ball and then killed by a cannon-shot passing through him and throwing him on me—a sergeant who extricated me had his leg carried off in the act—and a second cannon-shot passed through my horse on the ground. It was at this time that, passing on foot along what Mr Kinglake in his History calls " the Kitspur," a ridge thrown out from our position towards the enemy, I found myself suddenly almost enclosed by a large Russian force, before which our men, whose ammunition was exhausted, were retreating out of the Sandbag Battery. Being very lame from a recent accident, I almost gave myself up for lost; and after a vain attempt, in which the late Lord Balgonie of the Guards joined me, to rally some of our people, I succeeded with great difficulty in getting past the enemy and regaining our position. Subsequently I caught in succession two masterless French horses, both of which were wounded in the course of the battle. In the brevet given for this engagement, I was promoted to the rank of Major.

The commanding officer of the artillery of the army, Colonel Strangways, having been killed in the battle,

Colonel Dacres succeeded him, and I became his first aide-de-camp. In that capacity I continued to serve throughout the campaign, being present in the actions in the trenches and at the French battle of the Tchernaya, where I rode with the Sardinian cavalry.

Neither in the memoranda nor in 'The Campaign of Sebastopol' does he mention — and it is characteristic of his modesty — the part he played in the battle of Inkerman. Fortunately his friend Kinglake, in gathering up the incidents of the protracted struggle, gives him his due meed of praise. For when he brought up the guns which formed the half of Paynter's battery, he showed his tactical skill by acting promptly on his own initiative, and bringing them to bear with telling effect :—

Captain Hamley had come up with three guns, and he now so placed them in battery on the eastern slope of Mount Head, that, whilst commanding a great sweep towards the front, their left was well covered from the fire of the enemy's artillery by the crown of the hill. When our soldiery had so far drawn off as to leave a clear front for the gunners, it appeared that the troops which had fought against Adams were more or less hanging back, for none, or scarce any of them, as yet could be seen moving up towards Mount Head. Therefore bending his mind for the time to a column 600 yards off on the farther side of the Quarry, Captain Hamley plied it with round-shot, and presently saw the force break, then turn to its left, and drop hurriedly down into the shelter of the Ravine; but after a while, troops supposed to be part of the same force came climbing up on the right bank of the Ravine, and at length also some of the men who had combated Adams began to appear on the slopes. They moved cautiously, and hung in the brushwood, undertaking to skirmish a little, but attempting no decisive advance. Upon such of the enemy's people as were near enough to be worthy of fire Hamley opened with "case," and they were quickly repressed.

Preceded, as it was, by the withdrawal of our troops from the Kitspur, this happy use of three guns placed the contest for a moment on exactly that kind of footing which was desired by men basing their tactics on the strength of the Inkerman ground. With the means of extending their batteries to the Fore Ridge after the manner just shown them by Hamley, and some 4000 infantry either guarding already or else close approaching their heights, our people had resources enough for the defence of their natural stronghold in front of the Isthmus; and, if only they had resisted the lure of the Sandbag Battery—now loved more than ever, because in the enemy's hands—they must have been henceforth secure— not, of course, against the chances of war, but—against the necessity of having to fight under desperate conditions.

Except as regards the brief and successful operation thus conducted with three pieces of cannon by Captain Hamley, the commanders of all the three batteries which had been newly brought up found berths for their guns on Home Ridge, and there kept them in action alongside of the other artillery.

Necessarily the soldier who was perpetually under fire had many other narrow escapes, which are not recorded in his letters; and, indeed, it is a striking illustration of the chances of war that he was never seriously wounded.

On one occasion he was attending Sir Richard Dacres on an official visit of inspection to the trenches. The sergeant who guided them took a wrong turning in the dark, when, as they were retracing their steps, a shell exploded in the gallery they ought to have followed. The gallery collapsed, and had it not been for the sergeant's mistake the party would assuredly have been buried in the *débris*. No writer ever gave a more vivid idea of the dangers and difficulties of driving parallels towards a fortress—of the excitement of men plying their tools in the dark, who know that they may be mining over the matches in counter-mines, or piercing the thin partition which separated them from their listening enemies. Yet even these subterraneous scenes, where death came to the labourers in the most appalling shapes, he enlivens with a certain grim drollery. There is a good story of a gallant British general of Engineers who had gone to examine the Russian works from the nearest French parallel. As he peeped over the gabions and sandbags, all went tolerably pleasantly for a time. Then a concentration of Russian bullets made things more lively. The Briton heard the Frenchmen chuckling, and began to suspect something. Looking up, he saw a bottle on the parapet behind. The French had been in the habit of enlivening the monotony of trench-work by setting up empty bottles to draw the Russian fire, and now the marksmen in the rifle - pits were responding to the usual challenge.

Hamley himself had reminiscences of amusing interludes, which recalled the rollicking Peninsular experiences of Charles Lever's Hibernian heroes, of Old Monsoon and the capture of the King of Spain's sherry; as when a flying expedition of light cavalry and mounted gunners made a casual raid on the cellars of Prince Woronzoff. The Prince's celebrated Crimean champagne had become the prize of the war: each man had ballasted his holsters with a couple of long-necked flasks, and the expeditionary force, as it withdrew at a trot in the moonlight, might have been followed up by the fire of exploding corks and a trail bestrewed with empty bottles.

Before passing from 'The Campaign of Sebastopol,' it may be worth while to call further attention to it, as evincing the writer's remarkable literary skill. Indeed, had Hamley been less versatile, he would certainly have left a deeper and more lasting mark in lighter literary work than that of the professional strategist. Apart altogether from its value as a sketch-history of the war, from the picturesquely dramatic point of view 'The Campaign' is admirable. No trifle escapes the author which can assist the reader's intelligence, and as the panorama of the siege rapidly unrolls itself, we see each of the shifting scenes enacted. No scene is more impressive than that in the tragic prologue to the piece, in the gloom of the plague-stricken camp when the cholera had broken out at Varna. The man who, seeking relief from depressing thoughts, saunters forth for a stroll in the twilight, sees silent groups in all directions, digging shallow graves within musket - shot of the tents. On the land, at least, the living could bury their dead out of sight. But where the vessels were moored in Balchick Bay, the corpses too hurriedly committed to the deep would come up again in a ghastly resurrection, and float and decompose beneath the gangways. There is the welcome relief when the ships have their sailing orders. Then when the shores of the Crimea have been sighted, there are the nocturnal attempts at disembarkation in overloaded craft and stormy weather through the heavy surf. Had the Russians been prepared to meet the descent in force, it can hardly be doubted the attempts must have been a disastrous failure :—

At night the rain came down in torrents, and the troops

on the beach were drenched. Bad as their situation was, I envied it. At eight in the evening I had left the transport with another officer in a man-of-war's boat, which, assisted by two others, towed astern a large raft, formed of two clumsy boats boarded over, on which were two guns, with their detachments of artillerymen, and some horses—two of my own among them. The swell from the sea was now considerable, and made the towing of the raft a work of great labour. As we approached the shore, a horse swam past us, snorting, and surrounded by phosphorescent light as he plashed rapidly by. He had gone overboard from a raft which had upset in attempting to land. The surf was dashing very heavily on the sand, though it was too dark to see it. Fires made of broken boats and rafts were lit along the beach, and a voice hailed us authoritatively to put back and not attempt to land, or we should go to pieces. Unwillingly the weary oarsmen turned from the shore. The swell was increasing every moment, and the raft getting more and more unmanageable. Sometimes it seemed to pull us back, sometimes it made a plunge forward, and even struck our stern, while the rain poured down with extraordinary violence. It was a long time before we reached the nearest ships, which were tossing on the swell, and not easily to be approached. The first we hailed had already a horse-boat alongside, with Lord Raglan's horses, and needed assistance, and two or three others which we passed were unable to help us. By this time the raft was fast filling with water, and the men on it were much alarmed; and our progress was so slow that we took at least ten minutes to pull from the stern to the stem of the Agamemnon. At length a rope was thrown us from a transport near, whose bows were rising on the swell like a rearing horse; and, getting the artillerymen who were on board her out of bed, we hoisted in our horses and guns; but the gun-carriages, too heavy for our small number of hands, were lashed down to the raft, which was allowed to tow astern of the ship, and which presently sank till the water was up to the axles, when the Agamemnon sent a party and hoisted them on board, and the raft shortly after went to pieces. A horse, which had been swimming about for two hours, was also got safely on board. It was a grey, said afterwards to have been given by Omer Pasha to Lord Raglan.

After the victory of the Alma, when the jubilation was tempered by regrets for fallen comrades, follows the description of a field of battle. We see the dead lying in swathes as they had fallen, cut down by the cannon-shot or mutilated by the shells :—

Where the struggle was hottest on the part of the French, our allies left a stone inscribed "Victoire de l'Alma," with the date. The English left no monument on their fatal hill; but it needs none. The inhabitants will return to the valley, the burnt village will be rebuilt, the wasted vineyards replanted, and tillage will efface the traces of the conflict; but tradition will for centuries continue to point, with no doubtful finger, to the spot where the British infantry, thinned by a storm of cannon-shot, drove the battalions of the Czar, with terrible slaughter, from one of the strongest positions in Europe.

The advance over the Katcha and the Balbek tells the sad story of a peaceful population suddenly surprised by the unfamiliar miseries of a hostile occupation. At that time, after the long peace, those incidents for readers in England had the painful sensation of novelty. But certainly no war correspondent except Hamley would have dwelt sympathetically on the troubles of the domestic favourites. He admired the cats who clung with "feline tenacity" to the forsaken hearths, calmly suckling their kittens in the sunshine, and indifferent, so long as mice were plentiful, whether the village was held by Russians or English. Amid his graver preoccupations, he stopped to pick up one abandoned orphan, and carried a small black kitten on his holsters, feeding it with biscuits; but during one of his temporary absences the little creature gave its benefactor the slip. So nothing can be more pathetic than the picture of the sufferings of the starved and overtasked horses when the siege was dragging out its weary length :—

Perhaps the most painful feature in the dreary scene was the number of dead and dying horses scattered, not only round the cavalry and artillery camps, but along the various roads which traversed the position. Some had fallen and died from fatigue, some perished from cold, some from starvation. Once down, a horse seldom rose again. After a few faint attempts he lay still, except for a feeble nibbling at the bare ground; then he would fall over on his side, and, stretching out his legs, would so end his career, leaving a smooth space in the mud where his head and neck had moved slowly to and fro, or where his hind-leg had scratched convulsively before he died. Sometimes an ownerless horse, probably too lame and unserviceable to be worth inquiring after, would linger about the neighbourhood of an encampment. Day after day he would be there, waiting patiently, wondering perhaps why no hay nor corn came, getting thinner and thinner—nobody could relieve him without robbing his own horse, on whose strength and condition his own efficiency depended—until, after wandering to and fro over the barren spot, if no friendly hand could be found to send a bullet through his head, he would drop and die there a lingering death. It was impossible to traverse the position in any direction without seeing many carcasses—some swollen and bloated, some mere skeletons. Here and there would be seen the curious spectacle of a horse's bones covered only with his loose, collapsed hide, all the flesh, muscles, and even ribs, having disappeared—which would be explained presently, when, on passing the next carcass, a gorged dog would put his head out from the hollow arch of the ribs, and, after looking lazily at the comer, return to his horrible feast. These spectacles never ceased to be painful, though custom diminished their effect; for, a few months before, the sight of a dying horse would have haunted me for days.

These sights, and others that are described, on the skeleton-strewn plateau, remind us of Alp's walk round the walls of beleaguered Corinth, for Hamley in his faithful and literal descriptions always showed no little of the imagination of the poet. There is a terribly realistic chapter on the disposal of the invalids, and the lamentable state of the ambulance transports and the Scutari hospitals. We are told how those of the sick who were in the worst extremity were sent from the front to the ships, tied on to broken-down cavalry horses, which could ill be spared from the provision and ammunition trains :—

Few sights can be imagined more melancholy than that of a troop of cadaverous, feeble, suffering beings, wrapped up in their blankets, swaying to and fro in the saddle, or crouching on the necks of the horses which bore them slowly towards the longed-for haven, where they might hope for some remission of their misery.

That haven was in the distant hospitals at Scutari; and as to what they were, before Miss Nightingale with her corps of ministering angels revolutionised the overcrowded wards and the kitchens, it will be best shown by an extract from 'The War in the Crimea.' It would be difficult in a few concise sentences to make us more sympathetically realise the fate of those who had thought themselves most fortunate :—

Scutari, the longed-for haven, was for weeks the very climax and headquarters of suffering — crammed with misery, overflowing with despair. In those large chambers and long corridors lay thousands of the bravest and most miserable of men. Standing at the end of any of the galleries, one looked along a deep perspective, a long diminishing vista of woe. . . . The tenant of each bed saw the pain reflected in the face of his comrade opposite; fronting each was another victim of war or cold, starvation or pestilence. Or frequently the sick must read in the face before him, not the progress of fever or the leaden weight of exhaustion, but the tokens of the final rest to which he was himself hastening. With each round of the sun nearly a hundred gallant soldiers raved or languished out their lives.

The writer's irrepressible sense of humour will break out in these pathetically graphic letters; but besides that, there are rifts in the gloom and occasional gleams of brightness. Hamley, in his single-minded attention to his immediate purpose, might have shown himself indifferent to scenery when shooting quails in Ontario with his friend Bent; but the horrors around Sebastopol gave infinitely enhanced charm to the rare enjoyment of the beauties of nature. He describes with the enthusiasm of an artist, when defining the Allied positions, the rosy-coloured cliffs which buttress the domed roofs and the minarets of the Monastery of St George; he paints in lurid colours a stormy sunset seen on the eve of an impending assault, when the fast-repeated flashes from the opposing batteries were mingling with the luminous glare of the blazing tints on the horizon. Superstition might well have taken the menacing vision for an omen of the carnage that was to come off on the morrow. But we may turn for relief to the more cheerful recollection of a spring ride along the verdant downs to the eastward of Balaklava. Doubtless, as he says, the long suffering and deadly monotony on the dreary heights of Sebastopol enhanced the beauties of the view. A smiling May, within the last week or two, had been scattering flowers broadcast over the landscape :—

Below us lay the valley of Baidar, stretching from the edge of the sea-cliffs on our right to the distant mountain-range, where it wound round out of sight. Like the fabled vale of Avilion, it was "deep-bowered, happy, fair with orchard-lawns"; flowery meadows, sprinkled with trees and groves, reminded me, in their fertility and expanse, of the Vega of Granada, as seen from the mountains behind the city. Two red-roofed villages, embowered in trees, stood at some distance apart in the midst of the valley, but no inhabitants, nor cattle, nor any kind of moving thing, gave life to the scene,—it was beautiful as a dream, but silent as a chart. No corn had been sown for this year's harvest; the only tokens of agriculture were some farm-waggons discernible through the glass at a distant point of the valley. The villages were not only deserted, but, as some visitors had ascertained a day or two before, quite denuded of all tokens of domestic life.

As that brilliant narrative of the war not only appeared in 'Blackwood,' but was subsequently republished, I have only endeavoured to indicate its most impressive features. But extracts from two of the rare private letters may perhaps be appropriately introduced by way of supplement. The first of them is dated from Eupatoria, on the 13th September 1854 :—

My DEAR BLACKWOOD,—The combined forces left Balchick for the Crimea on Thursday the 7th, and to-day at 3 P.M. we have anchored off Eupatoria, which either has or of course will surrender forthwith—and no great conquest either—without firing a shot.

We have had capital weather across the Black Sea. . . . The coast is low and level, and easily swept by the ships' batteries, so that there is no doubt of our effecting our disembarkation without loss ; but I don't think 'twill be commenced this evening, as 'twill be dark in less than two hours, and a small part of the army, if landed, would be liable to be overwhelmed by the Russians in a night attack, supposing them to have a force on the march to oppose the landing. We were visible yesterday from Sebastopol, and perhaps forces from there or about there may be now on the way to contest the disembarkation. I sincerely hope they will do so, as on a flat beach like this we should meet them at an immense advantage, backed by the heavy guns of the ships, which could throw a far greater weight of shot than anything they could bring by land to oppose us in the way of artillery. Late though it is in the season, I see no difficulties in the way of an advance on the fortress : whether we shall be able to take that by assault is another matter, but I hope and think we shall.

Our right, I should suppose, would rest throughout the march on the sea, thus securing that flank of our communications with the ships, on which we rely for provisions and stores, and their support in case of a battle. I should suppose there would be at least one great action in the open field before we invest the town, which is thirty miles from here, and in the field 'twould be heresy to doubt of success. The English three-deckers and part of the rest of the squadron—French, Turkish, and Eng-

lish—sailed past us last night to keep the Russian fleet
in Sebastopol from molesting our landing. . . . We are
weak in cavalry, having only, I believe, brought four
light regiments and the French none. To-morrow we
shall be on Russian soil, and shall commence what must
be, I should think, a most remarkable and bustling campaign. If I get safely through it, you shall have fullest
particulars for 'Maga' at the earliest moment.

The next passage proves that at that time
neither Ministers at home nor the best-informed
men in the expeditionary force had contemplated
the possibility of protracted operations :—

One way or another, it must terminate soon, for the
weather is already cold, and winter will be upon us in
earnest with the end of October. But to beat the Russians
in the field,—to invest and storm Sebastopol in spite of
the forces doubtless assembled around it, and to destroy
the fleet in the harbour there,—'twill be a glorious business
if well carried out, and if any troops can do it ours can.

His opinion of the quality of the troops was
more than justified; yet almost exactly a year
afterwards we come on another note written from
the camp before Sebastopol. It is dated September 7, and most men in the circumstances
would have been preoccupied with their own
affairs, and probably deferred their correspondence. Hamley begins by quietly and pleasantly
congratulating his friend on the birth of a
daughter, and goes on :—

My dear Blackwood,— . . . This is the eve of the assault: at noon to-morrow the French go at the Malakoff, and as soon as their success is evident we attack the Redan, and the French on the left enter the works before the town. The task of the French is much easier now than on the 18th June, as they are only a few yards from the ditch either of the Malakoff or the bastions before the town; but we are pretty much where we then were, owing to the stony nature of the soil. But this time we shall have a fierce cannonade from daybreak to shut up the Russian guns, and as we shall not advance till the French are in the Malakoff, I have great hopes that to-morrow will see us in possession of the south side, or at any rate of some of the most formidable works. My place will be with General Dacres in the trenches. I wish the garrison would quietly slip off in the night and save the butchery. I believe the poor devils have been suffering a good deal lately from want of provisions, and this tremendous cannonade must have made the town a great shambles. I don't quite see our way when we have got the south side, as their formidable batteries on the north side will render the occupation of it unpleasant, but hope that the Czar will no longer think it worth while to prolong the contest here, and either make peace like a wise man or leave the Crimea.

CHAPTER V.

IN SCOTLAND.

RETURN FROM CRIMEA—CRIMEAN HONOURS—LEITH FORT—FIRST MEETING WITH JOHN BLACKWOOD—DE QUINCEY—'THE RECENT CONFESSIONS OF AN OPIUM-EATER'—REVIEW OF 'BOTHWELL'—LITERARY ACQUAINTANCES—THE STURGISES —EDITING 'TALES FROM BLACKWOOD.'

HAMLEY came back from the Crimea in January 1856 with a high reputation. Except when detached on a brief mission to Constantinople, he had never been absent for a day from active duty, and he had been present in every engagement, even in that of the Tchernaya, where he rode as an amateur with the Sardinian cavalry. As he has told us in the memorandum already quoted, after Inkerman he got the brevet majority, and the Duke of Cambridge, who commanded his division, made honourable mention of his services in a special letter to Lord Raglan.

Various honours were awarded him on the conclusion of the war. He received the brevet of Lieut.-Colonel, the Crimean medal with four clasps, the Sardinian and Turkish war medals, and the orders (Companion) of the Legion of Honour and the Medjidie. General Dacres, who was his staunch friend as well as his immediate chief, pressed his claims repeatedly for a Companionship of the Bath, which would appear to have been unreasonably and inexplicably delayed, but which was eventually bestowed for those Crimean services. On the whole, he had come off well. He might deem himself happy in having escaped death or mutilation, and his constitution had stoutly resisted the incessant strain of hardships and privations. Probably that was owing to habitual temperance, and to the admirable digestion which could accommodate itself to rough and scanty fare. Yet he carried away one unpleasant souvenir of the campaigning in the sleeplessness which often troubled him in after years.

It might have been supposed that in the Crimea his rare hours of leisure would have been amply occupied by the war-letters which regularly appeared in 'Blackwood.' Nevertheless he contrived to find time to contribute two other articles. One of these came in naturally enough.

It was a review of the 'Poetry of the War,' a little volume which he had welcomed in his hut on the plateau. But the other was on a subject altogether apart: it was a revival of the old literary recollections which have been alluded to, and a tribute to the memory of one of his boyish idols. John Wilson had died, and the death suggested to his ardent admirer a delightful essay on "North and the Noctes." Had the Professor been spared for a few months longer, the two men who had so much in common in their love of literature and their passion for sports would have met. For by a somewhat singular and very fortunate Providence, the battery Hamley commanded on his return was ordered to Leith Fort. Then the editor and contributor for the first time came together, and the regard which had been rapidly strengthening through their correspondence quickly ripened into closely affectionate intimacy. Their subsequent letters increased in number, as has been said, year after year, and Blackwood could have given no more conclusive proof of the value he attached to Hamley's friendship and judgments. For few of his contributors had reason to complain of his troubling them with any superfluity of communications. Meantime, however, nothing passed between them in the way of correspondence but frequent invitations to dinner, and even these speedily ceased. Blackwood had more than his share of the old Scottish hospitality, and Hamley knew he was sure of a welcome at all times and seasons in the house in Randolph Crescent. Then Professor Aytoun, who lived hard by, was wont to drop in on a similar footing ; and De Quincey was also an occasional guest, although at that time the intimacy with that strange, eccentric, and capricious genius had cooled down to a certain extent. De Quincey was then residing in a suburban village to the south of Edinburgh ; but though his family affairs were under affectionately careful management, he was by no means free from the pecuniary troubles which Burton has humorously described in 'The Book-Hunter.' Nor did he ever hesitate to seek from his friends the assistance in any shape which he would readily have given had their respective situations been reversed. William Blackwood, the present head of the publishing House, remembers his first introduction as a boy to De Quincey. He chanced to be at his lessons in the bathroom of his uncle's house, Randolph Crescent, which was fitted up as a small sitting-room, when one of the servants introduced an odd-looking little gentleman, who was far too excited to stand on ceremony. With unlooked-for agility, he sprang into the empty bath, begging that the cover might be drawn over him. It was De Quincey with the bailiffs at his heels, and he lay *perdu* in the bath till the quest was over. It seems odd that Aytoun did not make use of the incident in one of his humorous 'Tales from Blackwood,' which used to delight the editor. Perhaps the author of " The Glenmutchkin Railway " and the creator of the impecunious Dunshunner shrank from violating the sanctities of that hospitable roof-tree. But the humorous side of the Opium - Eater must have struck Hamley forcibly and at once, for it suggested the first of his contributions from Leith Fort. It took shape and form in the inimitable parody which appeared as " The Recent Confessions of an Opium-Eater." The " Confessions," with their pleasantly incisive satire, should be read in connection with the thoughtful and serious essays on the philosophy of Carlyle, with his mannerisms and affectations. For Hamley could wield with versatile address the various weapons of wit, ridicule, or mockery, whether in kindly play or in sober earnest. Here the local colouring is exquisitely apposite, for the scene is laid in a garret in those crowded rookeries of the Old Town which always impressed Hamley as powerfully as Scott. A practitioner in the out-of-doors medical school of Burke and Hare

stumbles across the dreamy philosopher, and in-
vites him in all good-fellowship to come in and
partake of refreshments. The generous host, under
the guise of port, fills a flowing bumper of lauda-
num; his seasoned visitor, draining it, awakens to
the suspicion that he has fallen into a trap, but
finds his faculties wonderfully brightened. There
is an exchange of glasses and liquors while the
entertainer has stepped aside, and it is the acolyte
of the anatomical theatre who drops beneath the
table. A line before he threw off the sparkling
story shows the thought and care Hamley
bestowed on his lightest work, rapidly as it
was written :—

Thanks for the loan of the 'Opium-Eater' and 'The
Selections, Grave and Gay,' with a view of catching the
old gent's style and executing the little *jeu d'esprit* we
planned over the poldowdies. That little note you sent
me of his was quite characteristic, and I shall preserve it.

When he had left Leith for Woolwich in the
spring of 1859, the letters became frequent.
There are warm thanks for all the kindnesses
he had received, and many pleasant allusions
to the friends he had made in Scotland. There
was no one of them whom he liked and admired
more than Aytoun, and many are the references,
more or less intelligible, to lively evenings with

the Professor.   There is a note written afterwards, accompanying a review of 'Bothwell':—

Sunday Night.

MY DEAR BLACKWOOD,—Here is a short review of
'Bothwell,' *all* of which I have written for publication.
The fun is of a sort that Aytoun himself will smile at,
and it will probably attract readers more than grave
eulogy.

The Cavalier himself asked me to notice the perpetual
fixing of the Editorship on him.

It appears that the staff in Blackwood's printing-office had presented him with an address on
the occasion of his leaving.   He writes in
March :—

I regret that I omitted to mention how obliged I felt
for the assistance which those charged with the printing
and correction of my manuscript have always rendered
me. Despatched as the sheets generally were at the last
moment when it was possible they could arrive in time
to be printed, they were nevertheless given to the public
with scarcely the displacement of a comma.

The praise was undoubtedly well deserved, for
the compositors and readers in that office can
do nearly as much for the most crabbed hiero-
glyphics.   But Hamley's handwriting, under all
circumstances, was so remarkably clear that even
novices could scarcely have taken serious liberties
with it.

If he had been given a choice of stations after Leith, he could not have pitched on more agreeable quarters than Woolwich, and afterwards Dover. In the one he was almost resident in London ; at the other, within easy reach of it. The writer of the narrative from before Sebastopol would for many reasons have been welcomed by distinguished men of letters. But introductions from his friend Blackwood landed him at once among the old connections of the house, and in the inner circle of contributors. One of his first visits was to Delane, " when the great man gave me far more time than I could reasonably have expected." In fact, Delane took a strong fancy to him, and their relations never ceased to be cordial. It is the more remarkable that he never became a contributor to the ' Times,' although latterly his letters on military and political matters had the honour of leaded type. Some years afterwards Mowbray Morris, who then managed the journal, was so delighted with the humour of " Our Poor Relations," that he eagerly inquired as to the anonymous writer, saying that he would be worth any money to the paper. Morris and Hamley knew each other well; but the inquiry led to nothing in the way of business.

One of his first visits in London was to Samuel Warren, who received him " with such cordiality as I had no right to anticipate," and having given him an exceedingly agreeable dinner, insisted on his coming back to dine again next day. 'Ten Thousand a-Year,' although some of the sentiments are satirised by Thackeray in the Snob Papers, as it is one of the longest, was one of the most brilliant novels that ever were written. It makes law proceedings light, and party politics entertaining. Hamley laughs genially in his confidential letters at the humorous traits in the character of the clever novelist, whom he always styles the Q.C. Once he mentions that he has been obliged to decline an invitation because he has engaged himself for two or three days to Sir Edward Bulwer Lytton. That was the first of many visits to Knebworth, and Sir Edward used to drop in frequently on Hamley when he had established himself in chambers in the Albany. Then there is a lively note, telling how he made the acquaintance of Katie Stewart (Mrs Oliphant). Mrs Oliphant said that Hamley had been charged with 'Katie Stewart,' as she had been taxed with 'Lady Lee's Widowhood'; whereupon he politely remarks that the exchange of *rôles* would have been all to his advantage. There are numerous allusions to pleasant dinners with Thackeray, to whom Hamley was indebted for his fortunate introduction to the Sturgis

family, in which he always found a second home,
and where he was at once adopted as one of the
circle.   There is mention in a letter to Blackwood
of an exceptionally successful dinner given at
Greenwich by Hamley, at which the great novelist was in his most genial mood, and the life and
soul of a lively company.   Indeed guests and host
were so loath to part, that the symposium was
prolonged into the summer morning.   The acquaintance ripened into mutual esteem, and
Thackeray's surviving daughter has a grateful
remembrance of Hamley coming as the first
visitor, with simple and heartfelt condolences,
upon her father's sudden and lamented death.
Hamley had the most cordial admiration for
Thackeray's genius, although it never appears
to have influenced his own style, or rather the
forms of his humour, like some of the best and
earlier of the novels of Dickens.   In fact, as Scott
had been the passion of his boyhood, so Dickens
was the delight of his maturer years.   He would
dramatically repeat whole scenes and pages without misplacing a word ; and when he threw himself into the parts and characters with enthusiasm over the dinner-table, you might fancy that
Bob Sawyer or Micawber had come to make one
of the party.   Highly respectable members of
the Athenæum might be named whom Hamley

insisted on identifying with the portraits by the master, and the comical illustrations of Cruikshank or Phiz. With Dickens likewise he was on terms approaching intimacy, and references to their social intercourse will be found in some recollections of Hamley by his friend Mr Locker Lampson, which have been kindly placed at my disposal.

About this time are the first allusions to the Sturgises, through whom he had the privilege of making the acquaintance of some of the most distinguished Americans, for Mr Sturgis had been the American partner in Barings' house. In Mount Felix, "their beautiful place on the Thames near Walton," he was carefully nursed through an anxious illness; and the elder son of his earlier friend was left one of his executors.

Mr Julian Sturgis writes that there is little to say of the days at Mount Felix, simply because they passed pleasantly and uneventfully. But what he does say gives a most engaging picture of the genially-minded soldier who was so steadfast in his friendships, and who was never so thoroughly happy himself as when making the happiness of animals or children :—

His visits there were times of rest. He came often, and was amusing and amused ; and I remember him once saying, with a moment's regret, that he was always very idle there. His friendship for my parents was very true and strong. In his last letter to me he reminded me that my father had said to him that their friendship had endured for thirty years without a shadow. He was introduced to them when he had just come back from the Crimea by Thackeray, who spoke of his rare union of conspicuous gallantry and cleverness. Many years later he introduced my father to Dickens, to their mutual satisfaction, giving them a dinner at his club. The friends he made at Mount Felix, and whom he would not be likely to meet elsewhere, were eminent Americans—Mr Motley, Mr Charles Francis Adams, Mr W. Story, and others. One may suspect that his friendship for Mr Motley and Mr Story, whom he knew best, was a distinct gain to him, modifying a certain prejudice against Americans, more common in his youth than now.

He always came at Christmas, and entered with zeal into the business (it was characteristic of him to treat it with more apparent gravity than the serious business of his life) of amusing the children. One Christmas he appeared as Father Christmas himself, disposer of gifts; another, he invented the character of Mincepie, "grandson" of Father Christmas, who was represented by the youngest son of the house. Mincepie delivered a long rhymed address which Hamley had taught him.

For all the children, as for all the dogs and cats of the place, he had names of his own, so that new acquaintances waiting for words of wisdom from him or comments on some great battle lately fought, would be surprised by very grave inquiries for the " Good Excellent" or the " Hodiglio." In the book which I made from my father's papers there is the story which Hamley often told of Thackeray's wiping his eyes at the sight of Howard's delight at his first Christmas-tree.

Writing playfully, as he always wrote to Mrs John Blackwood, in July 1857, he says :—

At Monckton Milnes' I made the acquaintance of Lady Morgan, a very singular and highly diverting old person, who used formerly to get frightfully abused and called shockingly unparliamentary names in the Magazine, but she don't seem to bear malice.

That he fancied the elderly " wild Irish girl " might have owed him a grudge, shows how thoroughly he had identified himself with the Magazine. Next day he entertained a party at Greenwich in honour of Mr Stephens, author of ' The Book of the Farm,' who, owing probably to some association with turnips, is always styled the Swede, and who " conscientiously tasted and compared twenty-two different sorts of British fishes." There was an illustrious novelist in " a state of great hilarity, who affectionately took leave of me eight times on parting."

But notwithstanding social distractions and military duty, he found time not only for literary work, but for something like literary drudgery. He had undertaken to select and edit the stories which formed the first series of the ' Tales from Blackwood,' and he resolutely bestowed infinite thought and trouble on the selection. He had mapped out the whole programme of the twelve numbers, and carefully weighed the rival attractions of an embarrassment of claims. Had he been bred a publisher he could not have discussed more practically considerations of length and the wisdom of variety. He goes on : " Some good papers which are of doubtful tone, like ' Charles Edward,' it will be better to postpone till the *prestige* of the series is assured." And on reference to the arrangement of the tales in the volumes, we see that his advice was almost implicitly followed. He received substantial proof of his labours being appreciated. He writes on March 26 a characteristic letter of thanks, which indicates that as yet he had no superfluity of riches :—

March 26, 1859.

MY DEAR BLACKWOOD,—Your too generous estimate of my small services reached me yesterday as I was starting for my cottage, and on getting there I found myself destitute of writing materials, or I should have acknowledged your kindness at once, as I much desired to do. To say truth, the supply was very welcome, as I don't know how I should else have come down with the ready on starting as a householder. I sincerely hope that a magnificent success for the speculation will quite justify your liberality, for which, as for all your warm and constant friendliness, I feel more your debtor than I can well say.

The first number is very prepossessing outside and in. The only additions I can think of as desirable are very slight, and such as I am no better judge of than the multitude of your readers—such as Aytoun's name after the " Glenmutchkin " on the outside cover; and a fly-leaf

with the name of the next tale interposed between the
stories, which would have the effect of the white tablecloth with the empty and clean plates between the courses,
keeping the fish from treading too closely on the heels of
the joint, and the latter from being too familiar with the
pastry. I drank success to the series and its projectors at
dinner to-day, which meal I took at the club, having returned to town after my lecture to make some few last
purchases before finally settling to rustic life. I feel
quite like a country gentleman already, and shall hardly
be surprised to find myself Justice of the Peace committing poachers to prison and lecturing rural Lotharios on
the heinous offence of getting trustful young women in
the family-way. I am rather pleased with the cheerful
though somewhat quaint aspect of my abode, but shall
withhold my self-congratulations till they are authorised
by the seal of Mrs Blackwood's approbation, as I trust
they shortly will be, for I shall consider all my arrangements incomplete till you and she have come under the
roof.

I will revise a set of lectures forthwith as for publication, and send them to you. I rounded off the first set
to-day, and they have been very well received.

Puck's constancy to my memory in recognising my portrait after an interval which to her immature ideas must
seem longer than the time Penelope waited for Ulysses,
is honourable to the sex and touching to me.

There is another letter on the 10th April,
which proves that the series had been eminently
successful from the start; and indeed it has made
the most sparkling of the tales as familiar as the
most popular novels which have been passed

through the Magazine. Yet the strategist was alive to the advantages of advertising, and in subsequent notes he reverts to the propriety of pushing the series in all directions, and enlisting the sympathies of an interested press. Possibly the opening paragraph in the following communication may refer to some other piece of work :—

10th April 1859.

MY DEAR BLACKWOOD,—I am most agreeably surprised at the result of the division of plunder, and not the least element of my satisfaction is to think that our past enterprises are not altogether unprofitable to you. I hope we may yet make many more successful forays with still more brilliant results.

I return Mr Hardman's[1] capital letter, and shall do my best when next in his neighbourhood to become acquainted with so eminently agreeable an old gentleman as I expect to find him. It will be a good move to put what he says of Coleridge at the head, as you propose. I shall be very curious to see the sonnet. Do you think the English public are sufficiently aware of the publication of the series? Scarcely any advertisements of it have caught my eye. I should like to make a few corrections of my tales,—what do you think of a few prefatory remarks?

From the quantity of reading necessary for exactness, some of it not very easily attainable, and the difficulty of writing and reading coherently while unsettled just before I came here, I find myself still going on in a hand-to-mouth sort of way with my lectures. I can't endure the

---

[1] Author of "The Student of Salamanca," and some admirable Spanish stories—all published in the Magazine.

idea of offering anything to my class which is crude or flimsy, and therefore they are not evolved so rapidly as I could wish. But as soon as I have got a fair breathing-space I will revise a set of lectures exactly as I should wish them published, which will be a little different in parts from what I address to my class, and send them to you, unless you are here in the meantime with Mrs Blackwood, an event I am looking forward to with the greatest pleasure. I think you will find me pretty snug for a wretched outcast of a bachelor—in fact, I'm afraid Mrs Blackwood will look on it as a piece of impertinence for one in my forlorn condition to presume to get on so smoothly. . . .

CHAPTER VI.

PROFESSOR AT THE STAFF COLLEGE.

LIFE AT SANDHURST — HAMLEY'S LECTURES — THE DELANYS—
WORK FOR 'MAGA'—STUDIES OF CARLYLE.

THE last letters are explained by their being
dated from Sandhurst. The early spring of 1859
saw the commencement of Hamley's connection
with the Staff College. It had been established
as a separate institution in the previous year. It
had taken the place of the Senior Department of
the Royal Military College, which had been latterly carried on under the superintendence of Sir
Patrick MacDougall, and it was to be conducted
in the new building with similar objects—namely,
to qualify exceptionally capable officers for Staff
duties. The change was effected on the recommendations of a commission, sent to examine and
report on similar institutions on the Continent.
The commissioners were Colonel Yolland, R.E.,
Colonel Smythe, R.A., and the Rev. Mr Luke,

who was subsequently Dean of Durham. They visited the École Polytechnique of Paris and the military colleges of Berlin and Vienna,—and Mr Luke, after parting from his colleagues, paid a visit to Turin. The report spoke so strongly of English deficiencies, and its recommendations were so sweeping, that the Secretary at War hesitated to accept it; but its recommendations, in the end, were substantially adopted. At the suggestion of friends, Hamley, with some hesitation, applied for the Professorship of Military History. Although he had made his mark with intelligent soldiers by the 'Letters on the Crimean Campaign,' he had not as yet turned his particular attention to the systematic study of scientific soldiering. And we fancy only the few who were in the secret knew that some remarkable military articles in 'Blackwood' were from Hamley's pen—though the review of De Bazancourt's 'Narrative of the Campaign' had been so highly esteemed in the War Department at Berlin that it had been promptly translated into German.

Strangely enough, Military History had been only then introduced as a subject of study. In fact, the College seems to have hitherto occupied itself with anything rather than the science of war. General Napier, who was commandant when Hamley received the appointment, writes with regard to that :—

Military History being a subject to which the attention of officers had not generally been much directed at that time, including, as it does, a knowledge of strategy and tactics, it was necessary to select an officer of talent and of more than ordinary acquaintance with the subject, able also to point out to the students the objects of the various campaigns on which he was delivering the lectures, as well as the manner in which these operations were conducted, showing when and why they were successful, and where and why they failed.

Such an officer was found in Lieut.-Colonel Hamley, who was accordingly appointed Professor, and who filled the post for six years with the greatest advantage to the officers, as will be allowed by all who studied under him, and who listened to his lectures with rapt attention and interest. How well he was qualified for such an appointment will be evident to every one who reads his work on 'The Operations of War,' which is still the text-book for the College, and is acknowledged to be the best work upon the subject in the English language.

I am sorry I have no record of the various campaigns upon which Hamley lectured, but they embraced all the most important campaigns of Napoleon, Wellington, and others. He visited many of the fields in person. I myself, when commandant of the College, had the advantage of going over with him the fields of Napoleon's campaigns of 1814, one of the most remarkable campaigns of that great soldier.

No appointment could have suited him better. At Sandhurst he was again established within pleasant reach of London, and of the society on which he began to be more dependent. His attention was not only directed but compelled to those professional studies in which he always took the keenest pleasure, and in which he must have had the consciousness of superior insight, although assuredly he did not foresee the methodical development his genius was destined to give them. Moreover, although essentially a London man, and a man of society who loved the sharp contact of flint and steel in the flashes of sparkling conversation, he was inclined, as he says in one of his letters, to be the dilettante country gentleman. The surroundings of Sandhurst are singularly charming. He was never happier or more content than among the sights and sounds of the country. He was in sympathy with the whole animal creation; he watched their habits and studied their idiosyncrasies. But he was no mawkish sentimentalist, and he delighted in shooting, fishing, and hunting. He shot well, and, with the characteristic determination which defied bad weather and ill-luck, had always been a skilful and successful fisherman : with the rod he beguiled many an hour that might otherwise have been very weary, in the wilds of Asia Minor and the Highlands of Albania and Macedonia. As he sketched and painted besides, his out-of-doors resources were endless. And with his many-sided character he made himself thoroughly happy in the company of his country neighbours. He hated fools, he had no tolerance for presumption, and he could never endure self-complacent bores. But no one so intellectually gifted had so little of intellectual pride; and as for personal vanity, or the arrogance of official position, he had nothing of either. Like Dr Johnson, he could talk runts on occasion, and indeed he had found a sympathetic affinity in the jovial author of 'The Book of the Farm.' He was always at home with each sporting and hospitable squire, in the farm, the stable, the cookery, the cellar; and his interest in all these matters was far from affected, for there was no mistaking his uncompromising frankness. With the bookish parson he was still more in his element, and all the more if, like Love Peacock's Dr Opimian, the parson prided himself on his port, so as to show that he had Christian charity for the foibles of the flesh. It is not to be doubted that he was the scholarly Captain Fane who beat up the quarters of the Rev. Josiah in 'Lady Lee's Widowhood,' nor that he had been as a subaltern the original of the light-hearted Bruce who entertains the venerable bookworm at mess.

As more than enough has been said by way of preliminary, Hamley may be left for a time to go on very much with his own story. His life as the Sandhurst lecturer was uneventful. He did not help to make history, as at Tel-el-Kebir; nor was he laying out the lines of future political geography, as when he was tracing the new frontiers of the shrunken Turkish empire. But the letters written in sequence to the same trusted friend are really autobiographical. Their charm is that they are the easy letters of a modern school, without the elaboration and polish of a Walpole or De Sévigné. Their style is the man: they are dashed off without reserve, without arrangement, and it might almost be said without thought, for the thoughts had been matured and came intuitively. In their way they are all the brighter reading on that account, and they show the writer in a clearer and pleasanter light than any amount of formal biography. Those who called Hamley cold and cynical will see reason to change their opinion. He did not wear his heart on his sleeve, yet he laid it very open to his intimates. Some of his free remarks on his contemporaries must in prudence be suppressed, lest they should ruffle unnecessarily the susceptibilities of survivors. But the satire is genial and never ill-natured. And what can be more humorously delightful than the picture of celibate domestic bliss when the student and "cynic" is at home with his dogs, his cats, his owl, and his squirrel? He had the magnetic touch that makes all the animated creation akin; and had he chanced to have been born in a different sphere, he might have rivalled Van Amburgh in the education of lions, or made a competency by winning the affections of performing dogs. With it all, he might have taken Strafford's "Thorough" for his motto.

Two things must strike one especially in his letters—the zeal he brought to his professional work, and the infinite pains and labour he bestowed even on anonymous and fugitive articles in a periodical. Unfortunately, the Blackwood correspondence for six months is missing. So the first allusion to the new appointment is incidental. "The opening lecture went off very well, and was extremely well received by the authorities. The class was interested and attentive."

The next note, which must have been written afterwards, has no date. It contains the first notice of the three Essays on Carlyle, to which he devoted immense attention — the matter is roughly drafted in his commonplace-book—and of which he perhaps thought more highly than of anything he ever did, 'The Operations of

War' scarcely excepted. He had been reading much and writing rapidly, as was his custom. Blackwood had been urging him to send an article for a particular number. "I had no time to read over the article, which you will see was finished in great haste, as the matter rather grew on me, and there were several screws in it which would have been the better for tightening, so that I quite tremble to see it in print."

SANDHURST, 22d *April* 1859.

When are you and Mrs Blackwood coming to see me? I wish you were here to enjoy the beautiful weather, which I am basking in under my own fig-tree. I have been putting flower-seeds in the ground,—an operation which has been watched with great interest by all the numerous small birds in the neighbourhood, who will probably promise themselves petunias and sweet-peas for breakfast to-morrow.

I am surrounded by rural sights and sounds: a strong band of nightingales performs every night, a cuckoo is hard at work just now, and I have just been obliged to leave this to help in driving out a sow with a young family that had made an inroad into the kitchen-garden. So domestic have I become that I haven't been in London these three weeks. . . .

Mr and Mrs Delany will take the greatest care of you and Mrs Blackwood when you appear.

Mr and Mrs Delany were a worthy couple who superintended the Professor's bachelor establishment, and there are many friendly references to them in subsequent letters.   Hamley was a kind and most indulgent master, and he had always the happy art of attaching his servants.   He reaped his reward, as we shall see, in his last lingering illness.   The Delanys would seem to have deserved his regard.   Mr Delany got on in the world : he speculated in house property to advantage ; and ultimately he became the. proprietor of his master's cottage *ornée.*

20th May 1859.

Cayley has been very sultry this past week.   The grass field in front has been cut, and added greatly to the general fragrance.   I took out the squirrel to show my governor last Sunday, and he bolted in among the laurels, and while I was in pursuit of a frog, which I mistook for him in the shade of that retreat, he made off and was lost for some hours, creating general consternation—Mr Delany distracted, Mrs Delany in tears, Rebecca a small Niobe, Rarey wringing his hands, and Tabitha apathetic : finally he descended from the summit of an oak on Mr Delany's outstretched arm, and restored calm to the household.

By that time the Blackwoods had paid their promised visit, and made acquaintance with his family in fur and feathers, and with his servants. "Rarey wringing his hands" was a figure of speech, for he and Tabitha were a pair of favourite cats whose flirtations were to lead to a family scandal.

In the next note we may accept as a pleasant fancy sketch his representation of himself as the voluptuous lotus-eater. We are reminded of Scott protesting to Morritt that he was the most indolent of mortals, when he was driving half-a-dozen horses abreast, and bewildering the critics by his phenomenal velocity. His remarks as to reviewing 'The Dutch Republic' are among the innumerable proofs of the scrupulous conscientiousness he brought to his undertakings. Most men with the half of his reading and capacity would have dashed off the article incidentally in the ordinary course of business.

My place is still most pleasant—in fact, pleasanter than before, as the flowers are luxuriant; the may in the hedges is replaced by honeysuckle. I don't do much else than bask and enjoy myself.

We will think over the Carlyle parody when the weather changes. At present I am a kind of clean and unverminous lazzarone, and consider basking to be the correct way for an intellectual and responsible being to spend his time.

Sturgis asked me the other day if I thought you would review his friend Motley's 'Dutch Republic.' Probably the subject would suit well. I haven't read the book myself, and don't know how I should like it; besides, I don't know that I am at all a judge of historical subjects: but if you haven't any one at hand to do it, I'll read it if you wish, and see what's to be done. However, you have many much better up to that special work, and it is not exactly what I would choose.

There is nothing of " log-rolling " in the following letter, for the relations of Hamley with the Parson of Eversley were by no means intimate.   Probably " the atrocities " have reference to the philanthropic Radicalism, or Christian Socialism, of 'Alton Locke' :—

SANDHURST, 16th July 1859.

MY DEAR BLACKWOOD,—I hope you have so far forgotten the atrocities of Kingsley as to publish the enclosed: besides, it is not all eulogistic, and rather an essay on classic poetry than an encomium on Andromeda; and if there is too much praise, you can with all the better grace serve him out on another occasion without seeming prejudiced or bloodthirsty.

I am extremely obliged to you for your kind efforts about the terrier, but don't give yourself too much trouble about it.

I have read a vol. of Motley, and think with you 'tis most readable and entertaining. I don't know if I have much faculty in appreciating history (very necessary to a reviewer), but will see if the ideas for a paper on the subject suggest themselves.

I'm afraid I'm hardly sufficiently up in contemporary politics for the parody you speak of. At any rate, as my class returns on Monday after their brief holiday, I shall be too much on lecturing thoughts intent to have a minute to bestow on more amusing topics just now.

The Editor was propitiated, and the article pleased :—

22d July.

I'm very glad you like the paper. . . . It needed no sacrifice of honesty to put in a compliment to Tennyson, of whom I am a warm admirer; and if a notice of his poems should at any time be desirable for the Magazine, I would gladly undertake one which his best friends would consider laudatory.

For the conductors of 'Maga' had long before reconsidered the hasty judgment which North in the 'Noctes' had put in the mouth of the Ettrick Shepherd, that Alfred would always remain a promising lad. As for Hamley, in his later relations with the Laureate he had many opportunities of expressing his heartfelt admiration; nor did he deem it the least of his honours that Tennyson should have addressed him in the Prologue to "The Charge of the Heavy Brigade."

MY DEAR BLACKWOOD,—I haven't been so lucky as to hit upon any idea likely to work into a light paper for the present month. This I regret very much, as I should have liked above all things to respond to your wish; but I fancy that I can no more speak "upon compulsion" than Jack Falstaff could, and must be content to take the ideas on their own terms when they choose to visit me. . . .

I doubt if Motley's book is at all in my line, as I have never been quite able to appreciate the peculiar merits of an historian. Still I like the book very much, and on closer perusal may discover food for a paper; but if you have anybody ready and able to do it handsomely, I should advise you to set him to work.

The terrier is in high favour at Monte Felice. He seems of a reserved and shy disposition, and is always cutting away to the farm across the road; so at meal-times he is tied to the Commander-in-Chief's chair, and in the intervals is picketed on the lawn. He is delightfully ugly.

Mrs Sturgis requests you will send by an early opportunity his third pair of legs. He is called "Bruce," greatly to my disgust,—intended as a compliment to me, and at the same time an allusion to his Scottish extraction. I propose to change it to "Centipede," as more appropriate to his figure.

The "Commander-in-Chief" was Mrs Sturgis, for it was always a sign of love or of affectionate regard when Hamley called any one "out of their name."

15th September 1859.

MY DEAR BLACKWOOD,—Bulwer is a trump of the first magnitude. He wrote to my brother last week, offering him the Collectorship of Customs in the new colony of British Columbia, which he accepted.

14th October.

I have been reading Carlyle—not without disgust. He is an incorrigibly bad boy, and I think we shall have to birch him for his present offence.

18th October.

The Commander-in-Chief and Sturgis came down on Saturday evening to pass Sunday with me. We drove to hear your friend Kingsley preach: the Commander-in-Chief has a certain mysterious admiration for him.

I thought he did not particularly distinguish himself. We had a pleasant little dinner-party last evening, at which I heartily wish you and Mrs Blackwood could have assisted. This morning they departed, to the grief of the household—Delany's dog, cats, squirrels, and owl, not to mention mine.

The children — four-footed and two-footed — were brought in after dinner, and excited great interest. One of them, the owl, is much more like a cherub than most people's children, consisting almost entirely of head and wings. Rarey is an immense cat, and has taken advantage of his intimacy with Tabitha to seduce her.

SANDHURST, 12th November 1859.

MY DEAR BLACKWOOD,—You were right in ascribing my neglect in not immediately answering your letter to an intention to send a paper. I had begun one on Carlyle, but I find that to do it justice, and treat him as a writer of so much notice should be treated if any effect is to be produced, I must read the previously existing biographies of Frederick, and also some of Carlyle's former productions, which I have seen nothing of this long while, in order to show that by acquaintance with his writings and mode of thought I am qualified to do him justice. I can't get the books here, and must therefore go up to live in town for a few days and read them; and to do this so hurriedly as would be necessary for next number, would be probably to produce a paper which I should regret to find afterwards might have been much better. . . .

You will say (with an appeal perhaps to the infernal powers), Why didn't I read the necessary books before? But up to a few days ago I worked night and morning finishing my half-year's course of lectures, reading students' notes, and preparing questions—all against the approaching examination. For every lecture I write I have to read twenty *résumés* or parodies of it, and read them carefully too, as the credit affixed to each tells on the writer's place in the class. . . .

As to a story, I wish I could say I had one so far hatched, or even warm in the egg, as to be likely to flap its wings when Bulwer has done crowing in January.

It would be in vain to promise that; but this I will promise, to look up materials and try for a good subject immediately. These once arranged, I shouldn't be long doing something.

I wish I was fairly into it: the conception is much more bother to me than the gestation or accouchement.

The confession about the story is unfortunately significant. If he had gone forward as resolutely with works of the imagination as he did when he was riding to hounds, or when leading the 2d Division at Tel-el-Kebir, he would have added alike to his income and reputation, and the novel-reading world would have been so much the richer. But, as was said before, he had never patience to woo the fancies, which seldom come unsought, and still more rarely conform themselves to the exigencies of attractive fiction, without the systematic and laborious thought which is irritating or repugnant to the romantic temperament.

CHAPTER VII.

LIFE AT THE STAFF COLLEGE.

OFFERED A SEAT IN PARLIAMENT—HUNTING—THE AMERICAN CIVIL WAR—'WELLINGTON'S CAMPAIGNS'—"THE FIGHT FOR THE BELT"—CRITICISMS ON GEORGE ELIOT AND ON MRS OLIPHANT—W. W. STORY—DIFFERENCES WITH BLACKWOOD ABOUT KINGLAKE'S 'CRIMEA'—DEATH OF CHARLES HAMLEY—CAPTAIN CHARLES CHESNEY—APPOINTED TO THE COUNCIL OF MILITARY EDUCATION.

SOON afterwards he was engrossed by graver preoccupations. It appears that already he was entertaining the ambition of a parliamentary career; and had he broken himself to public life in 1860, there can be no doubt that his success at Westminster would have been greater. Overtures were made to him, through his brother, from the electors of his native town. The sitting member for Bodmin intended to retire, and for the next election had promised Hamley his support. He was tempted, and hesitated; but after weighing the matter deliberately, he came

to the conclusion that it would be wiser to decline. The chances at the time were bad or
doubtful; and, moreover, he was engaged in
preparations for his lectures and in mastering
the professional subjects which he had hitherto
studied desultorily. Consequently he decided to
wait for the more convenient season which was
not to come till time hung more heavily on his
hands and he was seeking some fresh outlet for
his superabundant energy.

That energy would always find vent in one way
or another. In February there is the first mention of his hunting, and very characteristic it is.
He had made the acquaintance of the Mileses
of Bristol, through his friend Lady MacDougall,
a daughter of the family, and had gone on a visit
to their beautiful place near Clifton. No one
enjoyed more heartily the luxuries of country
life, with fair sport and congenial company, and
in that house he was thoroughly at home: he
found "splendid scenery, fine pictures, and a
very pretty notion of comfort and hospitality."
"One object in going was to hunt with the Duke
of Beaufort's hounds. I took Laurel, who went
over the stone walls as if he had been used to
them all his life, though I don't know that he
ever saw one before, except that which bounds
my front garden." He was a heavy - weight;

he had a soldier-like seat, but he was a singularly bold rider. Weight or no weight, he would do his best to be well to the front; and his courage would have been rash, and almost reckless, had he not been in the habit of considering his horses.

About midsummer the Professor of Military History began to occupy himself over the American civil war. The playful passages in his familiar letters are interesting, as expressing, in free and unconventional fashion, the opinions deliberately expressed in his lectures. Many of the chapters in 'The Operations of War,' which led to correspondence with the most distinguished American generals, show how carefully he had looked into the matter; and it is but fair to remark, that afterwards he bestowed high praise on the subsequent strategy of the Northern leaders. For in the beginning science was on the side of the South. And there was nothing he despised and detested more than the bounce and bluster of civilian journalists seeking to explain away mistakes and mishaps after a premature chorus of jubilant crowing :—

The Manasses business certainly was the greatest joke in the world. Taken with the swagger beforehand, there is nothing in farce equal to it. I hope the Cavalier [Aytoun] will indite a ballad on the subject. The Confederates seem to be aware that they might possibly, if they were to attack a position, find no better enemies than the Federals. In fact, with such troops, the odds are immensely·in favour of the side which awaits the attack.

Grave as were the issues involved, and although the losses on either side were already appalling, he hesitated to treat the subject seriously. On 12th December he answers Blackwood's suggestion of an article :—

It appears to me that the calm judicial style is altogether unsuitable to the discussion of American affairs. If their proceedings—civil, military, and popular—met the derision they deserve, they might come to a more correct estimate of their own position ; and when they saw they were making themselves ridiculous, they might cease this absurd war.

And in more than one letter he proposes that Aytoun should throw off a set of American ballads *à la* 'Bon Gaultier' :—

"The Battle of Bull's Cousin's Run," "The Song of the Pennsylvanian Patriot," &c., ought to be as good as "The Snapping Turtle."

That only indicates that, like some of our shrewdest soldiers and most far-sighted statesmen, he had failed as yet to gauge the strength and earnestness of the Americans of the North. As for their dash and courage, Laurence Oliphant, who had been present as a correspondent in both wars, used to compare them with the Germans in the French campaign, and to the disadvantage of the latter. Hamley felt the contempt of the professional strategist for the ill-directed efforts of heterogeneous masses of undisciplined levies. Nor, as Julian Sturgis remarks, was he altogether free from the popular prejudices against our American friends. Long before the termination of the war, he had come to the conclusion that the Northern American, like the Gascon, could plan and fight as well as swagger; and he learned to distinguish more dispassionately between types and classes when he had been privileged to enjoy the friendship of some of the most illustrious Americans resident in England.

In the spring of 1860 he found a more sympathetic subject in two articles on " Wellington's Campaigns." They were the outcome, of course, of synchronous lectures at the Staff College, and of another which was the first he delivered at the United Service Institute. They were intended to give a bird's-eye view of the campaigns as a guide to the intelligent perusal of the bulky military histories, and they are models of masterly analysis and condensation. The pains the writer bestowed on their revision was extraordinary. With a view to their republication he directs attention to the most trivial mistakes; and if some unimportant word fails to convey his exact shade of meaning, he insists on having it altered. That is worth noting, to prove that although opinions may be disputed, in all his work on military subjects he is thoroughly reliable in the most minute details. The criticisms on the Waterloo campaign, which are repeated with striking effect in 'The Operations of War, display his invariable independence of judgment, and must have been something of a surprise and a shock to idolaters of the Iron Duke who had been educated in the profound belief in his infallibility. Ségur and others have told us that the *élan* of Napoleon's genius had been broken by long strain and confirmed ill health; but in the chorus of praise on Wellington's generalship, perhaps no English writer of serious reputation had hitherto struck a discordant note. Blackwood seems to have been startled by the audacity of Hamley's strictures, and his letter elicited this answer:—

SANDHURST, *April* 1860.

MY DEAR BLACKWOOD,—I have studied everything that is recorded of any consequence about the Waterloo campaign, and you may rely upon the correctness of what I have written. The truth is, that neither the Duke nor Napoleon appeared at their best in it. The Duke's mistakes have always been glossed over by English writers, but the only effect of that is to diminish the value of the authority of those writers. Napoleon's want of vigour at several points of the campaign was remarkable in one usually so wonderfully prompt and active.

The same letter adverts to another famous international combat. The Professor of Military History regrets that he had no early intelligence of the movements of the combatants in the great battle between Heenan and Tom Sayers.

I am very sorry indeed that I missed the fight. Though it was known in London the night before that it would take place, yet no one was aware of it in the country. I reached Farnboro' about an hour after it was over. I would have given anything to see it. Motley and I were very nearly having a combat last night on the merits of the national champions.

Nevertheless, in mock heroics, he celebrated " The Fight for the Belt," and the courage of the champions, though deploring " the impotent conclusion which left the laurel in suspense."

About the same time he sends his comments on George Eliot's last novel. We fancy many people will be inclined to differ from him and the editor, or the editor's critic, on the comparative interest of 'Adam Bede' and 'The Mill on the Floss,' and not a few may dispute the dictum as to the inferiority of the aunts and uncles to Mrs Poyser.

For, as to the very best of Mrs Poyser's sayings, it generally strikes one that something of the sort has been said before.

SANDHURST, 2d *May* 1860.

I agree with your critic in thinking 'The Mill' superior in interest to 'Adam Bede,' and Maggie Tulliver a more captivating personage than any in the former.

If George Eliot knows the original, I should be glad of an introduction.

Bob Jakin is first-rate, especially as a boy; but none of the Dodsons come up to Mrs Poyser. Unlike most of the critics, I like the last volume best. It would never have done to let Maggie marry young Wakem; but I think she might, after a decent interval, have been allotted to Mr Guest. The flood scene strikes me as dreamy and unreal—wanting a few literal touches to make the reader thoroughly enter into its vicissitudes. Compared with the distinctness of the rest, it seems to me vague and fleeting. However, a second reading may alter my opinion.

At that time our military authorities were seriously alarmed as to the intentions of the French emperor. They feared that the war-frenzy of his army might force his hand, and that a declaration of hostilities in the following year was more than possible. There is a curious notice of a visit by a French admiral to Portsmouth, who had come over ostensibly to inspect the Queen's yacht, as Louis Napoleon intended to build a similar one. That gallant officer was hospitably entertained, and, apparently in a moment of expansion after dinner, he had confided to his hosts that France would assuredly attack us in the spring. Consequently, the invention of the Armstrong gun attracted special attention in military circles. Hamley went with his friend MacDougall—afterwards General Sir Patrick MacDougall, since, unhappily, dead—then the Commandant of the College, to witness the trials of the new weapon at Shoeburyness. They were conducted by Gordon, the brigade - major — the elder brother of Gordon of Khartoum — who had been Hamley's fellow aide-de-camp in the Crimea.

We had the gun thoroughly explained to us, and saw a number of shots fired. The performance exceeds what I expected; so does the simplicity of construction; and I feel pretty confident that no other Government could turn out a similar article, or one equally formidable. I wish both army and navy were thoroughly supplied with it, and then I think we might snap our fingers at our dear friend over the way.

The year 1862 and those immediately succeeding were uneventful. He was watching with keen interest the vicissitudes of the American war, which suggested subjects for the lectures and a succession of articles for the Magazine. But from the many letters in 1862, two interesting passages may be extracted. The first refers to Mrs Oliphant, of whom he was almost as warm an admirer as the author of 'Eothen,' who, to the very last days of his life, was always eagerly looking out for the latest of her innumerable novels.

'Salem Chapel' struck me as very like George Eliot's style, and I see many critics ascribe it to her. But the former story of Carlingford appeared to me indubitably Mrs Oliphant's, and as I suppose both your lady novelists would not write under one title, I conclude that this is not George Eliot's, but a very successful imitation, of which, indeed, I think I see traces in the story. If so, it is an additional proof of Mrs Oliphant's cleverness and ability for producing something much more popular than anything she has yet achieved.

As to the last sentence, it may be observed that, though Hamley had Scotch blood in his veins, he never seemed adequately to appreciate the early Scotch novels by which Mrs Oliphant first gained a reputation. Yet there were a freshness, a brilliancy, and a pathos in 'Mrs Margaret Maitland' and 'Adam Graeme,' which have surely never been surpassed in any of her subsequent work, save possibly with the exception of 'The Minister's Wife.' By a letter of 29th September, we learn that it was he who introduced Mr Story to 'Maga,'—he usually styles Mr Story "the stone-cutter,"—of which the versatile American sculptor was soon to become a valued contributor. Although at first, strangely enough, the connection hung in suspense, and might have been abruptly severed, had Story been less persevering. Perhaps because the brilliant author of the 'Roba di Roma,' like Hamley himself, had broken ground in poetry in place of prose. In subsequent letters Hamley reminds Blackwood that Story is still awaiting an answer to offers of a tale or other articles :—

29th September 1862.

MY DEAR BLACKWOOD,— Mr Story, the American sculptor, who is here, read to me yesterday a poem of his which I thought very good, and likely to suit the Magazine ; and finding that he would like much to offer it to you, I volunteered to submit it. He has written a good deal, I fancy, for the 'North American' and other Transatlantic periodicals, and would like to send you a contribution now and then from Rome, where his studio is, having a proper respect and admiration for 'Maga.' He is a very clever and very good fellow, the artist of the Cleopatra and Sibyl, the two most successful statues at the International ; but he is a red-hot Northerner.

We may imagine that the two friends had many a warm argument at Mount Felix, for Hamley was then a red - hot Southern sympathiser. In his letters his hopes and wishes were fathers to his thoughts, and he is frequently predicting that the drain of men and money in the North must dash the enthusiasm of the dollar - loving Yankees, or drive the Western States to follow the South into secession. On that subject he was in cordial agreement with the line taken by the Magazine ; and, indeed, most of the articles on American affairs, whether political or military, were written by him. But in January 1863 there was a passing difference of opinion with the Editor on a subject on which the soldier was specially well informed, and in which both were deeply interested for various reasons. Blackwood had brought out the first volume of Kinglake's great work. It was natural it should be sent to Hamley for review, for he was not only the most competent of possible critics, but being an intimate friend of the writer, had frequently discussed the Crimean campaign with him. Nevertheless he saw objections to undertaking the work, for, with all the admiration he was willing to express, he could not indulge in unrestricted eulogy. As a master of strategy he differed from Kinglake on many essential points ; and setting aside the honesty of conviction with which he could never be persuaded to tamper, he had too much regard for his professional reputation to let opinions from which he dissented pass uncontradicted. Moreover, as a man of the world, he suggested that, even in regard to the financial aspects of the matter, the feelings in well-informed military circles ought to be taken into account, and as to these he could speak from personal knowledge. The correspondence, from which I give various extracts, which have as much interest now as then, does equal credit to both parties. Hamley stood manfully to his guns, at the risk of making some trouble with Kinglake; and Blackwood, who was nothing if not straightforward, had the sound sense to give the reviewer *carte blanche.* But the passages from the correspondence speak for themselves; and, besides, they give such a *revue intime* as even Hamley did not think it necessary to submit to the public.

Mount Felix, 28*th Jan.* 1863.

My dear Blackwood,—I was on the point of writing you about Kinglake's book. I think it the most entertaining history I ever read—the style brilliant, and every page interesting. A great deal of the matter, especially the military part, is worthy of all praise. But there are some of the opinions with which I cannot agree, and which, as a reviewer, I could not pass by without seeming very partial or very blind. The historian's dislike to the French Emperor, as we knew before, amounts to a craze, and it has led him into numerous inconsistencies, and rendered a great deal of the portion of his book in which he accounts for the motives of the war quite incorrect. The chapter, too, in which he describes the *Coup d'état,* besides being unnecessary to the history, is a lampoon. But at the same time it is quite as piquant and amusing

VOL. I.   K as the rest, and I should do full justice to the literary merits, though bound to except against some of the reasoning and conclusions.   With this exception I should have nothing but praise to bestow.

Now, as you have published the book, I do not know how far you would consider yourself bound to maintain its opinions in the Magazine.   It certainly would not have suited the Magazine, I imagine, to launch out in that personal and bitter way against the Emperor, nor do I think he deserves it; and had the book issued from another house, I should have had no doubt of producing a notice in which you would have concurred.   As it is, I should think a perfectly fair review might be perhaps better for the book than a purely eulogistic one, conveying an impression of candour, without in the least checking curiosity about it,—rather, in fact, piquing it.   If, then, this would suit you, I shall be very happy indeed to write the review, and should indeed regret not to do so.

Hamley, speaking according to what was known at the time, is severe on the famous chapter on the *Coup d'état.*   After the confessions of De Maupas and other authoritative revelations, it certainly cannot be characterised as a lampoon, although the scenes have doubtless been coloured by Kinglake's picturesque imagination.   But the author always maintained its substantial accuracy, and there was nothing he had written—'Eothen' not excepted—which he regarded with greater complacency, as nothing used to gratify him more than to lead him to discuss it; and it may be true that an old grudge against the Emperor, dating from the days when they used to meet in Lady Blessington's *salon* and elsewhere, gave an agreeable piquancy to his serene self-satisfaction.

16th Feb. 1863.

MY DEAR BLACKWOOD,—Since I despatched my MS. to you I have had an opportunity, which I had not before, of hearing what people are saying of Kinglake's book. The feeling about the attack on the French Emperor is very general: it is considered out of place, absurdly exaggerated, and mischievous. People say that he has been a faithful ally to us, and that it would be a misfortune to alienate him or the feeling of the French people, as these personalities are calculated to do.

Military people are also objecting in many cases to what is said about themselves. The Duke of Cambridge, I hear, is furious. The Scots Fusiliers have called a meeting to consider how best to contradict the statement of their conduct at the Alma. Everybody, however, admits the cleverness of the book.

As a narrative, I think, as I have stated, that it is excellent; as a history, violently prejudiced, and by no means reliable.

The article seems to have been held over for very deliberate consideration. There is a final letter—the longest Hamley ever wrote to Blackwood—which deserves to be quoted. It assures us that in cases where he appears to be unduly severe, at least he gave conscientious expression to deliberately matured convictions.

Blackwood was as firm in opinion as himself: neither one nor the other was free from strong prejudices, but both would give way gracefully on sufficient cause being shown.

Mount Felix, 20*th February* 1863.

My dear Blackwood,—When you desired me to take my own line in reviewing Kinglake's book—and if I had not done so I could not have honestly done it at all—I made it my first consideration to write what would suit the Magazine. I was not aware that your opinions about the French Emperor were so nearly like Kinglake's as they appear to be. At any rate, I had never seen anything in the Magazine which seemed at all to coincide with his views. I therefore wrote what I considered a perfectly just review in this particular—inclining, indeed, so far to the author, that nothing I have said at all adequately expresses what I believe to be the general feeling respecting that part of the book. But while wishing to write what would suit the Magazine, I also considered that it was perfectly right and reasonable that you should wish to have all the praise given to a book which you had yourself introduced to the world that it fairly deserved, and I therefore bestowed it in such measure as is not, I daresay, exceeded in any other critique. I now see by your remarks that your opinion of the merits of the work is much more unqualified than mine. I perfectly recognise its animation and entertaining quality and excellence as a composition and narrative. But I do not see how any one can avoid concluding that it is violently prejudiced, and that it is deficient in some of the essentials of history.

As to the attacks on Louis Napoleon, to call them unfair

expresses but feebly what seems the general verdict.   In accounting for what seems the personal feeling that dictated them, people talk of grounds of animosity, which are no doubt mere absurd rumours, but which serve to show that there is necessity felt to account for them in some way. . . . What your grounds are for supposing that he means to sell us I don't know.   I daresay if our interests and those of France were in conflict, he would not hesitate to sacrifice ours.   But hitherto there is no instance of bad faith that anybody can point to.   If he wished to injure us, what opportunity like the time of the Indian Mutiny, when we had not a soldier in England?—and in this American business it would have been easy for him to make political capital at our expense, but he has not done so.   What would follow if he were unseated nobody knows, but it is extremely unlikely that in the state of things that would ensue we should be more secure from the hostility of France or on better terms with her than we now are, while France herself would indubitably suffer. If this be admitted, it is impossible to see the good policy of exciting the dislike and distrust of the Emperor, as such a course, if generally taken, could not fail to do.

But I do not consider this the only fault of the work. For so clever a man, Mr Kinglake appears to me singularly deficient in judgment and logical power.   His opinions are no doubt often strongly and clearly expressed, but then they very often contradict each other.   There is hardly any positive view which he takes of an important point which might not be refuted from his own book. Moreover, he gives to many personages and incidents an importance quite disproportionate.   Look, for instance, at the biography of General Airey, given at a length and with a minuteness which would be almost extreme in the case of a great historical personage. . . .

These being my views, I dropt out of sight when I wrote the review all those which, while unfavourable, were not in my opinion absolutely essential to the justice of the estimate, and I was therefore in hopes that the paper would be approved by you throughout, as it was carefully considered throughout and carefully written.

There is no part of it which I should of myself have wished to cancel; but I am most desirous that we should be in accord, and of course we have in common the desire of making the paper as suitable as possible to the Magazine, and I will therefore consider your marginal suggestions seriatim. . . .

I have quoted the first part of the letter at length, merely omitting unimportant sentences. Such temporary disagreements left no shade of unpleasantness behind, for only a month or two afterwards came another amicable controversy which places both the correspondents in a singularly favourable light. It is an agreeable episode in the "amenities of literature" to see editor and contributor bandying a handsome cheque backwards and forwards; and the motive which led Hamley to lay himself under a pecuniary obligation is but another of the innumerable proofs that the most kindly and affectionate of hearts was beating under a cold exterior. Former letters are full of references to his brother Charles. Captain Charles Hamley had contributed, like William and Edward, to the Magazine; and I have been told that John Blackwood used to say that, had he lived, he would have equalled, or even excelled, his brothers as a writer. I believe that from boyhood he had been Edward's favourite brother. He had served at sea with great distinction, but his dash and courage were combined with a singularly sensitive nature; his constitution had never been strong, and latterly his health had been failing. It is delightful to see how his brother always says for him what he was too modest to say for himself; how habitually the friendly editor is reminded that Charlie is disposed to self-depreciation, but only needs encouragement to do admirable work. Now he was lying on his death-bed at Plymouth, and Edward Hamley had hurried from Sandhurst to assist in nursing him. Till he had breathed his last, his devoted brother threw all business aside, and was always within call of the sick-chamber. The sad circumstances that drew them closely together strengthened the ties with his brother's widow, whom he had always regarded with much affection. Captain Charles had married Miss Hanbury Williams, whose cousin subsequently served as Hamley's aide-de-camp in Egypt; and whether he gave the dying man a promise or not, from that day he virtually adopted the little orphan daughter. He writes from Plymouth on May 14 to say that his

brother, knowing the end was near, was anxious
to set his affairs in order for the sake of his
wife and child.   For himself he was desirous that
his brother's last moments should be soothed by
the consciousness that all his worldly affairs were
in order.   So he asked whether further use was
likely to be made of the tales and articles which
had been published in the Magazine.   As a
rule, such contributions are of little or no further
value.   But Blackwood, though often a negligent
correspondent, never dallied when it was a question of serving a friend or evincing his regard
for an esteemed contributor.

PLYMOUTH, 18th May.

MY DEAR BLACKWOOD,—I cannot sufficiently thank you
for your prompt and friendly reply.   It will greatly contribute to set my poor brother's mind at ease.   He bids
me thank you warmly, and say how liberal and generous
he thinks your offer to be, and begs you to consider everything he has written your own; and in his thanks for your
most friendly generosity I wish warmly to join.

The remainder of the letter shows how entirely
the writer was preoccupied by his brother's illness, and how thoughtfully and affectionately he
was endeavouring to lighten the trouble of his
sister-in-law.   The next announces the death :—

22d May 1863.

Nothing could surpass the devotion of his wife to the
last, and she now shows no less admirable good sense than

feeling. It must be a great consolation to her to receive the sympathy that the event has called forth from all classes with whom my poor brother had any relation. The men and officers of his division, and all his acquaintance, and those any way connected with him, high or low, all testify the same feeling of uncommon regard. He was a thoroughly noble character, and I wish you could have personally known him. Some of his latest sentences were to beg me to convey to you the feelings which he was unable to express himself, for your ready and generous response.

In the autumn Hamley wrote again and at length, to explain that he had regarded the money received as a loan rather than a business transaction, that his single thought at the time was to ease the mind of a dying man, and that now his brother's affairs had been settled and sums had been unexpectedly received from other quarters, it was his own anxious desire and that of the widow that the advance should be repaid.

He sends a message from Mrs Charles Hamley :—

It has often dwelt upon my mind, and I always intended when the sum should be mine, to speak to you on the subject of repaying it. I shall be glad to hear that Mr Blackwood's ready generosity (the kindness of which I can never forget) had not resulted in loss to him.

Accordingly a cheque is enclosed for the amount

with interest. The cheque came back by return of post; and there, it may be presumed, a transaction equally honourable to both was closed, so far as the mere pounds and shillings were concerned.

As Hamley had the interests of the Magazine warmly at heart, he was in the habit of exercising his sagacity in detecting the literary promise of writers who had still their spurs to win. Blackwood was indebted to him for not a few invaluable introductions. We have seen that he had stood sponsor to Mr Story, and in the years 1864 and 1865 successively he was the means of opening communications with two soldiers of genius who were both to make themselves names in literature. Hozier, the historian of the Franco-German war, belonged to a Lanarkshire family, and was not unfrequently to be seen in Edinburgh; so Hamley writes :—

19th Feb. 1864.

MY DEAR BLACKWOOD,—If you meet a man named Hozier, formerly in the Artillery, now a lieutenant in the 2d Life Guards, I should be glad if you become acquainted. He is a pleasant fellow, passed through the Staff College lately with great *éclat*, and might become a useful contributor, especially as war correspondent.

The forecast was fully realised, and the Magazine was indebted to him for many valuable contributions. Shortly afterwards his services were engaged by the 'Times' as its war correspondent with the Prussians, when they crossed the Riesengebirge into Bohemia, and the result was his history of the Seven Weeks' War.

In the following spring Hamley gave the second introduction, which placed the Magazine in connection with the Chesneys :—

I enclose a letter from Captain Charles Chesney, R.E., my successor in the Professorship at Sandhurst, who, I believe, wants to become a contributor. He has written a very good account of the war in Virginia, has very clear and sensible views, and doubtless would be a very useful auxiliary.

Captain Charles had won Hamley's warm approval as the author of various important works on military topics. Two or three years afterwards his gifted brother—now General Sir George Chesney—enrolled himself among the contributors. It may be interesting, although perhaps slightly irrelevant, to advert to the episode which at once placed Sir George among the first in the foremost rank. The answer to the suggestion that he should send a military story was "The Battle of Dorking," which, as I have reason to know, was thrown off with extraordinary rapidity. A new generation has risen up since it was written, but Blackwood and his Magazine seldom made a more happy hit. The brilliant *jeu d'esprit* was read and talked about by thousands who scarcely appreciated the rare dramatic power, but were irresistibly impressed by its vigorous realism. It brought home to a nation of peaceful and money-getting islanders the domestic and pecuniary risks they ran in the event of a successful invasion; it did much to revive the dormant military spirit of a people who are essentially a warlike race; and it gave an extraordinary impulse to the volunteer movement. Besides that and many anonymous articles, Sir George Chesney passed three of his novels through the Magazine, and experts have pronounced that the best pictures of the Indian Mutiny are to be found reflected in the scenes in the first volume of 'The Dilemma.' It was pleasant to see the pleasure and pride which Blackwood took in his pet contributors. He seemed to regard them affectionately as indulged members of his family; but I never remember his face beaming more brightly than one forenoon at the Burlington Hotel, when the author of "The Battle" had dropped in, and was of course impressed for luncheon. He stole look after look at the man he admired, and the liking was blended with gratitude and admiration. So at another quiet luncheon at the "Garrick" he had welcomed and regaled Sir Garnet Wolseley on his return from the Red River Expedition, which its commander had chronicled in contributions to the Magazine. But on that morning at the Burlington, Blackwood had a double reason for being in high spirits. For he had triumphantly produced the first part of 'Daniel Deronda,' bought at a price which he did not regret, for he was sanguine as to the reception of the novel.

From the passage recommending Captain Chesney, it will be seen that Hamley had ceased at that time to be Professor at the Staff College. It was retirement, not resignation. In the previous year he had written :—

15th April.

MY DEAR BLACKWOOD,—I am sorry to say that I have been told officially that on my promotion to regimental Lieutenant-Colonel, which will be immediately, I am to join the regiment. I knew there was a regulation to that effect, but I did not think it would be acted on, because there are already more lieutenant-colonels of Artillery than they know what to do with.

The authorities here have made pressing application that I should be allowed to remain ; but the same request having been refused in another similar case, it could not be granted in mine. They have now applied to keep me here till the end of this term (June), and as it would be very inconvenient for the College that I should leave in the middle of a course of lectures, it will perhaps be allowed.

I am just going to town to learn what my destiny is to be—Woolwich, I imagine, in the first instance.

He was gratified to know that the military authorities were reluctant to part with him, nor could he foresee the flattering circumstances under which he would be recalled. His destination, as it proved, was Dover, and he hoped he should like his new quarters.

As it turned out, he found more leisure there than he had expected, and, consequently, threw himself with redoubled energy into his work on 'The Operations of War.' Doubtless it gained greatly by being thought out assiduously while the recollections of the Sandhurst lectures were still fresh in his mind. There is much correspondence about the arrangement of the book—indicating how carefully the most minute details had been considered—and especially as to the choice of an attractive title, to which he attached no little importance. He talks of hunting two days in the week, but otherwise he seems to have lived as much in seclusion as when writing 'Lady Lee' at Europa Point.

The citizens would be little flattered by his impressions of their venerable Cinque Port, and he found nothing to tempt him down from the heights in the well-intended overtures of its society. But the period of his probation was limited to the time that was needful for the completion of the *magnum opus*. In a letter of

December 1865, intimating the despatch of the concluding chapters, he also announces that new prospects were opening. The Duke of Cambridge, without application, had nominated him to fill an impending vacancy in the Council of Military Education. "It would be a great addition to my means, as the pay is made up to £800 a-year, which is high as military appointments go."

There was some vexatious delay, but Colonel Elwyn having decided to retire, Hamley received the appointment.

23d March 1866.

My dear Blackwood,—I am sure you will share my satisfaction at being appointed member of the Council of Military Education. It is a better position in every way than my present one, and quite doubles my income. I must live in or near town. The Duke had a *levée* to-day, which I attended for the purpose of inquiring about the post, and was told very graciously that I had been selected. The Duke nominated me of his own accord, which was kind.

Nothing could be more antipathetic to his energetic temperament than illness or inactivity. But he always acquiesced in the inevitable with cheerful resignation, and before his death he was to have signal opportunity for proving the temper of his passive courage. So in the autumn he writes an amusing letter, making characteristic fun of a doleful state of things, and full of allu-

sions to the book he studied as a second Bible
and unfailing source of inspiration.   Doubtless he
had sought consolation in Shakespeare through
the weary days of slow convalescence :—

30*th October* 1866.

MY DEAR BLACKWOOD,—I have been humiliatingly ill—
unable to do anything in my own behalf except swear, and
given over body and limbs, and what small portion of soul
I had left, which is scarce worth speaking of, to a lady of
the Gamp persuasion, without whose concurrence I could
perform no function whatever beyond breathing. I am
now, however, beginning to take notice, as they say of
lively infants, can walk across the room in quite a respectable totter, and dine on fowl and mutton, instead of lemon-
ade administered through a spout. I seem to be reversing
the process of Shakespeare's seven ages; for whereas a few
days ago I was very like the usual representative of the
"last scene of all," I have now rejuvenated into the lean
and slippered pantaloon, my youthful hose exceedingly
baggy, and my shrunk shanks like anatomical preparations.
Under Mount Felix diet I expect to get back ere long the
fair round belly of the Justice, and when I have once more
retrieved my position as a soldier full of strange oaths, I
shall there remain.

CHAPTER VIII.

'THE OPERATIONS OF WAR.'

SCOPE OF THE WORK—DIFFICULTIES IN THE STUDY OF MILITARY
HISTORY—WARFARE IN THE DAYS OF CHIVALRY—COMMUNICA-
TIONS—CONSIDERATIONS PRELIMINARY TO A CAMPAIGN—QUES-
TIONS OF STRATEGY—THE INFLUENCE OF OBSTACLES—TACTICS.

No soldier need desire a nobler monument to his
memory than 'The Operations of War.' No man
could have written it who was not endowed with
a very rare combination of qualities. It can only
be adequately appreciated if we consider the wide
range of the field and the vast scope of the subjects. We are amazed at the firm grasp of memorable facts and suggestive points, at the effective
grouping, the assimilation, and the consolidation.
The powerful intellect has seized on each happy
illustration that suits the immediate end in view,
and the tenacious memory is ready with every
fact that may serve the purpose of comparison
or contrast, for enforcing an argument, for praise

or for condemnation. The whole progressive science of the modern art of war is comprehended in the great work,—not chronologically, which would have been far easier for the writer, although puzzling and confusing to the student, but throwing clear light upon each consecutive stage, so as to make principles and practice pleasantly intelligible. Intricacies and complications arising out of changing circumstances are disentangled, and everything falls so naturally into methodical arrangement that we may be almost inclined to underestimate the literary adroitness. Yet the chapter on "Outposts," of which, *apropos* to a field trial at Aldershot, a cursory sketch is given later on, may suffice to indicate the variety of conditions and incidents presented by campaigning in a single aspect. This comprehensive and exhaustive military history embraces everything to be considered in working out strategical or tactical problems,—from the temperament of the hostile commander and the *moral* and quality of his troops to the topography of the country, the state of the weather, and even the farming, the forestry, and the manner of fencing the enclosures.

In other words, the writer impresses on his readers that matters apparently the most trivial may influence or decide momentous issues, and that nothing can be unimportant to a responsible soldier. Consequently 'The Operations' illustrate the combination of gifts and acquirements which, when leavened by the instincts of genius, makes a great general. But Hamley dwells on the due distribution of responsibility, descending through successive degrees, so that each officer in charge accepts his share of the burden; and the whole machine is working smoothly and harmoniously, making the nearest possible approaches towards arriving at perhaps an unattainable ideal.

A great feature of the work is that it is divested of professional pedantry : it investigates the science of MODERN WAR, as it has been evolved and developed by the progress of civilisation, of industrial enterprise and scientific invention. Yet the preliminary glances at the mode of warfare under the feudal system, when Edward III. and the chivalrous Black Prince were carrying fire and sword into France and Castile, are so picturesque, that we are somewhat tantalised by the necessity for dismissing the subject in a few brief sentences.

In a biography of Hamley it is perhaps advisable, if not indispensable, to give some faint idea of the work on which his reputation is solidly established. Fortunately an incompetent civilian is spared much embarrassment by referring to his own eloquent and pregnant introduction, which elucidates his method with masterly precision. The preface to the fourth edition modestly indicates his special qualifications for the task. He mentions, though it seems superfluous, that he had carefully followed, with a view to revision in later editions, the course of all operations in recent campaigns. "The American Civil War, the Austrian War of 1866, the Franco-German War of 1870, have all in their turn furnished illustrations and subjects of comment." If little notice had been taken of the Turkish and Armenian campaigns, it was only because they suggested little new matter. For many years, he reminds us, as Commandant of the Staff College, he had enjoyed an advantage which, to the expositor of military operations, could scarcely be overrated. "It has been a most important part of the Commandant's duty to direct the exercises of officers studying at the College, on actual ground, and on a supposed plan of continuous operations, as if they were acting under a general in a campaign." So we may presume that he seized opportunities of rehearsing deliberately on a field of peace the operations which interested him in contemporary war.

The introduction begins by exposing the difficulties which had hitherto attended the study of military history. Such standard works as those of Napier and Jomini presuppose an amount of preliminary knowledge which the reader in all probability does not possess. Nor would he be greatly helped if he turned to elementary treatises, which are for the most part obscure in attempting to be scientific. "The earnest student is then in this dilemma, that he requires a knowledge of theory to understand the facts, and a knowledge of facts to understand the theory." From that dilemma it is Hamley's object to extricate him, explaining the principles and theories by presenting illustrative facts. He has succeeded so well that not a few of the chapters are most fascinating reading for intelligent civilians. He merely makes cursory allusion to obsolete systems. Organisation and discipline have now been brought to a high pitch of perfection; the improvement of communications and the introduction of rapid and assured means of transport have revolutionised all the old conditions of campaigning—in fact, the field of observation, though still embarrassingly broad, has been cleared for professional and even popular study on definite and recognised principles. In a few lines he supplies a key to his programme :—

Taking our stand, then, on modern military history, let us suppose that the field were *not* trackless. Let us suppose that paths were traced on it which should all lead to a result. Let us suppose, in fact, that from amidst the mass of records certain campaigns and battles should be selected which should be *representative* operations, each involving and illustrating a principle or fact, which, when elicited and fully recognised, will serve for future guidance. Here we should have the matter at once greatly simplified; and this is what has been aimed at in the present work. The reader will be required to take no opinions on trust: certain operations will be selected, detailed, explained, and what lessons they afford deduced, till in this way a theory shall be formed on facts and experience which the student may confidently use for general application. And these comments and selections are intended to follow each other in such order that, with each step, footing may be gained for a further advance.

He begins the work by fixing a starting-point. Allusion has been made to his brilliant sketch of the merciless mode of warfare in the days of "chivalry." Drawing on the romantic pages of Froissart, he describes how war used to be made to support itself by rapine, so that while the victims of the ruthless inroads were reduced to misery and starvation, the troops of the conquerors scarcely suffered less when operating in districts already devastated. Consequently, in the absence of magazines and of regular supplies from a base, the operations were necessarily crippled and limited. There could be no coherence, either in the defence or attack. Beyond the walled cities, which formed so many centres of resistance, the strongholds of the nobles were in the most inaccessible situations, and, where possible, on isolated or impracticable heights. The army was not an integer, but an aggregation of discordant or incongruous units, which seldom formed effective combinations except when mustered for a pitched battle, and which fell to pieces on slight provocation. When each peasant was in the habit of carrying weapons, and the raw levies were drawn from an agricultural tenantry, discipline, as we understand it, could scarcely exist. With the strengthening of the power of the Crown and the subjugation of the great feudatories, we have the origin and the nucleus of standing armies. It was to the soldiers engaged for fixed periods and receiving regular pay that Edward I. and his grandson were indebted for the battles they won in France and Scotland. As the countries were tranquillised, and some protection was extended to industry and commerce, communications were opened up. When efficient artillery could be transported along practicable roads, the walled towns ceased to be places of refuge. Then the engineer had come to the front. The great cities were converted into formidable fortresses, and other positions began to be selected for fortification which might impede an invader's advance or shelter a retreating army. Then we have the days of leisurely campaigning and long sieges, when the artilleryman was playing the deliberate war-game against the engineer; when armies, according to rule, would withdraw into winter quarters, and when the capture of a single commanding fortress was considered the satisfactory result of a season in the field. Next there was another stage, "as the military machine grew more manageable":—

It was discovered that it was more profitable to occupy an enemy's territory than to devastate and plunder it, and that the readiest way to bring him to terms was to beat his armies. Improved roads and vehicles enabled large bodies to move more freely—improved cultivation gave them more abundant means of subsistence. Fortresses were watched, or "masked," by detachments; and Frederick and Napoleon, preferring manœuvres in which they were confident of their skill, to the tedious process of sieges, moved deep into the heart of the theatre of war.

Napoleon, in the height of his prestige, owed his career of unexampled success to the unprecedented celerity of his movements. He reverted, so far as practicable, to the old plan of making the war support itself, and when advancing with scarcely a check, through rich and fertile countries, he could dispense with the cumbrous trains of provision-waggons. A system which set prudence at defiance and ignored the possibilities of defeat, could only have been carried out by that daring and self-confident genius who succeeded in inspiring his soldiers with his own faith in his star. In fact, it fatally broke down when he sustained reverses, and when his troops were campaigning under inferior leaders in the rugged sierras of Spain. But even Napoleon established magazines at the base of his rapid operations, and at certain important positions on the lines of his advance. As a general rule, " the first preparation for war was the establishment of great depots and magazines, and these were collected in places that were secured from the enemy's attacks, either by natural defence or artificial fortifications."

Many of the most suggestive illustrations are drawn from the great wars of the Consulate and French Empire, and even from the campaigns of Marlborough, in which unrivalled military gifts anticipated modern ideas or inventions. Indeed some of the most generally interesting pages are on the fighting in Flanders, on the Danube, and in the Peninsula. But all is arranged so as to elucidate the revolution that has been brought about by the multiplication of roads and railways, and the improvements in cannon and small arms.

Bringing figures and close arithmetical calculation to bear, Hamley impressively explains the reason for the adoption of a particular strategy which is somewhat puzzling at first sight, or seems to run counter to accepted rules. As, for example, had Napoleon, when advancing on Brussels to interpose between Wellington and Blucher, concentrated his forces on a single road, we are told that the interminable column would have covered nearly fifty miles, altogether irrespective of its baggage and stores. Moreover, the calculations, so carefully worked out, are instructive, as they show the exactness of the premisses from which he reached his conclusions, and they give force to his remarks as to the influence of steam in simplifying and facilitating operations by sea and land.

The effect of railways in modifying the conditions of war is made manifest in ways we are apt to overlook. Not only are they available for forwarding troops, as they have wellnigh superseded the unwieldy transport trains; but they relieve an army of its sick and wounded, and so "the commanders are lightened of some of their heaviest cares." The importance of assuring communications and supplies, and of everything that facilitates freedom of movement, is admirably expressed in a striking simile, which should be borne in mind as a commentary on many of the subsequent chapters :—

It is extremely difficult to persuade even intelligent auditors that two armies are not like two fencers in an arena, who may shift their ground to all points of the compass ; but rather resemble two swordsmen on a narrow plank which overhangs an abyss, where each has to think not only of giving and parrying thrusts, but of keeping his footing under penalty of destruction. The most un- practised general *feels* this at once on taking a command in a district where his troops are no longer supplied by routine; or, if he does not, the loss of a single meal to his army would sufficiently impress it on him. While distant spectators imagine him to be intent only on striking or parrying a blow, he probably directs a hundred glances, a hundred anxious thoughts, to the communications in his rear, for one that he bestows on his adversary's front. Perhaps no situation is more piti- able than that of a commander who has allowed an enemy to sever his communications. He sees the end of his resources at hand, but not the means to replenish them. Is he to spread his troops to find subsistence for them- selves ? How then shall they be assembled to meet the enemy ? Shall he combine them for a desperate attack ? How, if that attack fails, are they to be fed ? He will then have no alternative but to make the best terms he can, or see his army dissolve like snow.

Part II. deals with the considerations which must precede the opening of every campaign,— and these are often far from being purely mili- tary : with the arguments that must be weighed before deciding to assume the offensive or to stand on the defence : with the relative advantages of railroads to the invading and defending forces : with the selection of the governing object of the war and the choice of the most favourable theatre of operations. As usual, the writer's intimacy with history supplies copious illustrations. Even in the case of Continental nations the alternatives in selecting the theatre are sure to be sufficiently embarrassing. But with English sea-power the difficulties are immeasurably increased, and "much more," says Hamley, "is it incumbent upon England to summon her most sagacious chiefs to council before committing herself to one of the numerous avenues which her maritime ascendancy will offer for her choice."

In Part III., and in the subsequent sections, principles and theories are reduced to practice, and we come to the study of complicated questions of strategy. The writer lays down the general laws which should regulate operations in the manifold relations of opposing armies. He not only analyses the conduct of the commanders in memorable campaigns or engagements, praising or blaming, as the case may be ; but he indicates and discusses the various alternatives that were open to them. Nothing, for example, can be more interesting than his strictures and speculations on the Waterloo campaign; on the movements, actual or possible, of the French marshals, MacMahon and Bazaine, after the first German victories;[1] and of the fighting in America, when North and South were being schooled in warfare by bitter experiences. In a couple of paragraphs, he concisely describes his plan of arrangement, which is equally systematic and comprehensive :—

Strategical movements will be considered as having the following objects: 1st, *To menace or assail the enemy's communications with his base;* 2d, *To destroy the coherence and concerted action of his army, by breaking the communications which connect the parts;* 3d, *To effect superior concentrations on particular points.* And as, whichever mode a general may adopt, it is essential that he should always maintain his own communications with his base, so the part of the subject first discussed will be the circumstances by which the security of those communications will be specially affected. . . .

The circumstances which it is necessary to know in order to understand the position of the opposing armies at the outset of a campaign, are first briefly recounted; then the fronts, the bases, and the lines connecting them are defined; next the plans of the generals on each side are discussed. Then the operations of the campaign are related in the simplest and most methodical form, without comment; for not only is the course of the operations rendered clearer by keeping the commentary separate, but the student is thus at liberty to exercise his own faculties

---

[1] Criticised in the fourth edition of 'The Operations of War.'

in accounting for the movements.   Lastly, the situation at
each stage is commented on; and as every campaign fur-
nishes examples of many points of war besides that which
it has been specially selected to illustrate, these are noted
and discussed.   Deductions, which seem to be of particularly wide application, are presented in a definite form
for future use; but nothing is offered in that shape, unless
it is so far supported by fact and argument as to have a
title to the reader's assent.

Take, as a single example of his vigorous and
pointed method, an illustration of concentration,
as virtually multiplying numbers and increasing
striking power :—

So long as there is constant communication between the
supreme directing authority and his dispersed subordinate
leaders, so long may a coherent impulse be given to *all* the
portions of an army.   But when the intervention of a
hostile force destroys this communication, the action of
every part is checked.   Combined action is the aim of a
commander-in-chief, and combination is impossible when
concert is destroyed.   Nor is the apprehension which
paralyses a commander who is thus separated from his
colleague the result merely of uncertainty.   For had
Beaulieu from Voltri, or the Archduke from Teugen,
advanced boldly on the enemy, each would have en-
countered a victorious and superior army.   It would seem,
therefore, that, under such circumstances, the only prudent
course is to effect a reunion with the utmost promptitude,
and that the advantages of the concentric position of the
interposing army are substantial, and are only augmented,
not altogether caused, by the moral effect of the situation.

The importance and interest of Part V., on "The Influence of Obstacles," may be appreciated by a glance at the first chapter, which is introductory to the rest. It summarises, from the military point of view, the geographical configuration of some of the most famous battle-grounds in the world—of Northern Italy, Spain, and the Central States of the American Republic. To a great extent that configuration invariably confines operations to certain lines and certain definite limits; yet it is shown that this restriction offers rare opportunities, which may be turned to signal account by the instincts of genius and by prompt decision, — as in the memorable campaign of 1814, in Champagne, when Napoleon, withdrawing before overwhelming forces, nevertheless carried off the honours of the war. The natural obstacles,—the mountain - ranges, the rivers and the forests,—with the means and opportunities of using or overcoming them, are discussed from every conceivable point of view. But perhaps the most interesting and thoughtful of the chapters is that on the changing value and employment of fortresses, which is a summary of the history of modern fortification. It is explained how the strongholds, which from time immemorial had been the fiercely contested pivots of international warfare, began to lose their value, when invading armies with facilitated transport could pass them and press forward to decisive battles. After a Marengo or a Jena, all the enveloped fortresses would surrender to the victor without a blow, and their garrisons would be sacrificed as prisoners of war. Yet we are reminded that the scientific fortification of frontiers is still indispensable as ever, and the principles are carefully expounded on which modern defences must be devised :—

The student will find it an excellent lesson in strategy, and one taxing his acquirements, to take a map of any country—France, Spain, Turkey—and devise for it an efficient and economical system of fortresses, always remembering that these must be placed where they combine the conditions of security from attack with the command of those points in the theatre which are of chief strategical importance. For to place the fortresses in the most effective situations, he must know well the features of the country, and be able to recognise and deal with the many problems it may suggest, under various circumstances, as a possible theatre of war—problems such as it has been the object of this work to state and discuss.

The latter part of the work is devoted to Tactics. Tactics which go necessarily into technical detail may be supposed to be less attractive matter than the strategy, which is often the romance of sensational history. Yet the writer's literary skill is nowhere shown to greater advantage than when he indicates how old and well-approved methods had to give way to the irresistible forces of invention. Infantry, cavalry, and artillery were all constrained to recast their parts in an action, when the range of field-guns was being steadily increased, and the fire of the quick-loading rifles became murderous. If a general persisted in attacking in the old column formation, his steadiest troops took the matter into their own hands by scattering and seeking for shelter, if indeed it was not decided for them by virtual extermination. Under pressure of stern facts, venerated traditions gave way, and the solid columns were dissolved into swarms of skirmishers. Battalions, when broken up into scattered sharpshooters, offer no fair mark to isolated batteries. Cavalry, although horse must be opposed to horse, have fewer decisive opportunities than formerly on a battle-field; but they are of more service than ever as scouts, for requisitioning, and for drawing an impenetrable veil around the movements of the army to which they are attached.

Hamley strongly advocates the multiplication of corps of mounted riflemen, capable of performing the duties both of cavalry and infantry, while combining the swift mobility of the one with the formidable fire of the other :—

The nature of the service would render it especially popular with the active, the enterprising, and the ambitious; and (supposing we were desirous for once of devising something in war, instead of copying foreign examples in the way that Chinese artists copy Italian pictures) it would not be easy to lead the way more effectively than by organising a force of mounted riflemen.

CHAPTER IX.

THE COUNCIL OF MILITARY EDUCATION.

CHAMBERS IN THE ALBANY—CLUB-LIFE AT THE ATHENÆUM—
LETTERS FROM VON MOLTKE AND AMERICAN GENERALS ON
'THE OPERATIONS OF WAR'—COMMISSION FOR THE DE-
LIMITATION OF ELECTORAL DISTRICTS—REVIEWING KING-
LAKE'S 'CRIMEA'—APPOINTMENT AS COMMANDANT OF THE
STAFF COLLEGE.

THE Council of Military Education had been
established in 1857. It consisted of the Commander-in-Chief as *ex officio* President, a Vice-
President, and four members, of whom one was
a civilian. Of its numerous duties the principal
were,—the appointment of Examiners for the
Military examinations, and Professors and In-
structors at the Military Colleges; the conduct
of examinations of officers for the Staff College,
general Staff, and the advanced class at Woolwich. Reports of progress were to be laid before the Council. It was abolished in 1880, when
the present Military Education Department was
formed.

Hamley had established himself in comfortable chambers in the Albany, and for the first time he was living in London society. He took very kindly to the new life, and his rooms soon were the favourite resort of a few familiar and congenial friends. He had barely settled into his new quarters before he was elected to the Athenæum by the committee. He was highly gratified by the compliment, for which, he says modestly, he was greatly indebted to the good offices of his friend the Chaplain-General. He could hardly have foreseen at the time how much the Club was to be to him. Self-condemned to celibacy, he made it his home, and thenceforward it influenced and modified his habits. It has at least the exceptional advantage of bringing together distinguished men of every profession, or of no profession, who meet upon absolutely neutral ground, irrespective of wide differences of opinion. The mingling of castes, callings, and creeds exactly suited the new member. He might be ultra-Conservative in certain of his convictions, but he was catholic in tastes and sympathies. He was soon on pleasant and easy terms with acquaintances in all circles. His soldierly frankness recommended him to everybody with whom he had anything in common. Radical Ministers and members of Parliament smiled at his good-humoured abuse of themselves and their measures. In the billiard-room or smoking-room (though he did not smoke, he was constantly in the smoking-room) he would indulge in humorous licence of speech with the solemn philosophers whose writings were held in reverence all over the civilised world, but when he happened to take them seriously they listened to him respectfully. The truth was, he was fond of treating playfully the men whose genius and intellectual acquirements he most admired, and the subjects in which he was most deeply interested. His company at dinner was eagerly sought after. Hayward, and his old ally and strategical antagonist Kinglake, Chenery the accomplished editor of the 'Times,' the late Sir William Gregory, and the gifted Sir Edward Bunbury, were among his familiars. Of these, with perhaps the exception of Kinglake, there was no man he appreciated more highly than Bunbury. He was a frequent guest at Barton, the family seat of the Bunburys, famous for its Reynoldses and the collection of the Dutch masters, and it was always a rare intellectual treat to hear Hamley and Bunbury discussing the fine arts. He used his friend, besides, as a classical dictionary of reference; and Bunbury's unrivalled memory was an unfailing resource in verifying a quotation from Homer or Horace. After dinner he loved to take a lounge round the tables. Now he would be talking dogma —or, possibly, the contemporary drama—with a liberal - minded divine ; now he would be discussing politics or sport with a member of the Cabinet ; and again he would get so seriously interested with anybody over anything, that they would sit absorbed in conversation till the lights were turned down and the silence in the deserted dining-hall was otherwise unbroken.

In that and the following year he had more than one very gratifying proof of the widespread popularity and success of his ' Operations of War.' There are sundry interesting and flattering letters from American generals ; and, in especial, his somewhat severe strictures on Sherman's campaigning in Georgia led to a correspondence, and afterwards to what would have ripened into friendship had the soldiers lived within reach of each other.   Hamley writes :—

I have received a letter through the Secretary of the American Legation from Sherman, in which he thinks I might be induced to modify my chapter on his operations, for reasons which he gives. That was a very handsome way of meeting objections, for most men who have attained to such eminence are content to wrap themselves in their dignity and make no reply—not even "D—n your eyes!"—to their critics.

The letters may perhaps be most appropriately introduced in this place, with no strict regard to chronology.

A communication from Von Moltke may claim precedence. It was forwarded through Colonel Walker — afterwards General Sir Beauchamp Walker, since dead—who had been our military *attaché* at Berlin during the Franco - German war, and had accompanied the staff of the Crown Prince during the march on Paris :—

Saturday.

My dear Hamley,—I enclose you a letter from General Moltke. At the Foreign Office you will find a roll of maps, of which he begs your acceptance, so please send for them before they are lost in the all-devouring maw of that most ill-regulated office. I am particularly desired to tell you that they are as yet quite in the rough. Those published with the official account of the campaign will be lithographed, and will also contain the positions of the troops.—Yours truly, Beauchamp Walker.

The enclosure might have been written by an Englishman, and indeed the writer had married an Englishwoman :—

Berlin, *March* 15, 1867.

My dear Sir,—I have received from Col. Walker a copy of your work on 'The Operations of War,' for which I beg you to accept my very best thanks, and at the same time my sincere congratulations as author of so valuable and interesting a work.

It may not be uninteresting to you to have accurate maps of our late battle-fields: I have therefore sent a copy of all we have as yet published to Col. Walker, with a request to forward them to you through the British Embassy. I beg you to accept of them as a token of the pleasure your work has given me, and of respect for its author.—I remain, my dear sir, your obedient servant,   V. MOLTKE.

There is an undated letter from Colonel Walker, apparently written previously, but which was suggested by the correspondence on the 'Operations':—

MY DEAR HAMLEY,—You are quite right in what you remark about the reserves at Königgrätz. The only use to which they were put was to attempt to retake Chlum and Rosberitz with them.

If you like to send me the proofs of your additional chapter, I will do what I can to correct them; and if you want any information which I can supply, just note the points and you shall have it. General v. Moltke is very much pleased with your attention in sending him the work, and begs that I will give you his best thanks. You have done well to establish a good relation with this thinking man. He told me last night that the official account of the campaign would soon be ready.

Could you not get leave to see my despatch No. 96, of the 2d Nov. 1866? I really believe (with some errors) it to be as clear and nearly as correct an account as has yet been written of the events of 2d - 3d July 1866. Don't scruple to write if you want information.—Believe me, my dear Hamley, very truly yours,

BEAUCHAMP WALKER.

Would you like Benedict's *ordre de bataille* for the 3d July ? I sent a translation of it last week to Cooke.

On 14th June 1866 General Lee wrote to Mr John Sturgis requesting that a copy of the work might be forwarded to him.

His subsequent letter to Hamley is remarkable, as coming from that illustrious and dashing commander, who had played his conspicuous part in the war from the most purely patriotic motives. After some preliminary civilities he goes on :—

The subject of your book is one full of difficulties. Whatever can lessen or remove them will be of service to those who resort to the arbitrament of arms. Mankind would greatly gain if nations would refer to the judgment of reason, rather than the decision of the sword, the settlement of disputes.—With great respect, your obedient servant, R. E. LEE.

The first communication from General Sherman was indirect. It was addressed to Mr Benjamin Moran, the United States Minister in London :—

HEADQUARTERS MILITARY DIVISION OF THE MISSOURI,
SAINT LOUIS, MO., *March* 16, 1867.

B. MORAN, Esq.

DEAR SIR,—I take the liberty of mailing to you five copies of a report of mine recently printed by order of

Congress, which will be found in the series of the Reports of the Committee on the Conduct of the War, but a few copies were bound separate, of which I send you five: one for yourself; one for George Hooper, Esq., who sent me his volume through you; one for Col. Hamley, whose volume I received from you; one for the U.S. Club, and a spare copy. This is not a real report, but is a compilation of letters selected out of my letter-books, and designed to show how and when ideas and plans originated. The time is not yet ripe for History, but in time enough data will be collected convenient for the hands of our Napier when he turns up.

A good many of the English commentaries and criticisms err, because it is impossible for them to see why well-established principles of war had to be modified to suit the peculiar geography and forest nature of our country. Thus, I think, if Colonel Hamley were to visit the ground about Dalton and Resaca, he would modify his chapter treating of my dispositions there. Though I divided my force (generally, but by no means always, a violation of a rule of war), Johnston could not have fallen on M'Pherson without doing just what I wanted—viz., let go forts and parapets, and a natural position that might have cost me 20,000 men to have dislodged by a direct attack. Johnston could not make a detachment large enough to endanger M'Pherson, who, on the defensive, would have had the woods and range of hills at Snake Creek in his favour, and I had good roads by the rear to reinforce M'Pherson in one march.

I like to see these criticisms, however, as they show that the rest of the world is interested in our youthful imitations of their grand games of war.—I am, with great respect, your friend,   W. T. SHERMAN,

Lt.-Genl. U.S.A.

Hamley answered and acknowledged it on 12th April 1867 :—

General,—Permit me to thank you for your courtesy in sending me your report, which receives great additional value as coming from yourself and bearing your autograph. Permit me also to express my satisfaction, in the interests of military science, at finding that a commander so eminent is willing to discuss with critics his own successful operations.

The chapter in my book on the campaign in Georgia was written at a time when it was very difficult to obtain in this country accurate information of its details, and I became aware, soon afterwards, that some of these were erroneous.

Nevertheless, the errors were not of a character to prevent it from remaining an example (all the better for being recent and unhackneyed) of what I wanted to illustrate—namely, the case of dislodging an army by operating with a detachment against its rear.

Nor were these errors of detail, so far as I knew them, such as to affect the general estimate of the operations.

After having the pleasure of seeing your report, and also your letter to Mr Moran relative to it, I find that you had made dispositions on the 10th May to direct an attack through Snake Creek Gap with an overwhelming force. This is the course which, in my comments, I ventured to indicate as the right one. I shall in a future edition record this, and with great satisfaction, as showing that my opinion was supported by the practice of so great an authority.

With regard to the remarks which you have done me the honour to convey through Mr Moran,—1st, that it was not a fault to divide your force; 2d, that Johnston could not have fallen on M'Pherson without letting go his hold of his position; 3d, that a front attack on Johnston was inexpedient,—I venture to observe that, freely admitting all these points, I do not see how they invalidate the general conclusions.

It was said of Cæsar that "it was difficult to argue with the master of thirty legions." So I should find it hard to dispute the opinions or object to the practice of a general who has commanded a great army with such brilliant results.

I beg again to thank you for the great favour you have done me in sending your letters on the campaign, which I shall study with great attention, and I am sure with great profit.—I have the honour to be, General, your most obedient and obliged,   E. B. HAMLEY, *Colonel.*

General Sherman replied in due course :—

HEADQUARTERS MILITARY DIVISION OF THE MISSOURI,
SAINT LOUIS, MO., *May* 10, 1867.

Colonel E. B. HAMLEY,
   British Army, London.

DEAR SIR,—Mr Moran of the U.S. Embassy at your Court did me the favour to transmit your most acceptable letter of April 12, and I assure you that it gave me pleasure, as I did not expect the matter would engage more than a passing thought to you. In common with some of our best officers I had read your most valuable work, to which my attention was called last summer by some of the officers at the mess in Quebec, and Mr Moran soon after transmitted me a copy. I beg you will understand me as really complimented by treating our American campaigns as worthy of being grouped with those of your European world; and if ever I expressed a qualified opinion, it was because you had at that early date been compelled to use statements of facts derived from our current newspapers, instead of waiting for the slower but more exact official papers.

I have no doubt you in England appreciate the situation of our military officers. Our education at West Point resembles that at the École Polytechnique of France, and after graduation we serve as lieutenants in some small garrison, taking the chances of very slow promotion by seniority. It is seldom we see assembled under arms a full battalion ; and before our war of rebellion I had never commanded, save on parade, more than four small companies. After thirteen years of continuous service in an artillery company I had reached the rank of captain of the staff, the pay of which was so inadequate to the support of a small family that I was in a measure forced to resign and attempt their support by other means. So that when war was upon us and had to be met, most of us had only theoretical knowledge of "*grande guerre.*"

I don't think any of us claim to be great generals, in the strict sense of that term, or to have initiated anything new, but merely to have met an emergency forced on us, and to have ceased war the very moment it could be done.

I beg you will consider me as one who fully accords to you the right to criticise strictly anything that will illustrate the principles of our art, which we, as military men, must claim to be based on principles as everlasting as Time. Your work shall always have a place in my library, along with those of Napier, Jomini, and others of all nations who have afforded us, a new people, with models for imitation.—With great respect,

W. T. SHERMAN,
Lt.-Genl. U.S. Army.

In the summer of 1869 is the acknowledgment

of the receipt of the second edition of the book, with its revisions and corrections :—

HEADQUARTERS ARMY OF THE UNITED STATES,
WASHINGTON, D.C., *July* 29, 1869.

Colonel E. B. HAMLEY,
   British Army, London.

DEAR SIR,—I had the honour to receive yesterday your valued favour of June 30, with a copy of the second edition of your volume on 'The Operations of War,' &c. I beg to assure you of my sincere thanks for this act of courtesy, and am much pleased at the manner in which you have received my former letter. The change you have made in the text is more than satisfactory to me, and I shall be pleased to bring to the notice of the officers of our army a book that, in my judgment, is worthy its title and of our profession, which I am pleased to see you place among the highest. I agree with you perfectly that the modern improvements in the railroad system, in the telegraph, &c., in no manner qualify the great principles of war, but make their application the more important, and impose on all military officers the positive duty of studying these principles the closer, because by their means war will be more rapid in its inception and execution, leaving no time to study up after the event.

It occurs to me, and I mention it in your interest, that so valuable a book ought to be put in a smaller compass as to size of volume, without omitting a paragraph, or the least part of it; also, the leaves should be cut before binding; also, the maps should be bound in leaves the same as the text, even if you have to put two or three leaves where you now have one map.

It is the case with our officers, and I believe with yours on foreign stations, that the weight of baggage is limited, so that many line officers would be unable to carry with them so large a book.

Again tendering you my thanks, and offering to re-ciprocate in case you suggest anything subject to my control, I am, &c.,   W. T. SHERMAN,
General U.S. Army.

Finally, in 1870 there came a gratifying tri-bute from General Barry, Commandant of the Headquarters, Artillery School, U.S.A.:—

FORT MONROE, VA., *May* 27, 1870.

Colonel E. B. HAMLEY, Royal Artillery,
        London, England.

COLONEL,—Without the pleasure of a personal acquaint-ance with you, but simply as an act of professional comity, I take the liberty of addressing this note to you to say that, after mature consideration and previous experience with the works of Jomini, Dufour, and Mahan, it has been determined to adopt the second edition of your work on the Art of War as a text-book in the department of Mil. Hist., Art of War, &c., &c., as taught at this institution.

Discussing, as your work does, the salient military events of modern times, and from a more modern stand-point, discarding most of the useless trammels of the *ancien régime*, it possesses unusual elements of excel-lence, and commends itself as being altogether better suited to our purposes here than any other work.

I have caused to be ordered from your London pub-lisher about thirty copies for the use of the young offi-cers who compose the class at the Artillery School for this year; and hereafter I presume we will require about twenty copies annually.—With high respect, I remain, Colonel, very respectfully, your obedient servant,

WILLIAM F. BARRY,
Colonel 2d Regt. Artillery,
Bvt. Maj. Gen. U.S.A. Comdg.

What General Barry calls a " formal note " was accompanied by another, thanking the author of the ' Operations ' for a friendly and respectful notice. He expresses " the gratification which it is natural for a soldier to feel on finding his views and labours appreciated by a professional brother —albeit a stranger, and of another country.

Then Hamley writes to Blackwood in midsummer :—

Prince Frederick Charles, the Commander of the Second Army, has been here incog. I dined with him one day at the Junior, where he was Hozier's guest—very affable, flattering, and communicative, so far as imperfect English would allow.

A more ambiguous compliment, which gave him considerable annoyance, was paid by his colleagues of the Education Council. The authorities of the Royal Military Academy at Woolwich had petitioned the Council for the institution of a Professorship of Military History, and suggested that Hamley's 'Operations' should be the principal textbook. The Council, apparently after some hesitation, assented to the professorship, but declined to approve the adoption of the ' Operations.' Both their objections seem unreasonable enough, and, naturally, Hamley was satisfied with neither. The first was, that it would be improper or indiscreet to recommend the work of a colleague ; the second, that it was beyond the capacity of the cadets. Hamley sent in a protest against the decision, which, privately, he professed himself unable to understand, adding, however, that he suspected no unfriendly motives. But though a firm believer in the power of the press, and although he had recourse to it on future occasions as a last resource against — what he considered — injustice which could not be otherwise redressed, now he resolved to move no further in the matter. The Directors of the Woolwich Academy were still insisting, so his case would have been a very strong one. But he said that letters in the papers would be unpleasant to himself; they would probably annoy the Commander-in-Chief, to whom he was grateful for his appointment; and above all, it " would be detrimental to the public service of the department, which requires free and constant communication among us."

In a letter written from Bridport in October, we find him enjoying an autumn holiday at the public expense. He had been nominated one of the Commissioners for the delimitation of electoral districts under the provisions of the recent Reform Bill, and he would often talk afterwards of that pleasant outing in the western shires, when, with sketch-book and fishing-rod as parts of his luggage, he made acquaintance with much enchanting English scenery, and had hospitable welcome in many a picturesquely situated mansion :—

BRIDPORT, 3d October.

MY DEAR BLACKWOOD,—It's an ill wind, &c.; and certainly I did not expect, when we were canvassing and abusing the New Reform Bill in Burlington Gardens, that I should personally derive any benefit from it.   Benefit it is, however, so far, that I am getting air, exercise, occupation, and a pleasant holiday, and am paid for it to boot.   My colleague, Ollivant, is a crony of your friend Skene. . . .

We spend about two days in each town, exhaust the information about the borough, and then move on.   Whenever we get a chance we walk from place to place, and have footed it through some very pretty scenery.   There is remarkable apathy in all the places we have visited (Wilts and Dorset) on the part of the new householders to be admitted to their rights.

Although frequent applications are made for the extension of boroughs, they never come from those who would thus become part of the constituency, but are always made by other people from local party reasons.

The year 1868 was a somewhat idle one so far as literature was concerned : with a single exception, the only contribution to 'Blackwood' was a review of George Eliot's 'Spanish Gypsy.'   He says in his letters, after touching upon minor defects :—

All the writer's power of thought and style is put forth in the poem.   A great deal of the verse is excellent, though, judging from the songs, I should say that blank verse was not her strong point—the versification is not always good, but the songs are most musical.

The story I think open to some objections, though I shall not allude to them in the review. Several characters are elaborately introduced, but have no influence on the plot. Further, Isidor, who seems to promise to be a powerful agent, is not so, and the cast of thought and dialogue is essentially modern.

The other contribution was what he calls an " unlucky " poem of his own, which seems to have received sharp criticism from Blackwood. The poet may have been annoyed, but he took the criticisms in good part, and " Dreams in the Invalides " appeared in due course.

There is a good deal of interesting correspondence on the second instalment of Kinglake's ' Crimea.' Hamley expresses warm admiration of the style, but he took exception to some important statements. Especially, he said that " the Flank March " conveyed a false impression, owing to the desire to exalt Lord Raglan. He refers to his own letters on the campaign, which the historian seemed to contradict, although without actually naming them ; and he adds, " I shall certainly not correct the testimony of my own senses by the light of his theories."

Again, read my account of the charge of the Heavies, which I saw, and you will find he omits the whole episode of the Turkish guns firing on part of the Russian cavalry force. Yet it was surely as important a matter for a chronicler as the question whether a cut or a thrust was given by a particular swordsman. My idea of his method of work is that, with the assistance of strong prejudices and queer crotchets, he forms an arbitrary enough conception of any particular event, and accepts what coincides with his own view, rejecting all other testimony.

These objections were strongly expressed, with reference to the proposal that he should review the volumes in 'Maga.' The upshot was that, after intimation of his intention, and obtaining Blackwood's assent, he responded to the overtures of Henry Reeve, and undertook the work for the 'Edinburgh.' Subsequent articles on the History, with the exception of that on vol. vi., appeared in the same periodical. Very noteworthy articles they are, and Mr Reeve appreciated them highly as examples of incisive criticism, with exceptional knowledge of the facts. For Hamley was nothing if not thoroughly honest, and neither friendship nor self-interest would deflect him by a hair's-breadth from the straight path of conscientious duty. With regard to the first article, he felt that Blackwood might naturally be annoyed by its frankness—not only as clashing with his own opinions, but as likely to check the sale of the book.

I felt the strongest desire to find that I had nothing but praise for it. . . . But sorry as I was, on reading the book, to find so many things I dissented from which, had I seen them earlier, might probably have deterred me from writing the review, yet I could not but in conscience express my disagreement with many of the military views.

The following autumn (1869) brought an unpleasant change in his prospects. The Report of an Education Commission had recommended the supersession of the Council by the appointment of a Director-General. No doubt Hamley's feelings were strongly against a change which must oust him from a desirable post; but he likewise objected on public grounds, believing that it would open a door for jobbery, by transferring all the patronage of appointments to the War Office. That reason made him philosophically resign himself to the inevitable, as the step was sure to find favour with the military authorities. Early in the spring of 1870 the Council ceased to exist; but just as that door was closed, another and a more inviting one fortunately opened. He was ruefully contemplating the prospect of rejoining his brigade in a worse position than when he left it, when he learned that he had been recommended to the Duke of Cambridge, by the new Director-General and by the Secretary at War, as Commandant of the Staff College. Nothing could, of course, have coincided more pleasantly with his inclinations, but for some little time he was kept in suspense. The Commander-in-Chief, who had always been his very good friend, was understood to be hesitating lest the appointment of an artilleryman should give umbrage to the linesmen, though it seems only natural that such a post should be bestowed on a member of one of the scientific corps. Independently of his scientific recommendations for it, the arguments in Hamley's favour were strong. His seat at the Council had familiarised him with the systems of military education in their details, and as he had already filled a chair at the College, he could enter immediately on the duties with the knowledge which the most able outsider must take months to acquire. The press spoke out unhesitatingly in his favour, and he was always grateful to Mr Cardwell, who strenuously urged his claims.

Notwithstanding professional anxieties, that year he sent two notable contributions to the Magazine. The one was " Our Poor Relations," to which reference has already been made. With his affection for the brute creation, he put his whole heart into it, and a brighter *jeu d'esprit* has seldom been thrown off. One might say that every sentence sparkles : if the essence of wit is humorous surprise, the little book is witty in the extreme; and whether the passages are humorous or pathetic, we are struck by the quaint originality of the fancies. The article having had an extraordinary success, it was republished in book form, with grotesque illustrations by Ernest Griset. One or two were by Hamley himself, although he modestly expressed a fear of provoking invidious comparisons. The other contribution was the scathing review of 'Lothair,' which, as it clashed with a very general chorus of praise, excited all the greater sensation,—the rather that the great chief of the Conservatives was scarified in the staunch old Tory Magazine. Possibly dispassionate judges will be of opinion that this was a case of the two sides of the shield. The reviewers, who wrote *currente calamo* in the morning and weekly papers, were on the look-out for the beauties, of which there were very many, and were eager or willing to praise — the Conservatives from loyalty, the Liberals from a sentiment of chivalry. In the monthlies and the quarterlies, which more deliberately weighed the book, praise and censure were more impartially distributed. Froude admired it heartily.[1] The late Lord

[1] See "Reminiscences of James Anthony Froude," by John Skelton, C.B., LL.D., in 'Blackwood's Magazine' for December 1894 and January 1895.

Houghton's review in the 'Edinburgh' was a model of judicial severity tempered with genuine admiration. But Hamley evidently had been chafed by the affectations of the style and the Arabian Nights' extravagances, which he deemed to be strangely and grotesquely misplaced in a social novel of the period. He gave free rein to his satirical fancy, and having dipped his pen in vinegar or gall, was greatly pleased with the results of his efforts. He had written beforehand :—

'Lothair' seems to me such horrid trash that it cannot be taken seriously, and the only way to treat it is by *jeers.* I have just met Lord Lytton at the Athenæum. He has not read it, but he says that people who have spoken to him of it, friends of Disraeli, all talk of it as I did— viz., the gaudiest trumpery that was ever printed.

Delane at least, who was no bad judge, differed from these gentlemen ; and Disraeli—though they were then bitterly opposed in politics—seized the opportunity to write him a letter of warm thanks, not only for the favourable notice in the 'Times,' but for the opinions conveyed in a private note. But whether one agreed with Hamley or not, it was impossible to help laughing over the article, or admiring the easy play of wit, and the bitter mockery which reminds one of Voltaire.

It is certain that the novelist smarted under the stings, and Hamley writes Blackwood on the 6th July:—

As to the 'Lothair' paper, I never dine anywhere without hearing it talked of, and it is mostly ascribed to Lever.

CHAPTER X.

COMMANDANT OF STAFF COLLEGE.

THE SYSTEM—CHANGES INTRODUCED BY HAMLEY—HIS INTEREST
IN THE STUDENTS — HIS RECREATIONS — FRIENDSHIP WITH
THE LATE DUKE OF WELLINGTON — A BARGAIN IN HORSE-
FLESH.

IN 1870, with a lightened heart, he went back to
the Staff College as Commandant instead of Professor. There he passed seven of the happiest
and not the least useful years of his life. When
the obstacles which had opposed the appointment
had been smoothed away, he had no cause for
complaint. The authorities gave their confidence
generously, and he had practically a free hand.
He entered upon the duties of his command under
exceptionally favourable circumstances. It had
been understood that there was ample room for
reform in the system, and that radical changes
were highly desirable. His commission was
signed in July, only three months after the
issue of revised Regulations for the College,

which had been framed to give effect to the recommendations of the Royal Commission of 1868-69, on the education of officers. The Commission was at first presided over by Lord de Grey, and afterwards, from February 1869, by Lord Dufferin. One of the changes introduced was an increase in the number of students from thirty to forty. The experiences of the past had shown the necessity for an extension of the practical exercises of the officers on the ground, and it was at the instance of the Royal Commission that the Commandant was charged with himself directing these exercises. As to the manner in which he availed himself of his opportunity, I am enabled to quote an authority who can speak with special knowledge of the facts :—

This duty [that of superintending the field exercises] he accepted as a most important one, and under his guidance and personal direction the fullest development was given to this part of the instructions. Various improvements were introduced by him into the course of small reconnaissances made in the vicinity of the Staff College; and the system of extended reconnaissances, which had been somewhat curtailed from a reduction of the sum voted for their execution, was re-established. In one and all of these most valuable experiences for soldiers being trained to be practical staff officers in the field, Colonel Hamley (as he then was) brought to bear his thorough and practical grasp of the subject. The advantages that resulted, not only to the officers themselves but also to the public service, can hardly be over-estimated, and they are still in operation.   In 1871 we find him employed at the head of his officers, sketching ground, reconnoitring, and taking notes of the operations in connection with the campaigning during the autumn manœuvres of that year.   But it was not alone the training of the officers in these more practical portions of their duties as staff officers that underwent a lengthened development during Hamley's term of office.   As a past professor at the College (of Military History) he took a special interest in, as he had a special knowledge of, this branch of study, which he largely extended.   He gave, indeed, to all the work a personal impress, which was of the greatest benefit to all concerned—to professors as well as students; and good work or honest endurance was recognised by him, as surely as careless or indifferent work.   A man of reserved character and few words, he but seldom gave expression to commendation, but where blame was in his opinion attributable for careless or bad work, he did not shrink from awarding it.   If in passing such strictures upon officers his manner of address was sometimes blunt and even severe, this was attributable to manner alone, which seemed to be aggravated by the necessity for the performance of an unpleasant duty which he would far rather have avoided.   Behind it was a nature that never failed to be appreciated and admired by those who knew Hamley sufficiently well to get behind his reserve.   The short period of residence at the Staff College—two years—did not render this practicable for many at the time; but few can have failed to recognise the ability and practical nature and force of character of the Commandant under whom they were privileged to receive their training.

The Commandant's hands were strengthened by the fact that the students, for the most part, were zealous officers eager to learn, and they readily fell into the new ways, none the less that the revolution enlivened the monotony of their residence. I am indebted to General Montague, who was one of the number, and who was subsequently to distinguish himself in South African warfare, for another account of the former system, with the alterations then introduced :—

Prior to 1870 candidates passed through the College by means of marks—given, first by the professors for the essays set by themselves; second, by the College for work done in class. When a minimum of 1800 was gained, the pass was secured. This led to two evils. First, there was no incentive to further work when the 1800 marks were gained, except among the more ambitious, when a fierce competition ensued for first place among the chosen men. Second, many of the marks being dependent on the professors, men took to writing essays which they hoped would fall in with their views, rather than the more original work which was asked for. Riding was taught in a perfunctory manner, and those officers who did not wish to keep horses could hire for the day when the work was essential. This was essentially a false system for men educating for the Staff, a mounted service.

Colonel Hamley at once instituted many changes. Among others—

1. System of marks being published was abolished, men merely being noted as passing out in order of seniority of regiments.

2. Students could now pass " with honours," or simply pass.

3. The course consisted of four terms, each winding up with an examination on the whole of the subjects which had been taught during the previous term. A man failing to qualify at any of these examinations was dismissed.

4. The commandant took personal charge of the senior division in certain subjects out of doors.

5. Each student was obliged to keep a charger, to be passed by the commandant.

6. Students attended riding-school daily, to be passed by a cavalry officer, instead of twice a-week, during the whole two years.

7. Colonel Hamley met professors and students to fix the minimum necessary to secure the " pass " and " honours." This was much appreciated by all concerned.

8. Hunting was encouraged, leave from most classes being easily obtained for the purpose. The change in the riding-school method was excellent, officers exerting themselves to learn and get out of the school. After six months of the new system, four officers were dismissed as incompetent for Staff duties—one for his inability to ride, an event I believe never to have happened before.

Hamley's manner was unquestionably brusque, and sometimes he might have made a disagreeable communication more pleasantly than he did. But he expected to find in others the same inflexible sense of duty which actuated all his own conduct, and, as has been very justly remarked in the memorandum I have quoted, from sheer kind - heartedness he was in haste to despatch any unwelcome piece of business. There can be no question that, as Commandant, he was highly popular with all zealous students. As has been said, they knew that he spared no pains: they found him an entertaining and most instructive companion on flying expeditions; and they appreciated the inestimable value of his practical teaching in the field. The facility with which leave was granted when the hounds met, shows the wise administration of a man of the world, who knew that while books were all very well, the students of the College were being educated for action. And there is a passage in one of his letters which indicates the sincerity of his attachment, and how anxiously he followed the fortunes of his *protégés d'élite*. He complains sadly of some of his best men being used up in the malarious jungle warfare with the savages of Ashanti. A letter to Blackwood, written in the midsummer of 1871, expresses his feelings as to the work he initiated and thoroughly enjoyed :—

I am full of business just now, for the time is at hand for taking my flock on various expeditions. Towards the end of this month we ride in parties to the Thames, for an imaginary warlike operation. Then I shall be out with them under canvas in the September campaign, and after that into Suffolk on a military sketching expedition of ten days or so. The D. of Wellington talks of giving me some shooting, but I shan't have much opportunity of enjoying it, certainly not in September.

Again in the autumn :—

You might have observed in the papers that I had a busy time of it in the autumn manœuvres, having to play the double part of umpire and director of my young men who accompanied me into camp and were exercised in practical Staff business. We had a not disagreeable and very improving time. A few days afterwards we set off to Suffolk on our annual reconnaissance, and had dreadful weather—returning here a fortnight since. I am now at work again—cutting down trees, planting, turfing, &c., as if I were a country gentleman with a proper desire of handing down his estate in good condition to his children.

But however much he was engrossed by his duties, material comfort was by no means neglected. The Commandant had an excellent house near the College, and the veteran campaigner bestowed much care on the selection of his personal staff. He had a housekeeper and *cordon bleu* who received liberal wages, and who must have rather resembled Mrs Greene in 'Lady Lee's Widowhood,' save that she never got the upper hand of her master. He declared that he was lapped in luxury, and by way of constant companions, beyond his books, he had the dogs and cats that cumbered the hearthrug. He took infinite pleasure in his garden, and in many passages of his correspondence he talks of acquisitions to his territorial domains, measured by roods or yards, and of the extensive improvements he was carrying out on the property. In fact, as few men had so many resources, he was never at a loss for occupations that interested him, and so, in the sympathy of common pursuits, he made friends in all classes of the community. If his manner to some may have seemed austere or reserved, in reality he was the most sociable and unassuming of mortals. At Sandhurst and off duty, he led the happy life of a country gentleman. He was always a welcome guest at many of the neighbouring houses, and he delighted in arranging pleasant little dinners himself, at which the wines could invariably be relied upon, and where the *menus* had been carefully thought out. Breakfast-giving was rather a *spécialité* of his—especially when he had chambers in London. Notwithstanding the illustrious examples of Rogers and Lord Houghton, we hold it an uncomfortable form of hospitality, and it is to the credit of any middle-aged wit if he can be animated over tea or coffee at 10 A.M. But a *tête-à-tête* breakfast with Hamley was a pleasant beginning to the day, even in November fogs or December frosts. The host, fresh and radiant from bed and bath, was always at his brightest and best. The dishes were as good and original as the talk. For the enter-

tainer prided himself, with reason, on a system
of spirit-lamps, &c., by which the *plats* he had
elaborated or invented were transferred to the
table at the moment of perfection.   He was a
master in the manipulation of oysters, anchovies,
&c., and Mr Micawber could not have surpassed
him in the seasoning of a devil.   Knowledge of
any kind is sure to come in usefully sooner or
later, and his staff found the advantage of those
culinary studies over bivouac fires when employed
on delimitation commissions, and detached from
the cook.   None of the neighbours seem to have
taken more cordially to him than the late Duke
of Wellington; and when at a later period his
Grace offered a prize for the best essay on a
military subject, he requested Hamley to undertake the duty of umpire—a responsibility which
he accepted.   A letter of 11th June indicates the
interest the Duke took in the publication :—

MY DEAR DUKE OF WELLINGTON,—I have compared Mr
Hildyard's corrections with his paper [1]—they are all such
as will be at once made by the printer. I think, therefore,
it will be well to send the whole of the Essays forthwith
to Messrs Blackwood, with instructions to forward a proof
of each individual paper to its writer for final revision,
except Mr Hildyard's, which has already been revised by

---

[1] Mr Hildyard, now Colonel Hildyard, the present Commandant
of the Staff College.

him in proof,—these revised proofs to be returned direct
to Messrs Blackwood to save time, and to spare your
Grace unnecessary trouble. I will write a short paragraph
descriptive of the circumstances under which the publication was undertaken, and send it to your Grace—for
insertion, if you approve, as a notice to the reader,—it
will be too short to be called a preface.

Mr Blackwood, writing to me a few days ago, inquired
what had become of Mr Maurice's Essay, which he had
expected weeks ago. The delay, therefore, is due entirely
to the writer, not the publisher. If he does not make
despatch, the other essays will tread on the heels of his—
which will serve him right.

I was going to take my niece to Ascot to-day, but the
weather has defeated that project, and no doubt many
similar ones.—I am, your Grace's most sincerely,

E. B. HAMLEY.

He was asked to Strathfieldsaye to shoot outlying pheasants in the hedgerows in the opening
days of October—an invitation he was compelled
to decline, as he was engaged in Sussex for the
wedding of his friend Mr Harry Sturgis with
the Speaker's daughter. But the Duke, who was
fastidious and capricious in his friendships, had
come to entertain a great affection for Hamley,
whose humour he heartily appreciated, and thenceforth the invitations and visits to Strathfieldsaye
became more and more frequent. Hamley, for
the most part, found himself *tête-à-tête* with his
Grace, or in such select company as that of the

Lord Chief-Justice Cockburn.   Many a good story he had to tell of those symposia, and of the shooting and the *al fresco* luncheons which preceded them.   The Duke had an infinite fund of drollery; he was fond of dwelling upon a joke which hit his fancy, and would write Hamley a series of notes, elaborating it through a succession of stages.   Sir Patrick MacDougall was good enough to supply amusing reminiscences of what he calls their jolly companionship :—

The Duke's whimsical nature made him very congenial to Hamley, who used to return from his frequent visits to Strathfieldsaye full of the latter's stories.   I here select a virtuous specimen.   The Duke speaks : "At one time my father's extreme popularity was rather embarrassing.   For instance, on leaving home each day he was always intercepted by an affectionate mob, who insisted on hoisting him on their shoulders and asking where they should carry him.   It was not always convenient to my father to say where he was going ; so he used to say, ' Carry me home, carry me home ; ' and so he used to be brought home half a dozen times a day a few minutes after leaving his own door."

Some of the Duke's remarks about his heroic father may be discreetly suppressed, but there is another and characteristic anecdote which is worth repeating, though I rather think it has been published before :—

The great Duke had appointed a sitting for his picture for the morning of the day on which his brother, Lord

Wellesley, died. The artist appeared at the appointed time, saying he was not sure if he ought to have come. The Duke soon set him at his ease. "Yes," he said, alluding to his brother, "he is gone. An agreeable man when he had his own way."

No little inducement in going to Strathfield-saye was that the good old Chaplain - General was established in a house in the neighbourhood. The Duke, like his father, had a sincere affection and admiration for him. On the 26th November there is a lively account of a visit they paid to the Commandant at the College. He writes to Blackwood :—

I have had two of your correspondents—namely, the Duke of Wellington and the Chaplain-General—here from Saturday to Monday. The Duke is well pleased, quite elated in fact, by the success of the two volumes. I hope the second is doing well. He is a most cheery old gentleman, and very easy to amuse. The first day we dined at the Mess; the Sunday I had a little party for him here, and he was quite happy. He went to the College chapel to hear his particular friend the Chaplain-General preach, and slumbered throughout the sermon in full sight of the congregation. The Chaplain-General is looking wonderfully strong and well, and is as young in his mind and ways as ever. They saw the Kriegspiel played at the College. I asked Maurice and his wife to dine, and the Duke was much pleased with the winner of his prize.

Probably the Duke's last correspondence was with Hamley. He wrote him five notes in a single week, and the last came little more than a fortnight before the invitation to the funeral.

The friendship with Sir Patrick MacDougall began with the establishment of the Staff College in the new building. It soon became close as it was constant, and some of Hamley's last letters were addressed to one of his most cherished companions. Beyond strong personal sympathy, they were drawn together by common tastes — soldiering, fishing, and broad culture. Many were the trips they made in company; many the fishing excursions at home and abroad; and together they had gone over many of the European battle-fields. Sir Patrick wrote :—

Our first acquaintance was when I had been appointed first Commandant of the College, and Colonel Hamley, just home from the Crimea, and even then with a literary reputation, was my first Professor of Military History. From that day to the day of his death, our close friendship never suffered a moment's interruption. He took a house near the village of Sandhurst, where he used to assemble very agreeable dinner-parties. He was a perfectly ideal travelling companion, as I frequently experienced. One indispensable qualification of such a companion is that he must be unselfish, and Hamley had not an atom of self in his composition. We visited Antwerp with its pictures and history, and of course the field of Waterloo; afterwards Heidelberg, the Black Forest, carrying our fishing-rods and knapsacks to Wildbad. At this place Hamley, while engaged with a good trout, shouted out suddenly, "Bring me the landing-net," when a German, who was looking on, but did not understand a word of English, smartly picked up the net and gave it. Another excursion we made to Yorkshire; and I shall always preserve a fond memory of a walk from Keighley over the moors, when we talked Shakespeare the whole time, convincing me that he had entered more into the mind of the poet than most of the commentators—an opinion he amply justified when he came to write "Shakespeare's Funeral." Whatever the subject, he so informed it with instruction that it was a pleasure to listen to him. During these many journeyings to and fro, I had ample opportunities of observing how fortunate I was to have such a companion, with a sense of the ridiculous so acute that it made him delightfully entertaining, and with serious knowledge so various and extensive that it was a privilege to hear him lecture privately on painting and Shakespeare. Of modern writers, I think Dickens was his favourite, because his writings lent themselves to his sense of fun more than others.

Both Sir Patrick and Hamley were connoisseurs in horseflesh — otherwise the latter could never have described to the life the turf experiences of Bagot Lee and his sporting Mephistopheles; and one of Sir Patrick's recollections as to an unfortunate bargain is both amusing and illustrative, for Hamley cared little what he rode. In 1869 MacDougall was living at Winchester when Hamley was at Sandhurst.

The Commandant used to pay me frequent visits, either to try horses or to have a gallop with Mr Dean's harriers.

At that time the very celebrated character of the name of Mr John Tubb owned a splendid range of stabling at the back of the barracks, and his stables were always full of splendid horses to look at, but few of them were fit to ride on account of some trick of temper. " The vicious Rogue," called by Hamley Diogenes because he came from a " Tub," was bought by Tubb at Tattersall's for £16, and afterwards sold to Hamley for £60. I was much struck with the quiet, sensible expression of the Rogue's face, and I was told by a vet. whom I employed to look at the Rogue, that he was the most genuine horse he had ever known Tubb to possess. Having got so far, I resorted to a method I have always employed since I attained powers of discretion in making acquaintance with a new horse, by having some pieces of sugar and apple in my pocket to give him. The Rogue met my advances most affably; then I proceeded to mount him. I rode him over some small fences, and brought him back quite delighted. I sent for Hamley, who was greatly pleased; but he told Tubb, unless the horse would go in harness he would not suit. Tubb's expressive features showed some signs of dismay. However, he assured Hamley he went like a lamb in single harness. The horse was tested then and there : he really went like a lamb, and was passed and purchased.

The subsequent correspondence may serve as a useful warning to novices who fancy they have been exceptionally fortunate in picking up a good-looking horse for a trifle :—

My dear MacD.,—I am going to tell you a little history about our friend Diogenes, because experience in horseflesh is always worth acquiring.

As I told you, I rode him several times, reconnoitring

with the class, and he always went capitally. But one day I started alone; and he began, as soon almost as I left the stable, to stop short, and when touched with whip or spur, to become restive and show symptoms of fighting, as if it were a habit. Inquiring of the groom, I found that the equine philosopher had reared several times, as he expressed it, "frightful." Since then I rode him in the school, and at a field-day among rifle-popping and big guns, when he behaved perfectly well. His style of going seemed to improve, and I got more and more pleased with *it*, but the doubt about temper caused me to inquire at Tattersall's. I found he was sent up under the name of "Oxford" from Lord Macclesfield. I wrote to his lordship; and his note being pretty and to the point, I transcribe it:

" Lord Macclesfield presents his compliments to Col. Hamley, and begs to say that the horse ' Oxford' is the most *vicious rogue* that he ever met with, and that he very nearly killed one of his sons, and he would strongly advise him not to keep him.".

The worthy Tubb, no doubt, had an inkling of his character—hence his keeping him idle in the stable, and taking so many precautions about putting him in harness. Question is, what to do with Diogenes? Do you suppose the respected Tubb would buy him back?—at a low price, of course; or shall I send him to Aldridge's? Or is it justifiable to sell him at all, or to prolong his valuable life at the risk of others? Meanwhile I am like Mr Pickwick after the gig was knocked to pieces, " with a dreadful horse that I can't get rid of." — Yours ever,

E. B. HAMLEY.

The difficulty and the questions of casuistry were solved by what looked like a special interposition of Providence. The eccentricities of

Diogenes grew upon him, and his character became notorious in military circles in the district. Whereupon a daring young subaltern of Horse Artillery wrote from Aldershot, with an offer of £30, made in full knowledge of the offender's misdeeds. He and Hamley went together to Reading, where the horse was standing at livery. The livery-stabler was only too eager to get rid of him. He said he had nearly killed his best rider, and that no man in England could sit him, if he wished to throw him off. "Thus far Tompkins!" Hamley faithfully repeated the tale to the would-be buyer, saying that he would not sell, but would send the animal to Tattersall's. "The V. R. was then brought out by my groom, from whom, after several rears and kicks, he broke away, and went trumpeting about the public thoroughfares with the bridle trailing, and his tail not merely erect, but curling like a pug dog's over his back, with all the hair on it falling the wrong way." Notwithstanding, the venturesome lieutenant was pleased with his looks, and lowering his bid by a fiver, persisted in desiring to possess the horse. He said that if Hamley declined to sell, it would give him the trouble of attending the auction. "His ambition is to hunt him : if he fails, he says he will sell him at Tatt's, and lose nothing ; and as he seems a knowing youth, this is likely enough." So, remembering that there were rough-riders and brakes at Aldershot, Hamley salved his conscience, and somewhat reluctantly got rid of the "dreadful horse."

Another story of that period Sir Patrick relates, and Hamley's niece remembers how her uncle used to delight in it. Perhaps he had embroidered it in .the manner of his friend the Duke of Wellington, and it is a pity it was not turned into a "Tale for Blackwood." Briefly, Captain Brook, "a dear friend and comrade," was then the riding-master at the Cadet College. Hamley had christened him the Murmuring Brook, on account of his incessant complaints to the War Office. Desiring to enter one of his sons at Wellington College, and before he had made acquaintance with the localities, starting one day to walk to the College from the station, Captain Brook caught sight of the Broadmoor Criminal Lunatic Asylum on an adjacent height. Confounding one establishment with the other, he walked up and rang the bell. As Hamley used to tell the story,—

He asked the porter if he could see the Principal. When the latter appeared, Brook thought him a queer-looking figure for an instructor of youth. Brook said, "I wish to put my boy under your charge, if you can take him." "Oh yes," said the man; "is he a bad case?" "Bad case!" said Brook; "what the devil do you mean? There's not a better boy in England; the only thing I fear is, he may be too old." "Why, how old is he?" "He is eighteen." "Pish! we take them up to eighty." "Why," says Brook, again in high dudgeon, "if he does not come here till eighty, what time do you suppose he is going to get his commission?"

A reminiscence in different vein relates to a dinner some years later at Hamley's chambers in Ryder Street:—

I had the pleasure of meeting Kinglake and Count Strelécky, when the conversation turned on the resemblance between French and English fiction-writers, taking Daudet for the French, Dickens and Thackeray for the English examples. For instance, we may feel convinced that Daudet in 'Fromont Jeune,' when he wrote a description of the scene where Risler discovers his wife's guilt, must have had in his mind the scene in 'Vanity Fair' where Rawdon Crawley surprises Lord Steyne. Similarly, it is probable that Daudet in his charming creation of little Désirée had in his thoughts Dickens's Doll's dressmaker. In discussing the comparative merits of the three, I think Kinglake gave the *pas* to Thackeray; Hamley supporting Dickens, for the reason that his peculiar fun lent itself more readily to Hamley's humorous instinct than the other; while I held that Daudet was the equal of either.

Hamley had happened to remark on the number of French atheists always present in London, when Count Strelécky mentioned his experience of a meeting he had attended from curiosity in Leicester Square. After listening for more than an hour to several speakers, all of them launching out in furious tirades against the Almighty, a mild old gentleman with quavering voice meekly asked leave to say a few words in favour of "*le bon Dieu.*" The cry was immediate and unanimous, "*À la porte !*"

CHAPTER XI.

LITERARY RECREATIONS.

"SHAKESPEARE'S FUNERAL"—'VOLTAIRE' IN "FOREIGN CLASSICS"—LEAVES THE STAFF COLLEGE.

ALTHOUGH he was engrossed by his official duties, and with all the distractions of field-sports, horticulture, and friendly visits, in these years literature was by no means neglected. In the way of his professional work was a new edition of 'The Operations of War,' which was imperatively demanded by contemporary events. He had followed with the closest attention the Franco-German campaigns, with the latest developments of scientific strategy. The knowledge he had been imparting to his "young men" suggested new and important chapters, and notably that upon "Sedan and Metz." As he sat in his chair, or while carrying on the field practice at Sandhurst, he had been playing a single-handed *Kriegspiel*, and imagining how he would have directed matters had he been on the spot and in command. He was fond of relating how, during those critical days when the German armies were closing in upon Metz, he gave his ideas to two friends who were dining with him—one was Mowbray Morris of the 'Times,' and I believe the other was General Hozier—as to how Bazaine might have conducted a retreat with comparatively little loss. Afterwards he found his suggestions confirmed by no less a person than Von Moltke in the official narrative of the war, published at Berlin.[1]

[1] The Franco-German War of 1870-71. By Field-Marshal Count Helmuth Von Moltke. Translated by Clara Bell and H. W. Fischer. Battle of Vionville, Mars-la-Tour (Aug. 16).

The 6th Division of the Prussians had been sent forward to Etain, by Mars-la-Tour, to obstruct, *if possible*, the northern road to Verdun, on the supposition that the French had begun the retreat. The underlining of "if possible" is mine. The Prussian forces were then facing the East.

"The position of the French was one of great advantage. Their left flank was protected by the fortress of Metz, the right by formidable batteries and a strong force of cavalry. They might safely await an attack on their centre.

"Of course the march to Verdun, even under cover of a strong rear-guard, had to be abandoned. If the Marshal had been resolved to proceed, he would have had to engage and get rid of the enemy in front of him.

"It is difficult to decide, from a purely military point of view, why this alternative was not taken. There was hardly a doubt that only part, and probably only a small part, of the German armies could as yet have passed the Mozelle, and when, in the course of the day, the Divisions which had remained at Metz arrived, the French were decidedly the stronger. But it seems that the Marshal's first object was not to be forced away from Metz—almost his entire concern was for his left wing. By constantly reinforcing the flank, he

Among other things he had written his " Shakespeare's Funeral," which is not only, perhaps, his most brilliant piece of work, but is the expression of his intense poetical sympathies and of the profound thoughtfulness of his literary temperament. He worshipped Shakespeare's transcendent genius, though he did not scruple to criticise him freely in " False Coin in Poetry "; and, as Sir Patrick MacDougall has remarked in his ' Recollections,' he had steeped himself in his own interpretation of the inner meanings of the plays. Each of the creations was a veritable individuality to him, which he sought to realise and analyse. In short, he had searched his Shakespeare as we are told to search the Scriptures, and no one need undertake a pilgrimage to Stratford who does not admire and delight in " The Funeral." In brief space, and in indirect fashion, all the catholic characteristics of the bard are brought out,— his intuitive penetration, his broad and sympathetic appreciation, the flow of his genial humour, and the simplicity of the pathos. To the grand artist nothing was common or vulgar that might serve to illustrate the manifold types of humanity. The originals of the Shylocks and Dogberrys were

massed his Guards—part of the 6th Corps—in front of the Bois des Ognons, from whence no attack was made. We are tempted to fancy that political reasons alone induced Bazaine, thus early in the game, to attach himself to Metz."

to be seen within a stone-throw of New Place. So Hamley fell in with the master's humours, and gave prominence to the humble countrymen and town's folk who, irrespective of clime or speech, had furnished him with many an immortal subject. Genius had made us forget the almost ludicrous incongruity of transferring the uncouth Warwickshire rustics to Greece or the enchanted isle of the Tempest, as the dewberry, with its purely local name, was made to blossom and bear fruit in the hedgerows of Attica. There is an interesting letter, in which Hamley defends his own conceptions, in answer to certain objections :—

9th March 1873.

MY DEAR BLACKWOOD,—It would have pulled the idea to pieces sadly, and have taken some of the pith out of it, to have omitted them. Bearers are not, I imagine, chosen commonly for their respectability—funeral entertainments, like all others in those days, generally ended in a carouse —and it seemed to me a kindly notion, and suited to our idea of the poet, that he should name for the office (instead of leaving it to the choice of the sexton) those poor townsmen of whom he had already taken so much note as to put them in his works. The omission of this trait, as well as others touched on in the last scene, would have been, in my view, a dead loss. That last scene, too, was necessary to the rounding off of the idea as I had conceived it. I am therefore much pleased that on reconsideration you agree with me that it should stand. Except as bearers, there was no way in which these additional Shakespearian personages could have come into the paper.

But Hamley happily illustrated, with a cynical humour of his own, the circumstances which the poet had cheerfully accepted. Nothing can be more comically clever, or more touchingly true to the facts, than the picture of that sublime genius living apart in the unsympathetic atmosphere of the everyday world. Sir Thomas Lucy, the Justice Shallow of Charlecote, rides in to grace the burial of a man of decent estate, and who had a right to quarter the arms of Arden. His worthy son-in-law, "good Master Hall," confesses that he cares little for the fond extravagances of his well-meaning father-in-law, whom he regards with the contemptuous affection of a practical man; and even his loving daughter, like the good vicar of Stratford, is sorely exercised over the condition of the poet's soul. He had not only squandered time and talents on the plays that were but vanity, or worse; but, in his indiscreet charity, he gave alms indiscriminately, and was never neglectful of the vicious and the ungrateful. And *apropos* to the Kit Slys and the Bardolphs—the parish gossips, the paupers, and the loungers—what can be more Shakespearian than the scenes at the funeral, with the parade and simple self-revelation of selfishness, greed, and petty ambitions!

In the spring of 1874 he expresses his opinion as to the great Conservative victory at the elections. He always maintained that Lord Derby, as a statesman, and even as a party leader, made a fatal mistake when he took his "leap in the dark," and he held with Mr Lowe that no move in that direction should have originated with the Conservatives so long as the bulk of the new electorate was uninformed and uneducated. The dissolution had come as a surprise, and I believe Disraeli was the only leader of the Tories who had anticipated the probability. Coming up to town one day from Hughenden a few weeks before, he had declared emphatically that it was quite on the cards that there might be an immediate appeal to the country. Hamley writes on 13th February :—

What an astounding series of political events—from Gladstone's *coup* to Benjamin's majority ! It certainly looks as if the Caucasian had been justified in descending to look for his "residuum," but I don't believe in it for all that. Much of the reaction against the Liberals is terror at the warnings given us in France and Spain.

It seems to me that there is so much to separate Liberals and Radicals, foolishly classed hitherto as of the same party, and so little difference between Liberals and Conservatives, that a coalition of the latter is the right thing to give a strong Government and to discredit democracy and demagogism. The chief obstacle is in the leaders—who could scarcely be brought together with cart-ropes after blackguarding each other on the hustings in the discreditable way they have done. It is a great pity that my little plan of putting them in a bag together and dropping them over Westminster Bridge is not altogether feasible.

Thus he had already forecast the coalition of the Conservatives with patriotic Liberals, though no man could have foreseen the particular evolution which was to be the proximate cause of the alliance.

Again he says, on February 2d :—

The best thing about the Ministry is, not that we shall get better administration, for that may or may not be, but that it shows a change of feeling in the people, and is a guarantee that the shooting of Niagara is postponed.

Personally, the only man he regretted in the outgoing Cabinet was Mr Cardwell, to whom he was not only greatly indebted for his position at the Staff College, but for support and encouragement in enlightened reforms. A letter of 12th March refers to the Ashanti Expedition, which he had followed with interest, although the strategist had rather a contempt for semi-barbaric warfare. But not a few of his pupils had gone to Africa, and several of the most promising were on the General's staff. He pays a graceful compliment to Sir Garnet Wolseley :—

Most of my officers have written me their experiences from time to time. Wood, who came with despatches, is already in England. Maurice, who was considered of too weak constitution to stand the work, has passed through the ordeal almost better than anybody, being the only one who never was ill. The conduct of the Expedition is meeting with the praise it deserved, as being altogether excellent. It is the end of it, from the first battle to the march back, that specially signalises Wolseley's quality as a commander, resolute as well as careful.

He goes on to condemn the burning of Coomassie as a political mistake, if not a positive crime :—

Acts of destruction are dangerous precedents, and may easily become very inconvenient. The charges of treachery against the Ashanti king are simply childish: there is no evidence of any deceit except such as has always been considered praiseworthy in the case of one defending his country and capital from invasion.

In a letter of the following week he says again :—

It is pleasant to see the unanimity with which the press praise Wolseley, whose conduct of the business was as good as possible. They got away just in time —there was a deal of sickness at the end. I met one of my late officers the other day. He went out a strong young fellow, and has come back an elderly cripple.

Another letter touching upon a friend's tragedy —which he was naturally inclined to view with favour—shows that he had reflected on the principles of dramatic criticism, and formed decided opinions of his own. It may be remarked, by the way, that afterwards, when an involuntary idler in London, he was not disinclined to accept the position of dramatic critic to one of the leading journals, for he was a regular frequenter of the theatres, and loved to assist at first nights.

My notions about a tragedy are, that the subject and personages should command sympathy—that the situations should be striking—that the story should appear in the most vivid light—and that it should afford ample scope for poetry. At any rate, some of these conditions appear indispensable. It is hardly necessary to say a word as to the subject and personages of "——"; and if my friend has made a bad choice, what shall we say of the setting ?

On the other hand, he gives warm praise to Sir George Chesney's novel of 'The Dilemma':—

I don't know that any novelist has ever before made the course of true love run over such obstacles. The whole work strikes me as superior to all of the day.

At that time he was bringing the whole strength of his conscientious energy to bear upon a little work of his own. Seldom has more scrupulous care or more anxious thought been bestowed on so small a volume. Blackwood had been following up his series of the Ancient Classics—a novel idea which has since been ridden to death—by a similar series devoted to the classical writers of the Continent. He asked Hamley to undertake 'Voltaire,' nor could he have made a better selection. Hamley's 'Voltaire' must strike one as a masterpiece of comprehensive condensation. Though necessarily and tantalisingly brief, the interest is marvellously sustained. The writer holds the balance steadily between the fanatical abusers of the misunderstood sceptic and his still more extravagant devotees. His own intellectual tendencies were severely analytical, for he was slow to receive on faith what was not susceptible of material proof. I would not be misunderstood, for Hamley accepted the great doctrines of the Christian creed; and I know that he always earnestly desired that his faith and hopes in the future might be strengthened. Latterly, nothing interested him more than the works of dispassionate and logical divines which treated with broad liberality that all-important subject. But he admired the brilliant audacity of the champion of free thought and frank speech. His own indignation was excited by the flagrant social and judicial abuses against which Voltaire waged unsparing war. He points out that the philosopher of Ferney was a sound Conservative so far as all things secular were concerned. He attacked neither the Crown nor the State as institutions. And in his assaults on the Church, as Hamley remarks, his earlier writings, if unorthodox, are not irreligious. His theistic views were less pronounced than those of Mr Mill. He set out by fiercely assailing the superstition, fanaticism, and corruption of the clergy, in an age when profligate laymen engrossed the richest benefices, and when members of the Sacred College and princes of the Church gave the worst possible example to the feudal autocrats in the provinces. As the struggle waxed warmer and his power was recognised, his bitter sarcasm became more and more envenomed : he launched out recklessly in blasphemous ribaldry, and so gained, not undeservedly, his reputation as the prince of mockers and scorners. All that is brought out with striking effect; and Voltaire is, besides, sketched successively as the man of the world, the dramatist, and the philosophical historian. Hamley prided himself, with reason, on the poetical translations, which reflect the spirit and sense of the original with a sufficiently close if not literal rendering. Voltaire's cynical humour had much in common with his own, and he undertook the volume as a labour of love, being already tolerably familiar with the Frenchman's innumerable writings. But he unhesitatingly declined a similar proposal as to Rabelais ; for, strange to say, he never appreciated the wittily grotesque extravagances of the jovial Curé of Meudon :—

It is very difficult to understand either his language or his wit in the degree necessary to do him justice. I never read any of his French, except so much as is quoted in the translations, but that shows how idiomatic and peculiar it is; and I should scarcely think that any but a born Frenchman would be competent to make him thoroughly intelligible. In fact, even with translations that exist, I have never succeeded in appreciating the humour which has made his name so famous.

7th December 1876.

MY DEAR BLACKWOOD,—You asked if I liked the notion of doing Voltaire. I have been working at it with great interest. I have made a good many translations of specimen passages; and if these are reasonably done, he ought to be recognised as a really good poet, of a type different probably in many respects from the popular English idea of him. . . . It will be better not to put in a sketch of his life complete, but rather to let it run on with his works.

No doubt publishers like zeal in an author, especially in so distinguished a specialist as Hamley, who might well be disposed to take things easily and trust much to his name and *verve*. But Blackwood, who had as little love for letter - writing as Johnson for clean linen, while the 'Voltaire' was in deliberate course of incubation must have been inclined to curse his friend's earnest enthusiasm. The letters with regard to the matter, and to emendations in the proofs, might have made up half-a-dozen similar volumes. He had taken infinite pains

with a subject that suited his taste, and his hopes
of a favourable reception were high. The publication only brought disappointments and mor-
tifications. He had forgotten that one small
member of a numerous family has little chance
of respectful notice. Not a few of the papers
ignored him ; others disposed of him in a paragraph among the minor critiques. It is more
surprising that some of the reviews were " slight-
ing " and others " insulting," for the book not
only sold remarkably well, but, as I have endeavoured to argue, may safely stand on its
merits. The reasonable conclusion is, that busy
reviewers merely skimmed the pages, and wrote
rather with regard to the Deist's popular reputation, than to this novel and intelligent conception of his real character and the veritable scope
of his work.

In the summer of 1877 Hamley's time at the
Staff College had expired : he was only continued
as Commandant till his successor should be nominated, and he had the cheerless prospect of
evacuating his comfortable quarters and quit-
ting a congenial occupation. About this time,
when the Russian army had failed again and
again to carry the position of Plevna, so stub-
bornly defended by the Turks under Osman
Pasha, Hamley was sounded as to his readi-

ness to take service under the Russian Government. But his sympathies were not with the Russians in their attack upon Turkey, and for this and other reasons he declined to consider the proposal.

Promotion to the rank of Major-General did not console Hamley much for want of employment—though, as he carelessly remarks, it did him no harm. "I have no prospect of an appointment" (22d October), "and scarcely expect, or indeed wish, for the Military Educational one" (for which several of the leading journals had advocated his exceptional claims)—"though I could not afford to refuse it. But there may be one on the cards before long that would suit me better." The post alluded to was that of Chief of the Military Intelligence Department, to be vacated by his friend General MacDougall in the following spring. "Most of the officers employed there have been trained by me, and my rank now qualifies me for it." The appointment was bestowed elsewhere. He broke up his home at Sandhurst, and sorely against his will came to London as a soldier in involuntary retreat. He writes Blackwood, from the Athenæum, on New Year's day : "Yesterday I exchanged my country mansion for a humble bedroom in this neighbourhood. My family is dispersed—Dandy gone to Gleig's from whence he came, the pug to a lady at Sandhurst, and my horses to Wokingham. The cat, Mr Ruffie, remains in Lady Alison's charge." For his friend Sir Archibald Alison had succeeded him as Commandant, and he had the satisfaction of knowing that the College was not likely to deteriorate under the new direction. As it happened, Colonel Alison only remained there for six months—though, in the expectation that he would serve his full time, he had relieved Hamley of his furniture. In the autumn Hamley made a flying trip to the Highlands, wandering about with knapsack, sketch-books, and fishing-rod; and in the winter he delivered a lecture on the defence of the Afghan frontier at the United Service Institution. Things have greatly changed since then, on the initiative and under the direction of Lord Roberts and Sir George Chesney; but few who heard him will forget the lucidity with which he demonstrated the complex problems of the situation, and indicated the comparative advantages of three possible lines of defence, finally falling back upon a concise exposition of the only plan which at the time was practicable. " I much dislike," he said, " any kind of public address; but being pressed by the Committee, I felt I could not refuse the challenge : if I call myself a strategist, I ought to behave as such." And in the brief discussion which followed the lecture, his views were generally accepted by experienced Indian generals, more or less familiar with the ground, and who had made a special study of the question. The manner of the delivery was singularly impressive: nothing was advanced without conclusive or plausible reason, and it was evident that the lecturer was giving expression to the deliberate convictions that had been carefully thought out.

CHAPTER XII.

THE SYSTEM OF OUTPOSTS.

THE HORSE GUARDS AND HAMLEY'S SYSTEM—TRIAL AT ALDER-
SHOT — PUBLICATION OF PAMPHLET — CHARACTERISTICS OF
THE SYSTEM.

BUT there had been an episode in the autumn of
1876 which demands something more than a passing notice among the comparatively unimportant
incidents of the year.   There had been many references in his letters to his ideas as to a better
system of instruction in outpost duty, to which
he necessarily attached extreme importance, as
ensuring the safety of armies when on the defensive in the field, and contributing greatly to
the success of offensive operations.   He had
been elaborately explaining the system in his
lectures, and had given a very lucid outline of
it in 'The Operations of War.' The Aldershot
authorities had arranged to give it a regular
trial on a certain day.   That was brought to

the knowledge of the Commander-in-Chief, who intimated his intention of being present. Subsequently came a telegram from the Horse Guards to change the day.

Had I been consulted, as in fairness I should have been, I should have chosen different ground for the test, and should have liked a rehearsal, as neither troops nor officers had ever tried it before. Nevertheless, the result was to convince me and everybody else who understood my system that it had proved its efficiency. Not so, however, the authorities of the Horse Guards, who did *not* understand it, never having even heard of my pamphlet.

With the Duke of Cambridge's ejaculation, overheard on the ground, Hamley would probably have cordially agreed. "If this is right, Airey, what we have been doing all our lives is wrong!" But he complained that at the close of the manœuvres, when men had gathered round the Duke to hear the usual comments, the opinions of the umpires were never called for. That was an altogether exceptional departure from the custom, but his Royal Highness spoke out with his habitual frankness, pronouncing strongly against the innovation. "Only in such a way as to show that he did not half understand what had been done. I was allowed, at Airey's instance, some words afterwards, and gave my view very decidedly, but that will hardly set the matter right." His system, as has been said, is fully explained in one of the most instructive and fascinating chapters in 'The Operations of War.' Although it had been practised to some extent in recent campaigns, and notably by the Germans in their invasion of France, yet, as he explains elsewhere in 'The Operations,' the conditions of even the Franco-German war had only necessitated its partial adoption. It excited so much interest among soldiers, that it was subsequently republished in pamphlet form under the title 'Outposts,' and the pamphlet passed immediately through two editions. It is at once so lucid and picturesquely illustrative of the various operations in modern campaigning, that it may be read with advantage and interest by any civilian who is interested in the study of military history. It graphically depicts the position of an army feeling its way and guarding against surprise or attack when advancing through hostile territory in face of a formidable enemy.

Though the work is strictly technical, there is nevertheless a suggestion of the romance of war in the presentation of the scenery of countries the most diversified in character, with the explanations of the various military advantages or drawbacks of hill and dale, woodland and marsh, or of highly cultivated districts, with their villages, farmhouses, and enclosures. In showing how outpost work may be modified by changing circumstances, the writer brings his own knowledge and strategical insight within the comprehension of the most inexperienced subaltern. First, he indicates the functions of the triple line of outposts,—the sentries, the pickets, and the supports. Theoretically all are supposed to be in ready touch, so that any pulsation in the outlying feelers is transmitted directly to headquarters. It is shown how by ready calculation on well-ascertained principles, and by rapid examination of the ground to be guarded, theory may be promptly translated into practice. Hamley points out how the available men may be economised, by making the most of natural obstacles. There is much in the choice of ground, and in the skilful use of the cover, which may be advantageous or the reverse, according to circumstances. He indicates when cavalry and field-guns may be profitably employed. He explains under what circumstances the outposts should fall back, and when it may be well to offer resistance, remembering always that the army must not be drawn prematurely into an engagement on ground different from that selected by the general.

These remarks merely give some idea of the

circumstances to be considered, and of the numerous difficulties to be grappled with. The essentials to maintaining an efficient guard are concert, coherence, and an intelligent direction, embracing the whole wide circle of operations. Under the old system these conditions were too generally ignored or neglected. The troops told off for duty were taken almost at haphazard from detached battalions, and the command of parties and pickets was intrusted to officers who took their turn of duty in the ordinary routine. Hamley held that, on the contrary, "the men and officers for the duty cannot be too much accustomed to work together. A line of suitable extent (say, two miles) would be best confided to an entire battalion, with its own colonel for commander. . . . In the case of large armies, each battalion should be taken from the corps or division placed in rear of the space to be covered by it." Each of the supports should furnish its own pickets and from different companies, so that the picket would rally on its own company. When the advanced-guards are over-fatigued, they should be relieved by a fresh battalion or other homogeneous body—the troops so replaced falling back into the reserve. Responsibility should be distributed among capable officers, selected for their special qualifications.

So the commander of outposts would only have to issue general instructions: for himself, he should occupy a fixed post, where he could always be found to give special orders; and "he should establish the most rapid possible communication with the main position, either by signals, telegraph, or relay." In fact, the dispositions are to be as the radiating threads of a spider's web, with the controlling force established in the centre. It will be clear from this brief *résumé* of the system that an impromptu trial at a camp like Aldershot, even if made with all due deliberation, could scarcely be a fair one. From the nature of things, such an experiment could not be satisfactorily conducted except with forces which had already been in harmonious training, and so, as we read between the lines of the pamphlet, we see that the materials were non-existent at Aldershot. It is but natural that he should have felt and expressed himself strongly on a hasty experiment foredoomed to failure, from circumstances he might foresee but could not control.

CHAPTER XIII.

THE BULGARIAN DELIMITATION COMMISSION.

VISIT TO ITALY—APPOINTED TO THE TURKISH AND BULGARIAN COMMISSION—THE POSITION OF THE FRONTIER QUESTION—COMMUNICATIONS WITH THE FOREIGN OFFICE—ARRIVAL AT CONSTANTINOPLE—THE COMMISSIONERS—DELIMITATION WORK—LETTER TO THE DUKE OF CAMBRIDGE.

IN January 1879, having no immediate prospect of employment, he took advantage of his enforced idleness to pay what he intended to be a prolonged visit to Italy. He had long desired to visit Rome, and he hoped to pass the spring in Naples and Sicily. But man proposes and Providence disposes, and all his plans were suddenly upset.

Before leaving England, Hamley had heard with regret that Colonel Home, the English Commissioner for the delimitation of the Turkish and Bulgarian frontier, was dangerously ill. At Genoa he saw the announcement of the Commissioner's death, but he had no idea at the time that the event immediately concerned him. He had gone on, and had spent a month in Rome under circumstances singularly unfavourable to enjoyment and sight-seeing. He wrote rather dolefully that the weather was phenomenally cold and wet,—that the galleries were gloomy, and the Campagna miry.

The climate did not suit him, and altogether he felt ill and out of sorts. Then he got a stimulant he did not expect, and we hear no more of languor or indisposition. On the 5th of March, as he was sitting down to dinner at his hotel, a telegram was handed to him. It was a despatch from the War Office, proposing that he should succeed Colonel Home, and asking for an immediate answer. The telegram had been accidentally delayed, and the answer was sent immediately. That same night he started for England, and on the morning of the 8th he was in London. A few days later he wrote to Blackwood : " I would rather have gone to Zululand or Afghanistan, but I am glad to get any professional employment of a respectable nature, and to have the offer of what is not distasteful I consider lucky." Certainly the authorities could not have made a more fortunate choice ; and beyond the flattering testimonials he received, the best proof of their appreciation of his services was, that he was continued in a similar capacity on two subsequent Commissions. His talents and his distinction in his special studies recommended him ; and he had an iron will, indomitable energy, a keen eye, and unrivalled aptitude for recognising the strength and weakness of positions. He had many opportunities of exhibiting his readiness of resource and his cool-headed promptitude in awkward emergencies. Yet he could be patient when necessity arose, and control himself under provocation. All that is said in these sentences is borne out by Colonel Everett, now the head of the topographical section of the Military Intelligence Division, to whom I am indebted not only for invaluable information, but for many good stories of the adventures of the Commissions. For Colonel Everett, like his late chief, is an excellent *raconteur*, and both had the happy knack of making the best of things and finding amusement in situations sufficiently serious. Colonel Everett says that Hamley's straightforward character soon asserted an ascendancy over his colleagues, and even over the Russian, who was practically commissioned to oppose him. Had he sought to meet subtlety with subtlety he would undoubtedly have been out-manœuvred. Occasionally, in the actual details of the delimitation, he might resort to a *ruse de guerre*, but that was all fair warfare. At the Council Board, or in consultation, he always spoke his mind, kept the purpose of the Commission before his colleagues—which was to assure Turkey a defensible frontier—and supported his suggestions with arguments which it was exceedingly difficult to refute. His position was a strong one, and he held to it tenaciously and with success. The Turk was naturally willing to be guided by him. The neutral Commissioners were honestly anxious to despatch their task quickly to the best of their ability; and Colonel Bogulaboff, who represented the Czar, could hardly avow that his veritable purpose was to keep a practicable road to Constantinople.

At that time neither the Czar nor any one else could foresee the subsequent development of events in Bulgaria. The Emperor Alexander made sure of the gratitude of the emancipated Bulgarians: he counted on their future ruler as the Governor of one of his own provinces, and regarded the country as a Russian outpost. Nor was it then surmised that Eastern Roumelia would be joined to Bulgaria in a few years by the force of patriotic or popular sentiment. Consequently, the neutral European Powers were inclined to strengthen a fortified natural barrier which would tend to assure European tranquillity. Consequently, too, the memorandum which Hamley drew up on the situation has lost much of its value. Still there are some points of permanent interest which I shall endeavour to select. In fact, he had begun and carried on to considerable length a narrative apparently intended for publication. It is continued to the end of the proceedings by a rough diary of daily incidents. As no one could describe better than himself, there is a strong temptation to transfer to these pages the fragment as it stands; but on the whole, and with regard to the sense of proportion, it seems more advisable to single out the more characteristic passages. Some of these tell the connected story of the mission, or indicate the difficulties that were successfully surmounted. Others give graphic and vivid descriptions of the Turks, and their relations to the subject races; of the condition of Bulgaria immediately after the War; of the scenery, from the picturesque and the strategic point of view, through which the Commission travelled; and of the romantic or ludicrous incidents which lent variety to monotonous work. Above all, the writer sketches with his habitual acuteness the notable dignitaries with whom he was brought in contact, and contrasts the fighting and sterling qualities of the Turks of the lower orders with the apathetic indifference of the ruling classes and the corruption of the Government. As to the abuses of the Turkish administration, his strictures were still more severe when he was sent to delimit boundaries in Asia.

The preliminary memorandum indicates the circumstances which induced the Powers to agree to the Commission :—

When Russia had advanced through the Balkan peninsula in 1877-78, destroying or driving back the Turkish armies and enclosing Constantinople in her lines, she forced on her defeated antagonist the Treaty of San Stephano. By this instrument only a small strip of European territory was left to Turkey, hardly a sixth of that she had possessed at the beginning of the war; and this strip, with her capital, would be at the mercy of the enemy in another war.

Not only the ancient traditions of the balance of power, but the instinct of self-interest, caused the Great Powers to meet in Congress at Berlin, in order to prevent Russia from gaining the vast accession of power and influence which the execution of the treaty would have bestowed on her.

When the Congress had roughly redistributed the conquered territories, skilled topography was essential for defining the new frontiers, and a committee of military delegates was constituted. New maps were to be made, for there was no reliable and official map of Turkey. The best in existence was by the Austrian cartographers, and as it only marked five miles to an inch, it was impossible to lay on it anything more than an approximate frontier line. That was the map used by the delegates, but the different frontiers were still subject to determination on the ground, so that they gave perpetual matter for dispute. Then the different frontiers to be traced are described; but that with which we are concerned had special importance, as it was to be regularly fortified for the defence of Turkey.

By the first article of the Treaty of Berlin, Bulgaria was constituted an autonomous principality, subject only to the payment of tribute, and the sovereignty was purely honorary. The Bulgarian Commission must be military, because the boundary was to be capable of defence. What it had to delimit was — (1) the frontier on the side of Roumania, from Rakovitza on the Danube to a point east of Silistria, and thence by the shortest line to a given point on the Black Sea. (2) The northern and north-western boundaries of Eastern Roumelia along the Balkans. (3) The boundary of Roumelia to the new frontier of Servia. The Commission had met at Constantinople in September 1878, and Colonel Home of the Engineers was then the English delegate. Preliminary difficulties brought the proceedings prematurely to a standstill. As Hamley puts it,—and no doubt he writes feelingly, for he had to face the same trouble himself,—

To the Russian diplomatic and military mind, it seemed that Bulgaria might be made almost as useful in a future invasion as if it were Russian; that the hostility of the races, being judiciously fomented, will always be ready to fructify into convenient quarrel; that when Russian troops should again cross the Danube, they would find themselves in the territory of a humble and devoted ally; and that it was therefore expedient by all means to conciliate and aggrandise Bulgaria.

When the delegates at last went slowly to work, they were obstructed by the fluctuating policies of the Powers, as well as by the objections gratuitously raised by the Russians. So the delimitation was little more than begun when the Commissioners agreed to go into winter quarters. It was to reassemble on the 15th April 1879, and then Colonel Home had been replaced by General Hamley.

On 20th March he received an official communication from Lord Salisbury, enclosing the Royal Commission. In acknowledging it, he made the following suggestions :—

Major-General HAMLEY *to the* MARQUIS OF SALISBURY.—
(*Received March* 20.)

LONDON, *March* 20, 1879.

MY LORD,—I have the honour to inform you that I have considered, with due reference to the information received from Commandant Lemoyne respecting the work done by the Russian topographers on the Bulgarian frontier, what number of officers it will be necessary to take. Being informed that I cannot count upon having the services of Lieutenant Chermside for the Commission, I recommend that four officers, in addition to Major Ardagh,[1] should be appointed for the work of verifying the Russian map, and of making good any defects or omissions in it. The difficulty and extent of the frontier render this number the smallest with which the work could be done with reasonable despatch.

It seems to me most desirable that the party, which with its servants, drivers, &c., will be of some strength, should be accompanied by an assistant-surgeon, who, by prompt attention to slight feverish or other climatic complaints, might keep the whole party in working condition, and obviate the sickness or invaliding of some of its members.—I have, &c., E. B. HAMLEY.

The Prime Minister and Foreign Secretary gave him several interviews.

Lord Salisbury was particularly and personally interested in the success of the Commission, having been one of our plenipotentiaries at the Congress. I received all the encouragement I could gain from frank confidence and assurances of support, but he did not conceal that he thought the situation dubious and unpromising. He spoke of the difficulties of dealing with Russia in this business, of which the course of her representative on the Commission gave sufficient evidence. He understood she was about to assert the pretensions of Bulgaria to the

---

[1] Major Ardagh was already chief of the Topographical Staff.

whole southern slope of the Balkans. The disturbed state of the country might cause serious obstacles; and, in fact, the Eastern Roumelian Commission had been compelled to desist from its work by armed Bulgarian mobs. The physical difficulties of country and climate were also looked on as formidable. Indeed all the conditions were so unsettled that he must leave me to do the best with them I could, after better acquaintance on the spot, for executing the provisions of the treaty.

In an interview with Colonel Stanley, the Secretary for War, he observed that he had always considered it expedient to have as Chief Commissioner an officer of higher rank than that of colonel, and who would consequently possess an influence more commensurate with the interest our Government felt in obtaining fair terms for Turkey. . . . I was treated with great liberality. All officers that I applied for were given me, and all necessary expenses were sanctioned.

It was known that Russia was making for her own purposes a survey of the new frontiers, and that the maps would probably be available for the purposes of the Commission. But whether they were such as would be serviceable to us, we had no means of knowing. I therefore asked for a staff sufficient to undertake a considerable amount of work in the absence of assistance from the other Powers, and which would in any case, if needful, serve to verify and correct the work of the Russian topographers.

The staff selected was strong and efficient.

Major Ardagh, who had resumed his employment at the Intelligence Department of the War Office, was to return as head of my topographical staff. He brought from that department Lieutenant Hare, a very accomplished interpreter, who spoke French thoroughly. Both these officers had been under me during my command of the Staff College, as well as Captain Douglas Jones, R.A., who now accompanied me as aide-de-camp. To avoid the objection of choosing none but officers of Artillery and Engineers, I was glad to be able to apply for Captain Everett, an excellent topographer, who had also been at the Staff College in my time. Being still in want of an officer, I applied to my successor at the College, and Captain Elles, R.A., a student there with whom I had no previous acquaintance, joined me at Constantinople.

As it seemed extremely probable that the services of a doctor might be in requisition, the party was completed at Constantinople by Dr Exham, a young assistant - surgeon from Netley.

Accompanied by Major Ardagh, Hamley left London, and their steamer anchored in the Bosphorus on the 4th of April. Off the plains of Troy they were boarded by Dr Schliemann, who came to fetch a fellow-labourer in archæological research. That visit, with its associations, may have suggested to Hamley the classical reflection in one of his letters, that in his ignorance of local feeling, and even of the physical features of the Balkans and the bordering districts, he was plunging like the Argonauts into the unknown.

Strange changes were visible in Constantinople since he had seen it twenty-four years before.

There were the same miscellaneous and vociferous mobs in the filthy and ill - paved streets; the population had been increased and the squalor aggravated, for the long war had left famine behind, filling Stamboul with troops of homeless fugitives. But cheap steamers were hurrying to and fro on the Bosphorus, to the imminent peril of the frail caïques, and the true believers had taken to travelling by tramcars drawn by steam-engines. " Perhaps the most interesting visit was to the English cemetery at Scutari, now a beautiful spot and carefully tended. Large grassy mounds marked the spots where I remembered to have stood by open graves, where the corpses of those who had died in the great hospital hard by were brought up by the cartload and buried wholesale." The Mosque of St Sophia in its dilapidation and decay seemed to have shared the fallen fortunes of the shattered empire. Sir Henry Layard was at the British Embassy, with Mr Malet (now Sir Edward) for first Secretary. General Sir Collingwood Dickson was military *attaché*, specially sent out during the war. But the high official with whom Hamley's mission brought him into more immediate relations was the British member of the International Commission for the Organisation of Eastern Roumelia. Few Englishmen can boast a more distinguished record, or have done more to deserve well of their country, than Sir Henry Drummond Wolff, who, after having made a brilliant reputation at home as a Conservative politician and statesman, has filled the most important diplomatic posts in Europe and the East, distinguishing himself by rare tact and ability in bringing to a successful issue the most delicate international negotiations. From the first, his intercourse with Hamley was cordial in the extreme. His counsels and oriental experience were of infinite utility, and as he warmly appreciated the value of Hamley's work, so he urged his claims for adequate recognition on the Government.

Hamley had gone from the great Mosque to pay visits of ceremony to some of the Turkish ministers :—

I observed the same tokens of decay in some of the public offices. There was evidently no money to spare for paint, plaster, glazing, and wall-paper. The ablest public servants of Turkey are for the most part either Greeks or Armenians. They, as a rule I should say, are rather subtle than wise—rather shifty than foreseeing. The Foreign Secretary, Carathcortory Pasha, thin, somewhat pinched of aspect, had not the presence or manner of a strong administrator, but was quite conversant with the business I had come upon, having represented Turkey at the late Congress. . . . He begged me to discuss the subject [that of arranging a defensible frontier] with the Grand Vizier and the War Minister (Osman, the defender of Plevna); but interviews with them convinced me that they had never thought of the matter, and had no views to impart. Osman, thick-featured, short-necked, heavy-shouldered, dull of expression, and changeless of attitude as the automatic chess-player, was the personification of an immovable Turk. His immobility may have served him well when it caused him to hold on so gallantly to the defence of Plevna, but showed its other side when he delayed his retreat so long that he lost his army.

The etiquette is for the newly arrived to make the ceremonial calls, and as his colleagues came dropping in, he received a succession of formal visits. But Commandant Lemoyne, the French delegate, had wintered in Constantinople. Hamley lost no time in paying his respects, and thenceforth they were always on excellent terms.

He was a Frenchman of the thin keen-featured type, and a painstaking, clear-headed man of business. . . . Baron de Ripp presently came from Vienna. Englishmen are always prepared to find in Austrian officers agreeable, courteous, cultivated men, and I esteemed him throughout the expedition a good comrade. . . . Major Count Wedel, the military *attaché* of Germany at Vienna, was a new member. When our proceedings began, he was seen to be more restricted than the rest by the instructions of his Government, according to which he was to support the Russian as a rule, except when the opinion of the majority might be against him, when he was to conform to it. This caused him to venture on few expressions of opinion, to reserve his vote frequently, and to refer often to Berlin.

Colonel Orero, the Italian, was a quiet and sensible man, who said little, and kept himself in the background, but was inclined to back Hamley. For the consultations generally turned on the conflicting views of the Englishman and the Russian.

The two members who, by common consent, were regarded as representing the chief opposing interests, Colonel Bogulaboff and myself, though often of necessity in disagreement in debate, always remained excellent friends. He was young for his rank, probably under thirty, had served in the late war and in Circassia, and had done a great deal of that diplomatic work to which Russian officers take so kindly. He was of a shrewd rather than a powerful intellect, with an expression of countenance more energetic than refined, and his tone in our discussions was often aggressive, owing to the confidence he felt in the support of his Government. But his object was always too clearly revealed, and he arrived at it rather by insistence than by *finesse.*

The Pasha did not take a part in our debates commensurate with the interests he represented. He was a plump, good-natured man, of grave aspect, had served under Osman Pasha at Plevna, spoke a little French, and had been in Paris. He was decidedly dull, but good-tempered and not bigoted. Stolid and inoffensive, he appeared to have been instructed to support my views, at least by voting for them.

With regard to the Pasha, Hamley has a good story which tells pleasantly against himself. Yet in circumstances when another man would probably have given serious cause of offence, few were inclined to take offence with him :—

Observing him sign his name as "M. Tahir," I said, "*Quel est votre nom Chrétien, Excellence ?*" "*Comment ?*" said the Pasha, with a look of surprise. I perceived my mistake, but did not mend it by changing the form of the question,—"*Je veux demander quel est votre nom de baptême ?*" "*Comment ?*" said the Pasha again, more gravely than before. I then recollected that I was as much out of time with my hearer as Portia when she talks to Shylock of the Lord's Prayer, and at length elicited by a question more aptly framed what his first name was—Mehmet.

The Pasha was attended by several officers for topographical purposes, and by a handsome and highly accomplished Armenian gentleman, who spoke French like the most refined Parisians, and was in the habit of thinking in that language. There were long and wearisome preliminary discussions as to how far the frontier might be settled, previous to actual inspection of the ground. Finally, unanimous assent was given to the resolution proposed by the Austrian delegate,—that the general tracing of the boundaries should be discussed, in order to determine what the disputed points might be, so that these might be referred to their several Governments by the Commissioners who had only restricted powers. On Hamley's proposition, communicated to Lord Salisbury by a despatch of 18th April, and concerted in an informal conference with his Turkish, Austrian, German, and Italian colleagues, general principles of the delimitation were agreed to. Briefly the *partage des eaux*, or watershed, was to be followed: the questions in dispute were likely to arise in including on the northern side of the southern boundary certain salient positions effective for defence.

Although snow still lay deep upon the hills, on the 29th April the English topographical party was despatched to complete the survey of the Balkans to the west of Samakow. Major Ardagh was in charge, and Hamley had found an invaluable interpreter in Mr Cullen, son of an English physician in Constantinople, who already knew the country well, and had been an eye-witness of some of the worst of "the Bulgarian atrocities." "I had purchased horses in Pera — small and strong—for the whole party, and I sold them at the end of the business at no great loss." Before leaving Constantinople himself, he found time to visit Baker Pasha, who was then engaged with nearly 40,000 Turkish troops on the lines of

Tchatchaldja, intended to protect the capital from invading forces passing the Balkans. That visit is described at length in a letter to the Duke of Cambridge, who had expressed a desire to receive occasional communications. It is unnecessary to give the letter in full, and I shall merely select some extracts as to the strategical and political importance of the lines, and the qualities of the men employed in constructing them :—

MAJOR-GENERAL EDWARD B. HAMLEY *to H.R.H. the*
DUKE OF CAMBRIDGE.

CONSTANTINOPLE, 12*th May.*

SIR,—At Tchatchaldja the position is viewed from the side of the enemy, who, having reached from Adrianople a long line of high and steep heights, crossed by very few roads and very difficult of passage, would then see it before him, across a flat valley from three to four miles wide.

As the heights on each side recede considerably from the valley, the defensive line is for the most part, in this portion of it, quite beyond extreme cannon-range from the heights reached by the enemy. The road from Tchatchaldja to the position runs across the valley through a marsh, which, according to the season, is from half a mile to a mile in extent, and is impassable.

The position, which, as the crow flies, is at an average distance of 35 miles from Constantinople, traverses a peninsula, which from the Sea of Marmora to the Black Sea is at this point about 26 miles wide. But as the flanks of the position rest on two lakes, each separated from one of those seas only by a sandbank, its actual fortified extent is thereby narrowed to about 16 miles. . . . From the main ridge parallel to the valley, a number of spurs run out into the valley: the position lies along the crests of the spurs, the lower parts of which form each an uncommonly perfect glacis. The general principle of the defence is to place a work on the crest of each spur, sweeping the glacis and the valley, and another farther back, where it can command the part of the valley which runs up between the spurs.

Describing the positions and armaments in detail, he pronounces the lines virtually impregnable, the points which nature had left comparatively assailable being strongly defended by triple works. As to the troops :—

These works have been constructed by the troops under the direction of Baker Pasha, who planned and traced them. The battalions are chiefly 'mustafiz,' or men of the last reserve, who, taken from their homes for the war, have been detained to labour on the defences. Nothing could have been more deplorable than the condition of these men during the winter,—in miserable tents on those bleak hills, the country everywhere deep in mire, rations and clothing very scanty, firewood fetched by the men from a great distance through the mud, and no hospital; and nothing could have been more admirable than the cheerfulness with which they continued their labours in these circumstances. In fact, their patience, energy, discipline, and uncomplaining spirit surpass what would have been displayed under such conditions by any other troops. Nor is their physical inferior to their moral excellence: although shabbily clad, they are now well fed, and a finer body of men it would be impossible to find,—immensely broad and deep in shoulder and chest, far above average stature, manly of bearing, and intelligent of aspect.

It would appear that beyond the mere military result, the existence of such a line of defences must exercise an immense influence on the affairs of Europe. An impregnable line of defence at that distance from Constantinople assures the existence of Turkey as a European Power. It may also be expected to produce a beneficial effect on internal affairs by affording that guarantee for national existence which is a necessary condition of national development.

CHAPTER XIV.

THE BULGARIAN DELIMITATION COMMISSION—*continued*.

TRAVEL IN THE BALKANS—PICTURESQUE SCENERY—VICTIMS OF THE WAR—FEELINGS OF THE POPULATION—ENMITY BETWEEN CHRISTIANS AND MOHAMMEDANS — ARRIVAL AT VARNA—DIFFICULTIES WITH THE RUSSIAN AUTHORITIES, AND EMBARKATION OF THE HORSES.

THE Commission set out on the 13th of May. With the attendants, equipments, and train of baggage animals, it made a formidable party. In one of his lively letters to his niece he describes an amusing *incident de voyage :—*

We slept at Adrianople—not in the city, however, but in the train. I saw somebody in red-striped trousers extend himself on the opposite sofa of the carriage, and, being half asleep, concluded it was Captain Jones. I thought his legs very short, and could not account for his head in relation to them. I also came to the conclusion that nobody ever snored so loud, and wondered how Mrs Jones could stand it. In the morning light, however, I discovered that my companion was the Pasha.

The second night was passed at Philippopolis,

the capital of the new province of Eastern Roumelia. " The singularity of this town is that it is built round the sides of a high steep rock, which crops up abruptly through the wide flat valley of the Maritza." Hamley had his lodging on the summit of the rock, in comfortable quarters placed at his disposal by Sir Henry Drummond Wolff. He looked down on the Maritza, which reminded him of the Thames, though storks in place of swans and the herds of shaggy buffaloes tended to dispel the fond illusion.

This city had been in the preceding year the scene of great cruelties practised by the Turkish governor. My interpreter, Mr Cullen, told me he had seen a procession of Bulgarians marched along the street under Turkish escort, and on arriving at a sign, lamp-post, or other convenient projection, a halt was made, a prisoner hung on the extemporised gibbet, and the march resumed to the next one. He described the Bulgarians as submitting absolutely without complaint or resistance, and had remarked that each was run up motionless like a stuffed figure, a grey shade which presently came over the uncovered face showing when life was extinct. A hundred and five had been thus dealt with at once. He had remonstrated with the Pasha, representing that all these men could not have been guilty of offences worthy of death,—to which the Pasha simply replied that to be a Bulgarian was a sufficient crime.

The strong cavalry escort was furnished by the Russians, and the real start was made on the

18th May for Tatar Bazardjik, where there was a large Russian camp.   In fact, the Russians insisted on taking excessive care of the delegates, considerably to Hamley's annoyance.   There was a guard of a dozen men in the courtyard of the house he occupied; sentries were posted before and behind, and he could not saunter out into the street without having an armed party at his heels.

As the Russians supplied the escort, so a Bulgarian official was charged by the Russian authorities with providing transport.

His zeal in our service was so great as quite to extinguish any sympathy he might have had for his Bulgarian brethren, whom he impressed most ruthlessly, along with their oxen and *arabas,* carrying them off from their labours in the fields, sometimes for days, while their families were left in ignorance of what had become of them. These *arabas* were often drawn by black and hideous buffaloes, with enormous flat curled horns and colossal limbs, and the picturesque procession moved slowly onwards to the melodious screeching of innumerable wheels.   A squadron of Russian dragoons, headed by the band with trumpets and kettle-drums, led the advance, and the rear of the cumbrous baggage-train was brought up by mounted Bulgarians.

Now that Eastern Roumelia has been annexed to Bulgaria, it is superfluous to follow closely the military itinerary, or to dwell on the defensive positions in detail. Nothing is less likely than that the Russians in our time will again march on Constantinople by the overland route, though it is certain that the Shipka Pass may still be of importance should there be trouble between Turkey and the liberated populations; so I shall chiefly confine myself to those incidents in the military promenade which have some personal reference to the subject of the memoir. It may be mentioned that the members of his staff often found their duties sufficiently arduous. On one occasion, for example, Captains Everett and Elles rode fifty miles over the roughest country, making a variety of topographical sketches in course of the ride. In some of the towns where the Commission was expected, though the escort held them in awe, the people were very menacing, and at Ichtiman, " a most filthy place," there was imminent danger of an *émeute*. For once, and as it happened when he needed them most, none of the escort was billeted in Hamley's quarters. He and his aide-de-camp dined with pistols on the table, listening to the uproar below the windows. The population were anxious to be included in Bulgarian territory, and believed that the English Commissioner, in especial, was opposed to their wishes. As for the peasants, they had no reason to like the Russians, who continued to carry matters with a high hand. One evening arrangements had been made for an early start, but in the morning all the enforced waggoners were missing, and had taken their *arabas* with them. Forthwith the dragoons were sent out to scour the country, and they impressed a sufficient number of unfortunates, who were put under stricter guard.

We rode over breezy downs, along the watershed towards a village bordering a stream. Here Major Ardagh and I, with one servant, pitched our tents in a meadow, procured some meat, and late at night supped upon it as cooked by the servant. Towards morning I was awoke by a young bull stumbling over the tent-ropes. The remainder of my party had encamped four miles from me. A waggon, loaded with baggage of the Italian officers, had rolled in the dark down a ravine, and Colonel Orero expressed to me much gratitude for the aid my officers had afforded in rescuing the articles and setting the *araba* again on the road.

Next day the road led up a deep gorge; the broken path kept crossing from side to side, and some twenty times they forded the Topolnitza, which flowed swiftly in the bottom. Emerging on the broad plain, they had left the lesser range beyond the Rhodope behind, and were in presence of the principal chain of the Balkans.

At the foot of the Great Balkans we were met by a deputation of Bulgarian notables, bringing a petition for respecting the boundaries of some village lands. They invited us to halt in a grove, where they had spread rugs and cushions for us, had cooked fine trout netted in a neighbouring stream, and roasted a lamb whole, by enclosing it in the hollow trunk of a tree. The animal looked somewhat grisly, but nevertheless tasted excellent; so did the trout.

Taking leave of our entertainers we passed on, and pausing beside a small mountain-stream to await our train, I got out my fly-rod, and caught a few brook-trout. My colleagues testified great interest in this small sport, especially the Pasha, who, usually apathetic, bustled officiously round me, and several times put me in terror for my tackle by assisting the landing of the fish. Next morning we ascended the Trojan Pass by a path zigzagged up the steep mountain - side, slippery with stones, and far too narrow for wheels, or for anything but a single horse.

Then he records an incident strikingly significant of his kindly generosity. He also alludes to it in a letter to his niece, characteristically saying nothing of his charitable gift. Everywhere he was painfully impressed by the pitiable condition of the victims of the war. For there was little to choose between Turkish and Bulgarian atrocities, and whether the Christian or Mohammedan Bulgarians had the upper hand, they ruthlessly avenged long - cherished grievances against the neighbours of a different creed.

When the Commission marched for Karlovo, I stayed with my Russian orderly and my interpreter to ride round the village of Teke. Being altogether Turkish, it was entirely deserted and completely ruined. When the Russian armies were approaching the Bálkans, the Turkish inhabitants, expecting no mercy, took to flight. Their property, left unprotected, was immediately pillaged by their Bulgarian neighbours. Their flocks were driven off, their crops plundered, their houses pulled down and the woodwork carried off. These proceedings were not altogether inspired by hatred or cupidity, but partly from a desire to prevent the Turks in any case from returning to their homes by leaving them no homes to return to. Mr Cullen, making a foray, as usual, in search of lambs, fowls, and bread, which the owners might be willing to sell, had found in this place some starving Turkish women, still haunting their ruined houses and fields, because they had no other refuge, and endeavouring to subsist on what they could glean in their devastated lands and gardens. Some of these veiled and black-robed forms were flitting furtively between the walls, and Mr Cullen learned that they could possibly subsist if they had a cow, which could be fed on the pastures round. I therefore left with them the few pounds necessary and rode onward. Our way now lay through immense tracts of roses, at this time in full bloom. Everywhere women were gathering them, and cart-loads were conveyed to the distilleries, established on the banks of suitable streams for the manufacture of the attar. Here enormous earthen jars in rows stood each over a charcoal furnace, and were connected by pipes with lesser jars, and these, sheltered by rough sheds in which lay vast heaps of gathered roses, with groups of peasants tending the furnaces, while *arabas* with fresh freights came in from the fields and forded the streams, lent singular interest and picturesqueness to the solitary valleys of the Balkans.

At a village beyond Kalofer, examination of the map showed a stream flowing from the mountain, and Hamley rode forth to reconnoitre.

Its aspect was most promising, and Mr Cullen awaited my return with a native, whose occupation was to scoop out trout with a hand-net. This functionary said there was an excellent spot about two miles up the stream, to which he would take me in the morning, proposing to bring his net, which he imagined to be indispensable. The interpreter assured him that if he disappointed us, and above all, if he brought his net, the Pasha (myself) would certainly hang him. Events had lent too much reality to a threat of that kind, and the fisherman, netless, wondering, and possibly somewhat frightened, punctually awaited me next morning.

In three hours he had caught upwards of five dozen trout, many above a pound weight. Many were killed in a deep gorge, where he was surprised by the bursting of a terrific thunder-storm, which brought down the river suddenly in a flood, much in the manner of the Morayshire Findhorn. Before the interruption of his sport, in

wending round a corner, I surprised a swarm of frogs sunning themselves on the stony margin, brilliantly attired, as Turkish frogs are, in green and gold and rose colour. Alarmed at my appearance between them and the stream, they threw themselves off, taking headers like schoolboys bathing, hands joined in front, heels in the air, so hurriedly that many struck against me before lighting in the water. . . . I sent all my largest trout to my colleagues for dinner, who, in return, bestowed upon me some bottles of beer which they had somehow become possessed of.

That stream had its source in a spur of the Shipka, and next day they ascended the famous pass, where Suleiman Pasha had sulked on the defensive, and which he very probably sold to the General of the Tsar.

The pass goes up from the village, and was traversed by a good road, twenty feet wide, made by the Russians, and now being improved by Bulgarian labourers. The summit of San Nicholas, the high point of the pass, is visible from the plains. We reached it in two hours and a half, and, from the summit of the peak, saw the road going steeply down along narrow crests till it vanished round a hill a mile off. Around were other craggy peaks, parted from us by deep and steep ravines; and all their rugged sides had been thickly strewn with Russian and Turkish dead in the long struggle for the pass. Below us was the Russian cemetery, so completely enclosed and commanded, that we made no difficulty of acceding to Colonel Bogulaboff's request that this graveyard should be left in Bulgarian territory, so strong a frontier being here assigned to Turkey as would, if suitably occupied, secure the pass.

In the altered political circumstances, the capabilities of the Balkans as a defensive line may be briefly dismissed in an extract from a letter to the Duke of Cambridge reporting generally on the work of the Commission. It was written from Buyukdere on the 7th July:—

The only passes where preparations for defence need be made are those of the Shipka, Hankivi, and Kotel. That these should be defended would appear a very proper measure, because the Balkans, being so difficult of passage, everywhere form a real and strong line of defence. But no expensive fortifications are needed. Earthworks would amply suffice both for infantry and artillery.

Beyond the Balkans the Commissioners were in a rich and fruitful country, with vineyards, rose-gardens, and fields of waving corn. Now there was no difficulty as to the commissariat, and supplies of all kinds poured in. Dr Exham went out with his gun, and with Don, the pointer, who had become an esteemed member of the Commissioner's staff, and he came back with bags of partridges and hares. The English members of the expedition stuck to their national habits, making a solid breakfast and a frugal lunch.

But our colleagues preferred their usual practice of beginning the day with coffee or bread and fruit, and at the mid-day halt a Bulgarian cook or steward, said to have been a captain in the army, would arrive on a horse, bearing all the materials for a substantial *déjeûner*—cold meat, cold fowls, salads, potted fish, and wines; and while we despatched the trifling matters which our saddle-bags contained, the foreigners, spreading a huge tablecloth in a woody glade or on a grassy meadow, would make a meal which was followed by hot coffee, and liqueur, and by some period of repose. The rest in the hot time of the day was welcome, for the sun now poured his rays as from a furnace. . . .

There was one mitigating feature in the sultry rides—namely, the fountains which were so frequently to be found by the roadsides, generally the grateful offering, as the inscription on a tablet mostly records, of some pious hadji or other devout Mussulman. Out of these always gushes cold, pure water, falling into a trough for beasts. These structures are of some size, and often very picturesque, the votive inscription in white or gold on a green tablet.

We had now left the rose-fields, and were journeying at the foot of slopes clothed in vines. A good well-flavoured red wine is produced, but the manufacture is rough and ready. Baron Ripp, who seemed to understand the subject practically and from a proprietor's point of view, observed to me that the conditions of soil and climate were excellent, and that by planting suitable vines and exercising the same care as in France or Germany, wines surpassing even the famous growths of these countries might be produced.

A few days afterwards they rode into a village, after a forced march of twenty-five miles. At nine o'clock, after weary waiting, they heard the screeching of the wheels of the belated baggage train, when it was too late to encamp, and when arrangements for supper were impossible. Next morning, and notwithstanding their fatigue, all the disgusted peasants had again disappeared, taking cattle and carriages along with them. So Hamley appears to have disposed of the time by noting down his general impressions of Bulgarian villages :—

A Bulgarian village differs from ordinary European villages in this, that it appears to be composed altogether of one class of persons, the tillers of the soil. There is nothing to be called a street, no small shopkeepers, no inns, no shoemakers or tailors, nor anything to distinguish some of the agricultural population as superior to the rest. Of course there must be diversities in degrees of opulence, but these do not make themselves apparent in greater comfort, better houses, or better living. Everybody lives in squalor: washing is, I should think, quite unpractised, and I concluded that men and women kept on their clothes day and night, for some indefinite period. Both men and women are destitute of good looks. Their houses are separated by spaces of ground—not for gardens, for I never saw the slightest attempt at cultivation : the wild weeds, generally tall camomile, grow up to the doors, and must in the decay of autumn be very unwholesome. The wide tiled eaves of the houses are supported on posts enclosing a balcony which is reached by a broad ladder. The ground-floor is reserved for horses, cows, pigs, and stores. In the room I used as a temporary habitation there was a large hole in the floor, through which the sweepings were cast into the regions below. All fare alike on the bread and cheese of the country, both, to our taste, disgusting—the bread clammy, the cheese soft, discoloured, and of horrible odour. Where each family makes its own food and drink, there is no opening for the shopkeeper.

The camomile spreads over the whole country, and our tents were often pitched on ground covered by it, so that my recollections of the expedition are always associated with the odour of the plant.

The special product of Bulgarian industry is embroidery. They have all the gift of colour and of fanciful design with which the people of the East are endowed, and the towels and coverings which the women adorn with their needle-work are now well known in England, owing to the distress of the Turkish population, who, crowding into Constantinople after abandoning their property, were driven to sell whatever they still possessed, in order to keep body and soul together. The Government lodged them, so far as possible, in great empty houses, such as are always to be found on the Bosphorus.

The Turks who remained, unwilling to abandon houses or lands, held their lives, like their property, on a most precarious tenure. One day, after camping near a lonely cemetery, and pitching the tents close to a new-made grave covered with thorns to keep off the jackals and hyenas, the Commission crossed a desolated tract of country to Verbitza.

I was lodged in the detached villa of a young Bey, about eighteen or twenty years old, whose father, a Pasha, was lately dead. Here was a lively illustration of the condition of Turkish proprietors who remained in the new Principality. The Bey's steward, an old servant of the family, told us that a fortnight before, as he was journeying with his master from a town at some distance, they were waylaid by a party of brigands, among whom they recognised many of their own neighbours and townsmen, and were thrown to the ground. The Bey, with a knife at his throat, was compelled to pay a heavy ransom. They had been menaced by notice with fresh violence, the Russians afforded no protection, and they quite expected to be murdered after our departure. I saw in the streets many loungers who looked quite capable of that or any other crime.

In the Verbitza pass the Commission separated, to meet again in Constantinople. A part of the delegates turned westward, to complete the delimitation in that direction, each Commissioner sending his adjutant to represent him where he was not personally present.

The division of duty was matter of friendly arrangement, and Hamley preferred to join the eastern party, as the eastern frontier embraced the issues directly leading from the north to Constantinople. The marches led through singularly romantic scenery :—

For days we had seen the chain of the Balkans, clothed in immense forests of beech, oak, chestnut, and pine, through the shady parts of which our road for the most part lay, emerging now and then into an open space whence we could survey the undulating woods as they covered hill and dale, pierced at the highest points by pinnacles of crag. From Dobral we again crossed the Balkans, at the pass of that name, halting at the Bairam dere. (*Dere* signifies valley of a stream, and may be the same termination as that of Scamander, Mæander, and other classical streams.) While our baggage next day took the road by the valley, we plunged into the woods, riding in deep shade, sometimes stooping under the boughs.

At the next camping-place Hamley invited the captain of the Russian escort to dinner on the following day. He desired the cook to make hospitable preparation, and accordingly a lamb and a goose were purchased, and hung up in the *al fresco* larder.

That night there was tremendous excitement among the village dogs, which had made a battle-ground of our green, with savage snarling and growling. One animal made himself specially obnoxious by sitting apart and plaintively howling. In the morning we discovered that the nocturnal engagement had been waged over lamb and goose, only a foot of the one and the bill of the other remaining to explain it. The dog that had howled was a stranger, debarred from a share in the feast.

Two days afterwards, from Petreo on the heights, they saw the Euxine shimmering in the sunshine beneath them, and following the ridge of downs bordering the water, after a ride of about 620 miles, drew bridle at last in the streets of Varna, sadly familiar to Hamley in the cholera time before the Crimean campaign. Two characteristic incidents marked the brief stay there. Prince Dondakoff Korsakoff, subsequently of Trans-

Caucasian celebrity, was directing affairs in Bulgaria, and had his residence in Varna. The Commissioners thought it but courteous to call: their Russian colleague, who must otherwise have presented them to the Prince, had gone with the other party. The courtesy was indifferently reciprocated. The Commissioners duly announced their names and functions. The reply of the officers in the antechamber was that the Prince was sitting down to breakfast, and they had better call again. Hamley was the last man to put up with a slight of the kind, especially when he was representing the British Government. He spoke for the rest, and sharply told the aide-de-camp that their purpose of calling on the Prince was fulfilled, and for himself, he would be unable to pay a second visit. The officer turned on his heel, and left the room without any form of leave-taking. The foreign envoys were loud in their indignation at what they styled the insolence of master and man. However, the Prince so far made the *amende* that in the course of the day Hamley found his card on the table. Had he shown himself more friendly, some trouble and embarrassment might have been saved. Hamley, who wished to get rid of his horses, had hoped to sell some of them in Varna, embarking the rest. He learned rather late that no horses could be shipped without a special permission from the Russian Government. This the shrewd Bulgarian horse-dealers knew, and as the steamer was to start at a given time, they thought they had the Englishman and his animals at their mercy.

He had successfully shipped the horses on lighters, but the lighters were intercepted by a revenue boat and compelled to put back. He hurriedly despatched messengers to obtain the requisite permission. The dealers were triumphant, and made a modest bid for the lot of much less than the value of a single horse. Hamley was not to be victimised if he could in any way help it.

It was dusk, and close to the hour of departure, when the permission came. I had requested the captain to send the steamer's boats, which he did; but the shallow water would not permit them to approach within some forty yards of the shore, and they would only hold half the number. The joy of the horse-dealers was great: they saw me in extremity, and expected me to capitulate on their own terms. I selected at once the horses I intended to take, had them led into the water to the boats' sides, when our grooms and servants, eight or ten in number, seized each horse, two or three to each leg, and by main strength lifted and tumbled them in. The interpreter's pony they carried the whole way, and pitched him in so abruptly that he got his legs scarred in a way which he still bears the marks of, if he still exists.

The remaining animals were brought on in another steamer in charge of Captain Jones, and so the grasping dealers were effectually baffled.

Retributory justice overtook another Bulgarian, whose sufferings were more acute, and Hamley, in very charity for his fellow - creatures, regarded and narrates them with a grim sense of humour :—

The sea was nearly motionless—there was an almost imperceptible heave in it. But this was too much for Tchitchagoff, who had never before seen the sea. He retired at once, in extreme distress, to his cabin, where he lamented, screamed, and even wept all night. The Bulgarian peasantry could hardly have desired a completer vengeance on their persecutor. Next day he staggered across the deck to the doctor, to whom he announced that he was dying, and then disappeared. Shortly afterwards, he returned with the information that he was not dying but actually dead—and, in fact, he fell below the binnacle in a motionless heap, and so remained till we landed. But the poor man was really so ill that I heard he never got out of his bed at the hotel, except to go straight back to his home in Bulgaria.

The story of the labours of the Commission may appropriately conclude with the last of the letters to the Duke of Cambridge. The first part is omitted, as its substance has been anticipated in the extracts from the diary. The rest is curious and interesting, as evidence of how the subtle Muscovite policy overreached itself, and of how entirely the Russians had deceived themselves as to their future relations with the co-religionists whose affections they had done much to alienate by arbitrary proceedings and an overbearing demeanour.   The writer was more clear-sighted:—

MAJOR-GENERAL E. B. HAMLEY *to His Royal Highness the* DUKE OF CAMBRIDGE.

BUYUKDERE, 14*th July* 1879.

SIR,—I have the honour to offer to your Royal Highness some observations on the condition of the provinces through which the route of the Commission has lain.

[After remarking that in his opinion the pastoral wealth and fertility of the country, even previous to the war, must have been greatly exaggerated in official reports, he goes on :—]

At the same time, the country has all the elements of riches in its soil and climate, and wants nothing but a period of tranquillity to develop them.

Whether such a period will be granted to it is now the problem.   The Russians have done a good deal to prevent it by the political ideas they have been inspiring, by organising and drilling a kind of national army, and by large presents of arms.   In every town armed bodies were being drilled, and in every cottage a breech-loader and bayonet might be seen.   Numbers of men were sometimes to be met with on the roads thus armed, and wearing a badge to show that they belonged to the militia.   These arms were left by the Russian troops, who were to receive others of a newer pattern on getting home.   Large quantities of ammunition have also been distributed,—we met a long train of waggons near Sliven which had been impressed at Bourgas, all loaded with ammunition-boxes. The Russians, I believe, justify this by saying that the Turks in Roumelia and Bulgaria have quantities of arms hidden away, which they only wait the withdrawal of the Russians to use. However that may be, there evidently exist in this armed and organised population sufficient elements of disturbance. I think, however, there is fair ground for hoping that quietness may prevail. Much of the excitement may cease with the withdrawal of the Russians, whose treatment of the Bulgarians has not been of a kind to make them popular. The population are naturally industrious and not naturally warlike, and may quickly come to see that they have everything to lose and nothing to gain in further troubles.

.   .   .   .

Instead of instilling political ideas, the people should be taught to cultivate the conveniences and decencies of civilised life. . . . The best government will be that which takes the best way to raise the country to the present European level and to develop its natural advantages. I hear from various sources that the new Governor of Roumelia is not likely to take the lead in any policy requiring vigour or capacity.

I have been emboldened to offer so many remarks by the kind encouragement of your Royal Highness; and trusting that the length of my letter may find excuse, I have the honour to be, &c.,   E. B. HAMLEY.

CHAPTER XV.

ON THE BOSPHORUS.

LIFE AT BUYUKDERE—DELAYS IN THE COMPLETION OF THE TOPOGRAPHICAL SURVEY—DIFFICULTIES SUCCESSFULLY SURMOUNTED—APPROVAL OF THE FOREIGN OFFICE—IS MADE A KNIGHT OF THE ORDER OF ST MICHAEL AND ST GEORGE.

NOTHING can be more enchanting than the banks of the Bosphorus in the spring and early summer, and Hamley passed the time very agreeably while awaiting the arrival of the other section of the Commission. Following the example of the Embassies and the wealthy residents, he preferred the country—or rather the suburbs—to the city, and took up his quarters with his aide-de-camp in the hotel at Buyukdere. There he was glad to rest from his active labours, and found pleasant occupation in boating expeditions to visit the palaces and romantically situated villages that fringe the shores of the Straits; in rides, or long excursions on foot over the bordering hills, when

the sketch-book was never left behind; and in
joining picnic - parties which were got up *impromptu.* Within doors and on wet days he
was busied in methodically embodying the results
of his late observations in memoranda which
were duly transmitted to the War Office. He
and Captain Jones happened to be the only Englishmen in their hotel, the rest of the company
consisting of Russians and Americans; but the
delightful residence of the British Ambassador at
Therapia was within easy reach, and there he
had always a warm welcome. As he writes to
his niece, he met his old acquaintance Laurence
Oliphant, who, although he had only arrived a few
days before, was already as much at home in the
house as if he had been the oldest member of the
family. With regard to that meeting, Hamley
would sometimes speak rather enviously of Oliphant's extraordinary faculty of ingratiating himself with all and sundry. Though he himself
possessed it in a wonderful degree in the case
of bright and clever women, when his manner
would soften insensibly and his face would light
up with smiles. But if Oliphant carried all before
him in society, he was less successful elsewhere
and in his immediate objects. Like Hamley,
he had also come on a mission; but he was
not clothed with official authority, nor did he

represent the dignity of the English War Office.
He had come to obtain certain concessions with
regard to colonisation and land sales in the
Jordan valley. He used to give most ludicrous
accounts of incidents more amusing in the retro-
spect than in the reality,—of his dancing attendance in the Turkish antechambers; of his being
bandied about from one minister to another; of
free-handed distributions of backsheesh, by which
he was never to benefit. He would ruefully
confide to Hamley how his suave diplomacy was
powerless against the apathetic courtesies of the
Pashas, and how his patience was only sustained
by his being prepared for the worst, and consequently fortified against delays and disappointments. Hamley soon had somewhat similar experience of his own. In respect to the Turks, as
he was doing his best to help them, he naturally
found them complacent enough and willing to
assist him in their dilatory fashion. But he had
to play out the *parti* with his subtle Russian
antagonist, who fancied he had a card in reserve
that should win the final trick. Hamley played
the game in his own manner, with firmness,
promptitude, and no little astuteness, and had
good reason to pride himself on the result.
His purpose all along had been to push the

arrangements through; the Russian's desire had been delay, and, if possible, to settle nothing definitely. The incident, important as it was, had only passing interest; but it illustrates Hamley's indomitable energy, and his readiness to accept responsibility. In brief, an extent of thirty-five miles still remained to be surveyed on the Macedonian frontier. Colonel Bogulaboff had undertaken that his topographers should do the work. On the reassembling of the Commission he calmly announced that the promised work was still undone, owing to the failure of the Turkish authorities to facilitate it, and he fixed two months as the time indispensable for the completion of the plans.

His colleagues were in consternation at the unexpected delay, and the discussion became stormy. They came to Hamley after the debate, in which he had taken a lead, expressing unanimously their indignation and despondency. Thus he was assured of their support in any steps he might take. As he says: "I had been sent out expressly to oppose the arrogant pretensions which the Russian Commissioner too often displayed. . . . The present blow, long delayed, had been resorted to as a safe and certain compensation for the many concessions which the Russian had been compelled to make. There seemed no possible way of averting it." For his own staff had been detached on a different piece of duty, and in particular he had to regret the loss of Captain Everett, who had been summoned away to his vice-consulate at Erzeroum. Moreover, the Russian added insult to injury, by pleasantly recommending Hamley to go on a two months' tour, when he might return to see how matters were progressing. Had anything been necessary to stimulate the sense of duty, it would have been a sneer of the kind. Hamley resolved on moving heaven and earth to make an effective practical retort, and Fortune favoured him in an unexpected fashion.

Just then he heard that Captain Everett, on his way from England to Trebizond, was actually in the hotel. He asked Everett if he would stop and do some work for him. "Certainly, sir," was the answer, "if you will get me authority." He immediately started to walk to the Embassy, and saw Sir Henry Layard going out for his ride. He had begun to run when the Ambassador heard himself accosted, and drew bridle. He preferred his request, but Sir Henry hesitated. He declared there was urgent necessity for Everett going to his post. "I observed that the occasion was an important and urgent one, and that on my getting Captain Everett depended whether I should or should not defeat the Russian plan for stopping the business of the Commission. It was certain that any step tending to defeat Russian designs against Turkey would have a charm for Sir Henry." Sir Henry asked if he would undertake to answer any further complaints from Everett's chief at Trebizond. The answer was unhesitatingly in the affirmative, and Sir Henry telegraphed to Lord Salisbury that the Vice-Consul was detained.

Simultaneously came a second stroke of good fortune, which gave him the services of Lieutenant de Wolski, R.E., a skilled topographer. Major Ardagh was put in charge of the party; Captain Jones, R.A., was to accompany it to arrange for the camps, commissariat, &c.; a Turkish officer was attached at the request of the Turkish authorities; and a suitable interpreter was found. All this was the work of a day or so. The next step was to obtain the formal assent of the Commission, and though greatly disappointed and annoyed, even Bogulaboff could not decently refuse. He expressed his vexation in no measured terms, but was suavely answered by Hamley that he was surprised at the spirit in which his offer had been received, being persuaded that the sole desire of the Russian was to facilitate the labours of the Commission.

Then came the consideration of how the topographers were to get to their ground. The Russian control of the country was so complete, that neither escort nor transport could be reckoned upon for the land route. The alternative was to send the Englishmen to Salonica by sea; but there seemed to be no possibility of starting for a week, and then by a slow coasting steamer. He hurried back to the Embassy to ask for one of the three English gunboats lying in the Bosphorus. The upshot was that he obtained the Bittern, on the understanding that he should again relieve the Ambassador of responsibility and bear Captain Pusey out with the Admiral.

At the *séance* of the 2d August the window of the room in which we sat overlooking the Bosphorus was darkened by a passing ship. This was the Bittern returning from her mission. I observed that this was the vessel which had taken the topographers of the Commission to Salonica, and the fact that she had been so employed evidently made a deep impression. In my despatch on the subject I observed, " The Commission cannot fail to contrast the manner in which the English Government endeavour to facilitate their work with the attitude taken towards them by the Russian." Consistent in his official attitude of

obstruction to the last, Bogulaboff made a final attempt
to have the work of his own topographers, when completed,
substituted on the map for that of the Englishmen. But
the other Commissioners unanimously refused to consent
to what could only be regarded as a gratuitous affront.

The following is the letter from the Foreign
Office expressing approval of the work of the
Commissioner and his subordinates:—

Foreign Office, October 23, 1879.

Sir,—I have to acknowledge receipt of your despatch
No. 91 of the 11th instant, announcing your return to this
country upon the completion of the operations of the International Commission formed under article 11 of the
Treaty of Berlin for the delimitation of the frontiers of
Bulgaria; and in so doing I gladly avail myself of the
opportunity to convey to you the cordial thanks of her
Majesty's Government for the valuable services you have
rendered to the Commission, and their high appreciation
of the tact and judgment which have characterised your
proceedings.

At the same time I request that you will convey to the
members of your staff my acknowledgments of the zeal
and efficiency with which they have severally discharged
the duties intrusted to them.—I am, sir, your most
obedient humble servant,   Salisbury.

By way of recompense he was made a Knight
Commander of the Order of St Michael and St
George. In private interviews he had the oppor-
tunity of reporting to his Lordship on the condi-

tion of the districts he had visited, the capabilities
for defence, and the feelings of the population.
Moreover, he was cordially thanked in less conventional terms; but the most satisfactory evidence of the appreciation of his work, as has
been already remarked, was in his being selected
on two future occasions for the discharge of similar duties.

END OF THE FIRST VOLUME.

PRINTED BY WILLIAM BLACKWOOD AND SONS.